Katherine Kovacic was a veterinarian but preferred training dogs to taking their temperatures. She seized the chance to return to study and earned an MA, followed by a PhD, in Art History. Katherine spends her spare time writing, dancing and teaching other people's dogs to ride skateboards. She lives in suburban Melbourne with Leonardo the borzoi, Oberon the Scottish deerhound and a legion of dog-fur dust bunnies. In 2012 she was longlisted for the Voiceless Writing Prize and in 2017 she was runner-up in the Australian Crime Writers' Association's SD Harvey Short Story Award. *The Portrait of Molly Dean* is her debut novel.

THE PORTRAIT OF

MOLLY DEAN

KATHERINE KOVACIC

echo

echo

A division of Bonnier Publishing Australia
534 Church Street, Richmond
Victoria Australia 3121
www.echopublishing.com.au

First published 2018

Printed in Australia at Griffin Press.
Only wood grown from sustainable regrowth forests is used in
the manufacture of paper found in this book.

Cover design by Nada Backovic
Cover image: lambada / Getty Images and Raftel / Shutterstock
Page design and typesetting by Shaun Jury
Typeset in Bembo

A catalogue entry for this book is available from the
National Library of Australia
    ISBN: 9781760409784 (paperback)
    ISBN: 9781760409791 (ebook)
    ISBN: 9781760409807 (mobi)

🐦 bonnierpubau
📷 bonnierpublishingau
🅕 bonnierpublishingau

Her faint, curv'd smile disturbs me: her long eyes,
Misty with secrets, creep around my heart.

'Merlin', Mary Dean

MELBOURNE, 1999

'FIVE GRAND, THAT'S IT.' I don't touch my wallet. Not yet.

'Nup. I've already sunk that much into this painting – I need more.'

'It's second-rate.'

'It's a David Boyd!'

'It's a crap David Boyd and you know it. Nobody's buying Boyd now anyway. It's all Olsen and Blackman.'

We both stand back and look at the painting again. Children with Ritalin eyes and feverish cheeks in a field of flowers, the whole thing a chunder of colour. But there are plenty of buyers for this sort of thing and business is supposed to be about the client's taste, however abysmal it may be.

'C'mon, five-and-a-half.' Dave is twisting his hands together now. 'I know you'll be able to turn a profit, mate.'

I snort derisively. 'Five-and-a-half ...'

His grizzled mug starts to crack with triumph, but I'm not done.

'... and you throw in the Scheltema.'

Dave's eyes glaze as he does the math. 'Mate.' He stretches both hands toward me.

I shrug and turn away.

'You always were a hard woman, Alex.'

I turn back, the cash already in my hand.

At that moment, an old lady with a scruffy black and tan terrier shuffles around the corner and freezes. She narrows her eyes and her head does that slow up and down thing as she takes in my black Docs, old torn jeans (not 'distressed'), vintage jacket and messy (not 'artfully tousled') hair. It's a look that comes off as trendy around the corner at Prahran Market, even at 8.30 on a Thursday morning in April. But here in the backstreets waving a wad of cash and about to shift goods from Dave's car to mine, it clearly reads as 'dodgy'. The old lady turns and drags her dog back the way they came. Dave and I stand there and watch her retreat before resuming our dealings. It's just another normal day in the office.

People like Dave inhabit the lower circle of the dealer world, a realm in which the First Commandment is, 'Thou shalt deal cash in hand', and the Second is, 'Move stuff fast'. Dave is quite religious on both counts. I'm already calculating how much profit I'll make selling these paintings up the chain to people who will think they're *quite lovely pictures.* People who would be discreetly pumping hand sanitiser and questioning the authenticity of the artwork if they were approached directly by Dave. A lot of my dealings with Dave and his compatriots happen in this neighbourhood because it's handy to a number of auction houses, such as Joel's, Christie's, Sotheby's and, of course, Lane & Co.

'Catch ya next time mate.' Dave drops an arm out of the driver's window in farewell then peels out, his car coughing and spluttering like an emphysemic Collingwood supporter whose team just went down at the final siren. I turn to my car and take a moment to wrap the two paintings in a blanket before returning them to the boot. Then it's a short drive through the narrow backstreets, lined with workers' cottages and one old corner shop still holding out against the convenience store tsunami. Five minutes later I pull up at Lane & Co. They have a viewing today for next week's fine art auction and I want to get in ahead of the crowd.

I try hard not to get noticed, but I'm barely in the room five minutes before I'm bailed up.

'Alex! Great to see you!' Rob has an auctioneer's honeyed tones, but he also has the volume.

'Rob, how are you?' I inch away from the painting I was really looking at and feign interest in a small McCubbin. 'A few interesting pieces this time.'

'Have you seen the early Smart? Stunning work!'

'Not yet. Where is it?' Any chance to divert attention.

We stroll across the floor of Lane & Co.'s auction room, which at this time of day is relatively empty of other punters. The single, vast space is broken up by a number of tall partitions that divide the room into quiet nooks and corners, while still deftly encouraging movement from one area to the next. The partitions, like the outer walls, are painted an unobtrusive bisque colour and on every vertical surface there are paintings. Some are bathed in spotlights, some tucked more discreetly in shadowed corners, but all represent the hopes of the sellers and the aspirations of the potential purchasers.

'Anything special lately?' Rob picks imaginary lint from his lapel.

'I've picked up a couple of early colonial watercolours, but

I already have a buyer for those. There's a lovely little Clarice Beckett I'm trying to get. If that comes off, it's yours for the next auction.'

Although I can quite easily sell the Beckett myself, it pays to keep the auction houses on side. Besides, I know Rob is also trying to work out what might have caught my eye from among Lane & Co.'s current offering.

We pass a Howard Arkley that transforms a Melbourne brick veneer house into a vibrant kaleidoscope of colour and pattern, turn left at a Streeton of Sydney Harbour gleaming with its own importance, and shuffle to a stop in front of the Jeffrey Smart. It is everything and more. Smart is best known for his freeway interchanges, traffic cones and isolated figures in desolate yet vividly coloured industrial landscapes. This painting predates those by a couple of decades, but you can see the promise of what was to come. The painting is simply titled *Garage*, and the viewer's perspective is from the unlit interior. Darkness dominates the foreground, although the brightly lit facade of a building beckons from beyond the workshop door. Between darkness and light, Smart has placed the hulking shape of a 1950s ute and the figure of a man. Man and car are all black, merely shadow, and somehow possess an air of menace. It's a gem.

I make all the right noises and we chat for a bit. Finally, Rob catches sight of one of his regular big spenders and summarily drops me like yesterday's art darling, managing to do it with all the charm of the consummate salesman. Exhaling, I turn and slowly wend my way back to the only thing I really want to see at Lane & Co. It is the portrait of a woman, Australian school, sitter unknown. But I know those brushstrokes and, more importantly, I have a fair idea who the pretty model was. The painter, Colin Colahan, was a member of an artistic circle known as the Meldrumites. Followers of the dynamic artist

Max Meldrum, they set Melbourne society on its ear in the '20s and '30s.

The painting is filthy and the varnish has discoloured to a nasty yellow, which is probably part of the reason Lane & Co. has failed to recognise the artist. But I can see the jewel tones beneath the dirt, and as I gaze at the lovely young woman with her short dark bob and mischievous brown eyes, I know I am staring into the face of Molly Dean.

I pull the painting off the wall to give it a detailed going over. First I tilt it backwards and forwards, looking at the surface under raking light. With light hitting the canvas surface obliquely, different details and textures show up. I can see more of the brushstroke and artistic technique, but importantly I can check to see if there are any distortions in the canvas or lifting cracks in the paint.

So far, my girl looks okay, and what I am seeing of the technique is still making me think of Colahan.

I pull a portable UV lamp out of my bag, ready to examine the portrait under black light. Sometimes a painting is small enough for me to basically make my own dark room by sticking it and my head under my jumper, but this painting is too large. I flag down one of the auction room grunts. I know her by sight and I'm sure she knows who I am, but I don't want her to dwell too much on the painting in my hand.

'Need to black light. Borrow your cupboard?' I'm already walking toward the broom cupboard that does double duty as a dark room. 'I think that woman by the Charles Blackman wants your help.'

The girl mouths a response but her blonde head swivels away from me immediately. The market for Blackman's work is really starting to heat up, and in a couple of years his paintings will probably be selling for a fortune.

The room's filling up a bit now, but I make it into the cupboard without anyone else noticing, keeping the painting held toward me, obscuring the subject. Tucked away in the cupboard next to a teetering stack of toilet paper, I flick on my UV lamp and kill the overhead light. Lighting up the surface of the painting, I look for dark patches that would suggest it has been touched up or altered in some way. Sometimes that's okay. If the area is small and insignificant, I can let it slide. But if there are vast swathes of overpaint, or if the discrepancy appears in an important area such as the signature or the face of a portrait, it can be a deal-breaker.

Or a deal-maker. You'd be surprised how many times a great work of art has been altered by some well-intentioned (but frequently talentless) person to make it more 'attractive'. Sky not blue enough? Let's fix it! Fancy a little more boob on your Brett Whiteley nude? No problem! Painted by Carrick Fox rather than Phillips Fox? A mere peccadillo! Then tastes change and that artist who was so unfashionable twenty years ago is now red hot. Misattributions, whether through the stupidity of the auction house or because signatures are missing or altered, have been among some of my biggest earners. I once bought a $100,000 landscape for $200 in a country auction because the painting was filthy and the signature was hidden under the frame.

Nothing shows up under UV, so I turn on the overhead light and examine the edges of the painting where it meets the frame. No obvious signature, but a few black spikes near the bottom right give me hope there might be something to find. The back of the painting has little to tell me. No faded auction number, exhibition label or convenient title in the artist's own hand. It sounds too easy, but sometimes it does happen. Most of the back is obscured by old brown paper, slightly tattered but largely intact. The only scrap of information is a timeworn label from a Melbourne framer that reveals precisely nothing. It identifies the company used by every half-decent artist from the 1880s right through into the post-war period.

But that doesn't matter, I've already decided I want this painting. The auction estimate is low – $400–$600 – because the sitter and the artist are unknown. There are some loose rules for valuing portraits: a well-known artist increases the value, a portrait of a woman is worth more than a portrait of a man (unless he's someone very noteworthy), a portrait of a pretty woman is worth more than a regal old dame, and if the identity of the sitter is known, add value.

Lane & Co. think they have a portrait of a pretty but unknown girl by an unknown artist. However, I am planning to buy a portrait by Colin Colahan of a girl who became famous for being the victim in one of Melbourne's most sensational murders; a murder that has never been solved. Her name is Molly Dean.

Monday's auction can't come soon enough.

'John?' I push open the studio door. I'm collecting a couple of minor paintings that had needed a bit of John's conservatorial TLC. One was just a clean up, but the other was a signature reveal. I'd picked up the second painting cheaply because the McCubbin signature was obviously fake and that had scared everyone away.

Strong northern light floods the old church hall, illuminating a myriad of colours. In the corner, a fan conjures a pleasant breeze from nothingness, making the papers on the desktop flutter. The sound of trams and traffic is just a distant hum, overlaid by the chromatic lushness of Debussy pouring from discreet Bose speakers.

From the doorway, it looks as though something near the far wall has exploded or at the very least collapsed, spewing a haphazard mass of canvas and frames across the floor. By luck or design, the artistic avalanche only extends about halfway across the bare boards; this side of the room is holding out against the advancing tide. Closer examination shows that in fact there is a system underlying the apparent chaos. Here a careful stack of nineteenth-century frames, there a serried rank of works in progress, and throughout it all piles of auction catalogues, signposts marking a path to the farthest corner. In the centre of the room stands an empty easel, waiting for the show to begin. I take a deep breath, inhaling the heady mixture of linseed, paint and turpentine and something else: an undefinable melange of scent with top notes of dust and smoke, a heart of genteel decay and a rich base of history.

'Alex!' The voice comes from right behind me.

'Christ! Was that really necessary?' My heart is pounding in my throat. John may be a brilliant conservator, but God he can be a dick.

'You're so inscrutable at the auctions these days, I had to check you're still breathing!' Laughing, he shoulders past me into the room.

'I've told you to crack a window when you're using solvents: you've finally killed off your few remaining brain cells.'

John is razor sharp when it comes to art, but he wears the guise of scatterbrained artistic type like a cloak of invisibility. Even when he talks people into paying him ridiculous amounts of money for his services, they come away thinking it was a bargain.

'Sometimes I think a paint-fume buzz would help me stay

sane when I'm working on all the second-rate shit auction houses give me.'

I can believe that. John is brilliant at what he does and all the big players like to use his services when they can. It's surprising – and depressing – how often they manage to damage paintings consigned for sale.

'Pour us a drink, will you?' John waves in the direction of the fridge as he plunges among the canvases. 'You're gonna be stoked.'

It takes only a moment to pop open a couple of cans of Diet Coke, but John already has a painting on the easel.

'Came up well,' John says, taking the Coke from me.

'For a Buckmaster.' Sometimes it pains me to handle these sorts of paintings, but there is always money in pretty-but-bland floral still lifes.

John moves to swap the painting, deliberately blocking my view of the easel. 'Forget Bucky. This makes up for the abundance of tat you drop at my door.'

He steps aside and a lovely country scene clamours for my attention. The not-McCubbin has benefitted from a good clean and John has also favoured it with a Thallon frame that embraces the canvas like a long-lost lover. What was two figures in a landscape is now a pair of school children in a paddock filled with golden gorse. They're confronted by a small creek and clearly debating the wisdom of their chosen path.

'Bugger me. Better than I thought.' Then I am across the room, peering at the lower left corner of the canvas. My shoulders melt. John has revealed the true signature: J. Sutherland. I turn to look at him. His shit-eating grin mirrors my own.

'Nice find, a Jane Sutherland.'

Jane Sutherland is an artist linked to Fred McCubbin's circle but until recently ignored by art buyers because *obviously* girls

9

can't paint as well as boys. Happily, since a couple of important exhibitions and publications in the late '80s and early '90s, early Australian women artists have been 'rediscovered'.

'It's only a small landscape but it should be worth, what? Fifteen grand? Maybe twenty if I can pin down some details?'

John nods. 'I checked a couple of the old catalogues just in case, but your library is better. Never been on the market though – at least not as a Sutherland.'

This sort of research is a big part of what I do. Not just filling in the background history of paintings, but also doing the reverse: tracking down important pieces that have fallen off the face of the earth. My personal reference library is the key, and it's taken me years to build it up to what it is now. I have shelves of art books of course, but it's the stacks of old auction records, files of clippings and extensive collection of original exhibition catalogues from as far back as the 1880s that give me an advantage.

'I'll get on it this afternoon.' I'm feeling jazzed by my success, but I put it aside because, right now, I need John's memory. 'Have you ever heard of a Colin Colahan portrait of Molly Dean?'

John narrows his eyes, partly because he's running through his mental database and partly because he knows me. 'Other than the nude?'

'Uh-huh.'

'Don't think so.' John's memory for art is phenomenal. Plus he sees a lot of paintings that never appear on the open market. 'You got one?'

'Not yet, but I think Lane's do – lot 186, Australian school.'

He reaches for his catalogue and flips pages. Grunts. 'Could be Colahan. Hard to tell from this picture.'

'Luckily for me they've also hung it incredibly badly, but when you see it in the flesh, it's right.'

Each week I spend a lot of time trawling the catalogues. Not just for Melbourne, but for interstate and even overseas auctions. If there's anything that sparks my interest, I always try to get to the viewing, even if it means hopping on a plane to Sydney or driving down to a quiet country auction in the Western District. It's necessary if I want to find sleepers – unrecognised or underappreciated paintings I can buy cheap and turn over for a nice profit – and I need to do it all myself. It didn't take me more than one or two stuff-ups to realise I should never trust anyone's opinion but my own.

Auction houses partly bankroll their executive retirement funds by employing graduates fresh out of uni, a lot of them blonde with names like Phoebe and Sybilla. Even though there may be someone with the exalted title 'Head of Fine Art', the grunt work of cataloguing the paintings is done by kids with virtually no hands-on art experience and minimal knowledge of artists beyond a dozen or so internationally famous names. These juniors may have degrees, but I'm sure they'd scrunch up their noses and say, 'Freud? Isn't he that shrink guy?' So I never trust their written descriptions. In addition, you can never tell the condition of a painting from a small image in the catalogue. Colours may be distorted or – ahem – enhanced, repairs, flaking paint and overpainting can be hard to spot, and don't get me started on dodgy signatures.

So far, 'my' painting ticks every box on the list of how not to catalogue an artwork for auction.

John tosses the catalogue aside. 'So why do you think it's Molly Dean?'

I shrug.

John nods.

I make my living – hopefully – by knowing more than everyone else about art and artists. John knows I'm playing a hunch, but the current validation of my gut feeling and professional eye is sitting on his easel in a Thallon frame.

'What's the plan? That bastard Rob will be taking bids from the chandelier if he knows you're interested.'

'Are you suggesting he'd deliberately fake bids just to raise the price on me?' I open my eyes wide.

'Mate, half the room will do that if they think you're on to something.'

'Usual plan,' I say. 'Fly below the radar, stand at the back where I can't be easily seen, low ball bids on a couple of other lots, then wait till the last possible second on this one.'

John tilts his Coke can in my direction. 'When you have her, bring her here.'

With the paintings stowed safely in the back seat, I point the Citroën toward Glen Huntly and home. I turn on the radio, twiddling the knob until I find a Bach keyboard concerto, and for a few minutes I'm lost in the exquisite symmetry of the music. The piece finishes and is replaced by something more orchestral, but I stop listening. Instead, I get busy mentally mapping out my research. The only thing is, I can't decide whether to start with Jane (a potential slam dunk given I already have the painting) or instead do a bit more work on Molly (the sentimental favourite).

'Molly Dean, where have you been hiding?' I realise I'm talking to myself again and slap the steering wheel, making my palm sting.

I'm weaving through the side streets now, past rows of yuppified Californian bungalows with the odd double-fronted-cream-brick veneer sticking out like a broken tooth in a perfect smile. Cruising the last hundred metres down my street, I know which painting has my attention. Finding out more about Molly Dean now will influence how high I'm prepared to bid for her portrait at auction. The better the story, the more profit I'll potentially make when I sell the painting on. I swing the car into the drive. Grabbing the paintings, I check the letterbox (bill, junk, charity, bill) and head up the rose-flanked path to my little house, thoughts of Molly Dean chasing through my head. I decide not to ask Lane's for any information about the painting: that would only tip my hand. Later on, when she's mine, I can try to find out who put Molly up for sale, but the lack of information in the catalogue tells me she's been tucked away for a very, very long time.

I prop the paintings against a terracotta pot and fiddle with my key in the lock. Hogarth is waiting and as I push the front door open, he immediately plants his paws on my shoulders and pokes his nose into my eye socket. As Irish wolfhound greetings go it's fairly restrained.

'Dude!'

He thumps back to the floor. His tail swings through such a massive arc that it's hitting both walls of the hallway, a steady andante tempo. I scruffle my hands through his charcoal fur. 'Had a quiet day so far, dude?'

He yawns in response then heads for the kitchen and the prospect of a late lunch. Living with a dog that is two metres tall on his hind legs is the only security system I need, and the company is a huge bonus. I retrieve the paintings from the front verandah, stash the Buckmaster in the spare room and hang the Jane Sutherland on a free hook in the lounge. One of the advantages of my work is the constantly changing display of artworks in my home. I always relegate contemporary stuff to a dark corner, otherwise I tend to find myself ranting about *artists today*. But I never rant about collectors with no knowledge and questionable taste; after all, they're some of my biggest clients.

I join Hogarth in the kitchen where he is loitering by the fridge, and after a brief inspection of its contents we settle on raw meat and three veg for him and instant noodles for me. Twenty minutes later, lunch is done and I'm in the study with chocolate and a mug of tea. The study is dominated by a French Gothic Revival desk, all dark oak, ornate carved edges and green leather top. The only things occupying space on its surface are the phone and a Mac PowerBook, looking surprisingly at home. I flip the computer open and while it's waking up, scan my library. Bookshelves line two full walls and run under the window. I have a couple of books that might mention Molly – a biography of Colin Colahan and a volume on the Meldrumites – but I don't expect they'll hold any significant information. Still, I pull them from the shelf and set them on the corner of my desk for later before grabbing my folder of notes and clippings on Colahan.

The first thing I need to do is to confirm I'm right and the subject of the portrait is Molly Dean. In my Colahan file I have a picture of Molly clipped from a 1930 copy of *The Argus*. It's an unflattering likeness, the sort of picture you'd expect to see on someone's driver's licence these days. At once doughy and stunned, as if she'd just woken up and can't understand why her picture is being taken. But the pleasant features are clear, and glancing between the catalogue entry and my clipping it's obvious I have the right girl.

Next I check through my collection of Colahan's exhibition catalogues. The early twentieth century was a dynamic time in Australian art and there were plenty of exhibitions. Luckily they were mostly small, so catalogues were rarely more than six pages. I also have a head start here, because I know roughly when Molly and Colin first crossed paths and I know when Colin left Australia, never to return. My window is 1929 to 1935 and I hit pay dirt in 1930. For thirteen days, Colin

Colahan was exhibiting at the Athenaeum Gallery and tucked in the catalogue, among *Scherzo in Yellow and Red* and *Suburban Arabesque* was number twelve, *Molly Dean*. Unlike the other works on offer, there is no price listed next to this painting. Instead, an asterisk and the tantalising footnote, 'enquire at desk'. Clearly, Molly was not for sale to just anyone.

I check the auction records for Colahan paintings in the latest copy of *Art Sales Digest*, but come up negative, so it seems the portrait has stayed with the same buyer or their family since about 1930. In the art business we often say paintings are sold for three reasons: death, divorce or debt. I figure that after nearly seventy years, the original buyer must be dead, which means an executor is behind the sale or a descendant needs money. Either way it works for me, because they don't know what they're selling. The reserve price will be low or non-existent.

'Thank you.' I'm not addressing anyone in particular, but from his jumbo dog bed in the corner Hogarth thumps his tail once.

It's nice to know my talent for remembering paintings also extends to faces. Molly Dean was attractive, but ordinarily she would not have been particularly memorable. She was only in my files at all because of her association with Colahan. But for a few months from 21 November 1930, Australian newspapers bristled with shock as they dutifully reported as much sensational detail and horrified speculation about her death as they could possibly manage.

Pulling the Mac closer, I connect to the State Library of Victoria's website to figure out which newspapers I'll need to look at. I'm assuming the details will largely remain unchanged from paper to paper, but publications like the *Truth* will have a decidedly more melodramatic spin on things. It's too late to go to the library, so I make a list of things to do tomorrow. Just as I'm finishing up with my notes, a large wolfhound head pushes under my arm and flips my hand from the desk. Hogarth has decreed that work is over and it's walk time.

An hour later, we've done several off-the-leash laps of the park, Hogarth has exchanged a few doggy greetings and I've made a decision. If I manage to buy the painting, I'll hang on to it long enough to try to uncover more of the story of Molly's murder. Holding on to a work for a while is not as drastic as it sounds. When a painting is put up in one of the bigger auctions, the world knows it's on the market and later, it's easy to find out if it was passed in or knocked down, and, if it sold, how much the buyer paid. When I buy a painting at auction, it has to fall into one of these categories:

1. I already have a client in mind who will pay more.
2. It has been wrongly attributed and I can buy it cheaply, do some research and immediately sell it for a higher price with the correct artistic details.
3. I'm prepared to keep it until the artist comes back into fashion. Could be years, so the potential pay-off has to be worth it.
4. The auction is off the main radar – a small auction house or a country sale – and I can sell the painting quickly, fresh to the city market.

Otherwise, if a painting goes through a more mainstream sale and turns up again too soon, it's burned. Everyone assumes there's something hideously wrong with it and if it sells again, it will only be for a fraction of its true value.

As far as the portrait of Molly is concerned, it's currently unattributed and once I positively identify her and the artist, the juicy story of her death will mean a better selling price.

The next logical step is to get to the State Library, read the newspaper accounts of the murder, then request the original coroner's report from the archives of the Public Records Office.

Until now, all I've really known is that Mary 'Molly' Dean's murder shocked Melbourne and had such a traumatic effect on Colahan that he ultimately left the country. Cynic that I am, I'd always felt his move had more to do with selling more paintings than soothing his delicate artistic soul, but who am I to judge? It can't be easy to pick up the pieces once the papers have forever linked your name with such a horrible crime and splashed your photo over the front page for good measure.

Back at home, Hogarth settles on the dog bed and I crack open the books dealing with the artist Max Meldrum and his circle to see what, if anything, they had to say about Molly. Skimming through, I decide some scepticism is warranted; the authors' opinions of Molly Dean could not differ more.

The first author, a man, portrays Molly as a naive but ambitious girl trying to find her way in the world as a writer. The second book I pick up is written by a woman who was a part of the 1930s Meldrumite set, and hers is an altogether more scurrilous – and bitchier – read. In this account, Molly was not only sleeping with Colin, but anyone who could further her agenda. It was Molly who persuaded Colin to engineer his own divorce, complete with prostitute, private detective, sleazy hotel, flash photographer and a couple of 'independent' witnesses. Just for good measure, the author quotes another woman in the group who claimed Molly's writing consisted of stealing other people's ideas and passing them off as her own. She wraps up her paragraphs on Molly by bemoaning the young woman's violent death as a great inconvenience, happening as it did just when the artists were about to open an ambitious group show. But then the author gives herself away, stating how she was personally very attracted to Colin Colahan. I can probably believe about 1 per cent of what she says about Molly. Where the guy writes about Molly's dark complexion, she calls it sallow skin. He sees a sultry gaze, she speaks of close-set eyes. Jealousy rolls off the pages in waves.

I make a few notes and mark a couple of passages in the books, then put Molly aside until tomorrow. The Jane Sutherland needs my attention.

Standing up, I put both hands into the small of my back, stretch out the kinks, then survey my shelves. Since John already ruled out any mention of the Sutherland painting going through auction, I head for the relevant bunch of exhibition catalogues.

'Dude, seriously?' Hogarth, naturally, has abandoned the dog bed and sprawled his hairy carcass directly in front of the section I need. I nudge a paw with my toe. He groans. Past experience tells me not to bother, so I brace my feet and let my upper body fall forward to the bookshelves, forming a bridge across the recumbent hound. Grabbing the folders I need, I give a hard shove that returns me to the vertical, miraculously without dropping everything.

'Thanks, you're a great help.'

I realise how gloomy the room has become. The evening has closed in without me noticing and the desk lamp is losing the battle. I decide to move to the dining table, where the light is better and I can spread out a bit more. It's a lovely old table, satiny Huon pine, with a golden honeycomb colour now darkened by a century of summers. The fact that I picked it up cheaply makes it even more attractive.

Opening the first folder, I start to read. Jane Sutherland did not have many solo exhibitions, and it doesn't take long to flip through the catalogues for those. I jot down a couple of titles I'll need to follow up, just in case they relate to my painting, then turn to the group exhibition catalogues. These are not big glossy books full of illustrations and details of everything on show. I wish. Even today, very few selling exhibitions include much beyond the title of the work, medium (oil, watercolour or whatever) and possibly the price, if the gallery is not trying to be too cute and discreet. All I have are listings of titles and prices. The problem is further compounded by the fact that even in the 1890s many artists had a pathological aversion to calling a spade a spade. Just about everything is *Nocturne in Pink and Gold* or *Tranquil Corner*. Sometimes I'd give almost anything for a *Departure of the Orient – Circular Quay* or *Collins Street, Five p.m.* I'm not finding anything useful. Sutherland's signature on the painting is great, but if I can pin down the original title it will be worth at least a couple of grand more.

Shoving that folder aside, I crack open my file on women artists of the Heidelberg School. Each newspaper cutting has the artist's name pencilled lightly across the top, so I quickly discard everything not related to Jane Sutherland. The pile I'm left with is depressingly small. Or pleasantly small, if we're talking about how long this is going to take. Now, rather than titles, I look for descriptions. Anything an art reviewer may have seen at a show or in the artist's studio that they've singled out for praise or derision. The florid journalistic style of the period is to my advantage here, as the writers tend to go into great detail about exactly what they love or loathe about a particular painting.

I strike gold in a clipping from an August 1890 edition of *Table Talk*, a Melbourne weekly that ran until about 1939. With its gossipy style and focus on fashion and the comings and goings of the socially adept, I'm just as likely to find a note on the hat worn by Miss Sutherland as anything about her paintings. But there it is on page twelve:

A very small landscape bearing the suggestive title of 'The Shortest Cut'. Two children, late for school, have left the road to follow a track across a gorse-grown paddock, but to their dismay find their progress stopped by the stream of water which lies in a hollow of the field. The strongest points of the picture are the gorse bushes bursting into bloom and the moist looking condition of the fresh young grass.

I go and get the picture just to be sure. The moist grass is a bit of a stretch, but then again I'm not sure where the writer got all that stuff about late for school from either. I am currently the owner of *The Shortest Cut* by Miss Jane Sutherland.

THE FOLLOWING MORNING I leave the car at home and catch a train to Museum Station. It's been called Melbourne Central for the past two years, but that sounds anodyne so I pretend it's still Museum. I cross Swanston Street and take the front steps two at a time, entering the State Library's foyer.

I'm very fond of the library. I could spend a day dawdling past the art collection, admiring the murals and soaking up the magnificent architecture. But not today. Today I head directly to the newspaper room and the microfiche readers. I've pre-armed myself with paracetamol for the microfiche headache I know will develop, but there's no way to prevent the nausea that comes from watching stuff roll past while I sit still. It's a wonder I've never seen anyone throw up or fall off their chair in here and I'm trying not to be the first.

I start with *The Argus* on the day of Molly's murder, 21 November 1930. She was found just after midnight, so there was plenty of time for the article to make it into that day's paper. For more than three hours I trawl through articles, often with my face inches from the screen as I struggle to decipher poorly scanned newsprint. After *The Argus* I move on to *The Age*, before I head outside to grab a sandwich and wash the paracetamol down with a disappointingly bad macchiato. Back at my microfiche reader, I load up the first spool of *Truth* and read my way through everything I can find there before starting on *The Herald*. With each newspaper I work right through the entire case, from the moment lead investigator Senior Detective Percy Lambell first arrives on the scene to the inquest and then the start of the trial. It's slow work, and I find myself getting distracted by some of the ads sailing past my eyes, fabulous fashions, a hernia truss, Hudson's Eumenthol Jujubes (The Great Antiseptic and Prophylactic! Contains no Cocaine or other Poisonous Drugs!). But ads aside, the more I read of Molly Dean's murder, the more I need to know, and I send the printer into overdrive trying to catch every last bit of information.

I'm getting to grips with the nuts and bolts of the case, but oddly I keep coming across things that make no sense. Even allowing for the journalistic standards of 1930, there are a number of points that come up repeatedly yet still seem too bizarre to be true. Molly's murder is like a B-grade slasher film except for one major detail: no one was ever tried for the crime. In fact, the only suspect had his case thrown out of court before it even began. My interest in Molly Dean's portrait may have started as a way to bump up the value, but this is more of a story than I ever expected.

It's almost five by the time I speed reverse the last spool back to its beginning and dump all the little boxes on the returns trolley. I gather up my stack of printing and my bag and hurry toward the exit. I only have to wait a couple of minutes for a train and I'm still ahead of the after-work crowd. As we roar out of the city loop, I listen to the Morse code double tap of the train on its tracks and wonder what the hell really happened to Molly Dean.

MELBOURNE, 1930

DESPITE THE PRESS OF other passengers, Molly had her notebook out and was writing furiously as the St Kilda train rattled into Flinders Street. As it screeched to a halt and a chorus line of red doors was thrown open, she tucked her pencil behind her ear and scooped up her bag, ready for the dash to her next platform. Her stylish chestnut bob stood out in the sea of homburgs and trilbys, cloches and sun hats, and more than one man turned for a second look as she whisked past, a trail of 4711 cologne and electricity in her wake.

'Molly! Molly!'

A round face popped briefly into Molly's view between the suited shoulders of Melbourne's businessmen, and moments later Sarah Fields pushed her way through to stand next to Molly at the edge of platform five.

'I didn't see you on the train!'

'You wouldn't have seen me if I'd been sitting in front of you. I didn't want to interrupt your writing.' Sarah stared at her for a moment. 'How do you always manage to look so smart?

No matter what time of day it is, you look as though you've just finished modelling at Buckley's!'

Molly struck a pose, pointing the toe of one double-strap pump, showing off her trim suit and patterned scarf. 'Not all of us look like Carole Lombard. You'd look divine if you were wearing hessian. I'm just trying to keep up with the competition.'

There was a surge of people behind them as a train rounded the bend and bore down on the platform. Sarah let out a squeak of surprise and grabbed at Molly, who simply dug in her heels, shot a glance at the wall of suits behind them and loudly stated, 'I know it's supposedly the busiest railway station in the world, but I had no idea it was the rudest.'

A small pocket opened up around them as the train was pulling in, more for the benefit of those getting off than because of Molly's words. Still, they managed to get aboard quickly and find seats for the short trip to North Melbourne. It would have been quicker to change from her earlier train at Spencer Street, but Molly always tried to snatch every free moment she could, and sometimes sitting on a crowded train could feel like a desert island. Molly jotted a few final observations in her notebook and shut it with a satisfied snap. Looking up, she saw Sarah watching her closely.

'You've had news, haven't you?' Sarah said.

Molly pressed her lips together but couldn't contain a broad smile. 'I'm published. Just a poem, but ...'

'Molly, that's wonderful; absolutely splendid!' Sarah bounced in the seat then bumped her shoulder against Molly's. 'Only twenty-five years old and you're already on the way to becoming famous. Show me?'

Molly rummaged briefly in her bag until she found the slim, blue-green journal and passed it to her friend. 'I'm trying to get a few extra copies, but it's only the second number, so they're still not printing very many.'

Sarah studied the cover of *Verse*, smiled when she saw 'Mary Dean' fourth in the list of contributors, then leafed carefully through to page eleven. She smiled again as she read the title, '"Merlin". I love this one.'

'I changed it quite a bit after you read it. Tell me what you think.'

Sarah began to read as the train pulled into Spencer Street. Their carriage exhaled a gaggle of commuters, only to catch its breath and replace them, a conjuring trick that left the casual observer wondering if these were really different people. The train was nearing North Melbourne when Sarah lowered the pamphlet, her eyes wide. 'The ending – you didn't have that before.'

Molly waited as around them people began to edge closer to the doors.

'This bit gave me goosebumps.' Sarah held the page out to Molly, pointing to the lines.

'"My doom is written thus, and now I take/ What might be stay'd for many crowded years./ Death will be a great darkness and a terror/ On my tired soul".' Molly's eyes were shut as she recited. 'I was rather pleased with that.'

They gathered up their things and inched toward the carriage door, Sarah following a chain of handles and hanging straps with her free hand, Molly absorbing the movement of the slowing train through her entire body.

Molly and Sarah stepped from the carriage and made their way out of the station. There was still plenty of time before the first bell, and as they made their way down Union Street to the dour brick school on the Queensberry Street corner, Sarah peppered Molly with questions about the poem, the journal, and in particular the rather dashing (so she'd heard) composer and editor of *Verse*, Louis Lavater. Sadly, Molly had only corresponded with Lavater so had nothing to say about his looks or charm, or whether he lived up to his reputation.

As they reached the school gate, Sarah put out a hand and stopped Molly. 'Let's celebrate at least. Let me treat you to Luna Park on Saturday night. We'll have a laugh – go on!'

'Luna Park?'

'Trust me. The weather has been lovely for September. I promise you it will be fun and if you absolutely hate it we'll have a milkshake and go for a walk instead.'

'I can't. I'm spending this weekend at Colin's.'

'The following Saturday then? Go on!'

'Why not? Thanks, Sarah. I think you're possibly the only person in Australia who could convince me, so Luna Park it shall be.'

The girls parted, heading to their respective classrooms to start chalking up new lessons. Soon, the discordant strains of 'God Save the King' could be heard reverberating off the brick-walled courtyard, heralding the start of the day.

FINALLY IT WAS FRIDAY night, and after an interminably long week with her class at the State Opportunity School in Queensberry Street, Molly hurried home, eager to shed her Miss Dean persona. Much as she loved the children, much as she felt a thrill of triumph when one of her more challenged students had a breakthrough, Molly was becoming more and more convinced that every moment spent in a classroom was a moment lost from her true path. This weekend – tonight – she would have a chance to be her true self. Molly Dean, the writer: creative, vibrant, witty. A star in the ascent.

She expected the regular crowd would be at Colin's for dinner tonight, which meant the usual combination of brilliant debate with the men and an icy wall of indifference from the women. Fortunately, Molly was largely immune to the snideness of her own sex. She knew men liked her precocity just as much as women hated her for it, but she preferred the company of men. Regardless, Molly could dress for the evening entirely to please herself, and she knew just the thing.

On the small verandah Molly paused before putting her key

in the lock. The semi-detached house with its smart red bricks and white trim looked pleasant enough from the street, but Molly tensed every time she opened the door. In her bedroom, she pulled a small case from the top of the wardrobe, ready to receive the few things she'd take for the weekend. She tucked shoes and underclothes into the bottom, added a thin wrap in case the evenings turned chilly, then pulled open the wardrobe door. Apart from a couple of plain day skirts and simple blouses, Molly was greeted by a row of empty wooden hangers, gently clacking together. She stared for a moment then spun around. A shape filled the doorway, a dark shadow that stepped forward and became her mother, arms folded, lips pinched.

'What have you done, Mother?'

'I've warned you about the company you keep, Mary.' Ethel Dean's words uncoiled like a snake. 'You're fooling no one but yourself. I know exactly how debauched and sordid your artist friends are, and it's high time you stopped behaving like a hussy. You'll not be going anywhere.'

'How ridiculous. You can't stop me from associating with my friends. They're creative and imaginative enough to understand me and my writing. Unlike you. You have all the artistry of, of… a dead fish.'

'I'm not prepared to watch you throw away a perfectly good job for some ridiculous fancy. Besides, if you carry on like this, no man will look at you, let alone want to marry you.'

Molly turned white. 'That's enough.' She spoke softly, emphasising every word as she struggled for control. 'Give me my clothes, *please*, or I shall find them myself.'

Ethel Dean took a menacing step toward her daughter. 'You'll do no such thing, my girl.'

Molly dropped her gaze and slumped in defeat, then as her mother relaxed she lunged to the right, managing to get past and through the door, feeling rather than seeing the grab for her mercifully short hair. She headed straight for the kitchen. One thing about her mother, she was entirely without originality. Molly yanked open the door of the pantry. Sure enough, her clothes were wadded up behind the canisters. She pulled them out and began to shake the dresses. Nothing seemed to have sustained more damage than a few creases, but the situation with her mother was clearly getting worse and it was wearing her down. She couldn't live with this constant state of tension, waiting to break her mother's next unwritten rule.

Molly hurried back to her room, fully expecting her mother to step in front of her at any moment, but for now it seemed she had won. She didn't want to linger, and it took only a minute to throw some of the clothes she held into the case and snap the latch. Everything else she left on the bed. Getting out was the only thing that mattered right now. Molly snatched up her red beret and clamped it onto her head, then took a final look around the room, wishing it could be for the last time, knowing there would be weeks, perhaps months, before she could leave Milton Street for good. On the threshold, case in one hand, Molly paused and plunged her free hand deep into her shoulder bag. Her notebook was there, as it always was, but she needed the reassurance of touch. It was only a school exercise book, its cardboard cover softened from use, but it held the key to her future. It contained everything from random ideas to complete poems, drafts for magazine articles (yet to be submitted) and the rough outline for a novel (yet to be written). Molly's notebook went everywhere with her. It was not just a matter of being able to jot things down as they occurred to her, it was also a case of keeping it safe from her mother. There was no doubt in Molly's mind that the interval between discovery of the notebook by her mother and it being consigned to flames in the belly of the kitchen stove would be very, very brief. It wouldn't be the first time.

Quietly, Molly made her way through the abnormally still house. When sun streamed through the leadlight panels of the front door, the plain carpet runner turned into a brilliant Turkish rug awash with crimson and blue. But now the narrow hall was full of shadows. She eased the door open and stepped out onto the verandah. The gate would creak, but by then she'd be on the street, and if there was one thing her mother tried to avoid, it was creating a scene in view of the neighbours. Mrs Goldstein in number 88 was always on the lookout. Small wonder; the arguments in the Dean house were frequently loud enough.

As Molly stepped out into Milton Street, she finally let herself relax and took a deep breath, filling her lungs with the salty tang of the ocean. The weekend was ahead of her and it would be good, no – marvellous. She'd have time to write, the company would be invigorating and of course there was Colin. Molly was too astute to believe he reserved his Irish charm exclusively for her, but for the moment they were a good fit. And for the next two days, Colin was hers. Thinking of him, the corners of her mouth teased their way into the beginning of a smile and her pace quickened. She didn't see the man who stepped out of the gateway moments after she'd passed. Didn't notice the hat pulled low or the coat, too heavy for a mild afternoon. Didn't realise she was being followed.

1999

THE AUCTION WAS DUE to start at 6.30 p.m., so I've timed my arrival for 6.45. The idea is that I look as if I don't care too much and, with a bit of luck, less of the competition will realise I'm even there – until it's too late. Two of the sharper heads in the room still swivel in my direction. The first belongs to dealer and bon vivant, Damien Savage (Savage Galleries, Sydney and Melbourne) perhaps best known for telling a journalist that anyone with less than half a mil to spend was a waste of his time. He jerks his chin in my direction. I incline my head in response. Damien probably isn't interested in the same lots, but with his deep pockets he may decide to bid if he clocks my interest, just on spec. Or to be an arsehole; it can be hard to tell with Damien.

The other person who notices my arrival I immediately discount as a rival; I can tell you now which lots he'll bid on. The brother of a famous Australian actor, he operates as his sibling's agent, only ever buying specific artists, but always prepared to pay top dollar. We nod politely.

The room has been completely transformed since last

week's viewing. Gone are the partitions and all of the paintings, except for a few works – too big to cart around easily – left on the perimeter walls. The lighting has already been dimmed. Spotlights focus on Rob's podium, the Lane & Co. logo behind him, and on a curtained corner to one side, where the canvas stars of the show will appear.

It's a good crowd, following a variety of dress codes from very casual to night-at-the-opera formal. The better dressed also seem to be the ones most likely to be clutching complimentary glasses of wine and champagne, while the shabbier among us know there is a very good reason auction houses try to get the bidders slightly pissed. I've only been here a minute and already the room feels too warm (another salesroom gambit) and the air is cloying with the mingled perfume and cologne of this expectant horde. I need to get into position.

Murmuring the occasional 'sorry' and 'excuse me', I ease my way around the edge of the room to one of my preferred spots. Standing at the back partly hidden by a pillar, I am less visible to the majority of the punters but easily seen by the auctioneer or one of his spotters when it matters.

Rob's opening spiel is just winding down. '... the fall of the hammer is final, although in the event of dispute, the auctioneer may reopen bidding.'

Translation: if they miss someone's waving paddle – someone they think is loaded, mind you – they can pick up the bidding again even if Rob has already sold the painting to another party.

The crowd shifts impatiently.

'And so, ladies and gentlemen, without further ado,' Rob has already been banging on for fifteen minutes, 'let me draw your attention to lot 1.' As he says this, the black curtain is pulled aside by an unseen hand and two gloved porters step through, thrusting the first canvas into the spotlight. A few heads crane, people keen to remind themselves what they'll potentially be blowing their money on. This is a Eugene von Guérard, a colonial landscape that speaks of wilderness and isolation; insignificant humans poised on the edge of an escarpment, dense forest as far as the eye can see.

Rob is waxing lyrical about the painting, but I drown out the rest of his patter and focus on the room, trying to scope out who is here, who has money. I see a grey cowboy hat bob through the door and ease back behind the pillar. One of my competitors is here.

The next couple of hours pass slowly. Rob runs at about sixty lots an hour, which is not bad, but the sale of a couple of paintings is drawn out by duelling bidders who hesitate, demur, murmur to their respective spouses, then dive in again. Still, the leisurely pace gives me a feel for the room and the rhythm of the auction. Phone and absentee bidders remain an unknown quantity, and one of the nouveau riche in the front rows could take an inexplicable liking to something I want, but otherwise I have the measure of the room. I also manage to discreetly slip my card to a disappointed *Ab Fab* type, all bleached-blonde hair and tottering heels, who'd underbid on a David Boyd.

We are now twenty lots away from Molly Dean and the first of my dummy lots is up next. If I get this at the right price, I can still make a good profit and if anyone notices it's me who's bidding, they'll hopefully stop wondering what else I'm after.

'Lot 167.' Rob casts his standard admiring glance at the painting held aloft by an aproned porter. 'Herbert Badham, *Bathers*. Dated 1934. Rare to the market and a lot of interest in this lovely Modernist work. I have some phone bidders ...' He looks to his right where five of Lane's bevy of grad. girls are lined up behind a table, phones pressed to their ears. Two of them nod in response to his unformed question. Rob returns his focus to the room and switches on, inviting his audience to come along for the ride, forget about how much they can afford, and think only of how much they want. Want this painting, want to win, and secretly, want to burst someone else's bubble.

'Shall we start the bidding at, say, twenty thousand?'

The room is silent, except for the murmuring of the two phone workers, breathily relaying information to their punters.

'I should be seeing dozens of hands at twenty, but all right then, fifteen.'

A few people shuffle their catalogues. One of the phones stiffens, half raises her hand, then shoots it all the way up. 'Sir.' Someone clearly can't control themselves.

'I have fifteen thousand! Twenty?' A paddle flicks above heads down in the front row. 'Thank you, madam. Twenty-five!' One of the spotters has alerted Rob to a second paddle over the other side of the room. 'Twenty-five against you, madam, and against you on the phone.' Rob looks at the girls taking calls. The one with the opening bid is clearly coaxing and cajoling, the other shakes her head. Her client has already called it a night.

'Thirty!' Madam down the front is back in.

'Thirty-two?' Other side of the room, trying to slow things down. Rob allows it with a gracious nod and pivots back to madam. 'Same privilege to you. Thirty-five?'

The lady quickly acquiesces with a flutter of her paddle. Meanwhile, if the girl's twitchy hand movements are anything to go by, her phone bidder is trying to jump in but has been sidelined by the fast battle between the two room bidders. Now she hesitates, listening hard to her phone as Rob takes the measure of his bidders.

I ease a little further out of my niche.

'The bid is with the lady at thirty-five thousand dollars!' Rob looks at his telephone acolyte. She slashes a hand across her throat. He turns to his current underbidder. 'Are you sure sir? Shame to lose it for just … one … bid.' He cocks his head. Someone in the crowd titters. 'No? Not likely to find another Badham of this quality easily …' His silky tones sing a siren song, but the man reluctantly shakes his head. Rob squares up behind his podium, ready for the finale.

I cock my elbow, raise a finger.

Rob's money-seeking eyes lock on me like lasers. 'Forty! New bidder!'

Heads turn as people crane to see who has jumped in, but I'm slouched against the wall, leafing through my catalogue.

'Madam?' Rob has already played the crowd for laughs on this one and he's ready to wrap it up and move on. 'Any further bids? Sold!' His smacks a small gavel onto the podium, makes a note of the buyer on the sheet in front of him. Normally, buyers need to hold up their bidding numbers at this point, but I am a known quantity.

While I wait for my next lot to come up, I do a few mental sums. Forty – plus a buyer's premium of 15 per cent – may seem like a truckload of cash, but this is only a mid-level work. More importantly for me, Badham *is* rare to the market and the last one sold over a year ago for $170,000. I'll live with Herbert on the wall for a few weeks then flip him to a private buyer in Sydney. Sydney buyers are very parochial when it comes to paintings and this is not just a beach scene, it's a distinctive Sydney rock pool. Deep golds and umbers, a steel-blue sea, stylised, angular figures all combine to create the impression of still air, baking heat.

I've been keeping up with the auction, noting the prices in my catalogue as lots are sold. You never know when that sort of info will come in handy. Now my next lot is up, a popping Margaret Preston oil. It's everything you want in a Preston painting: exploding with colour, dynamic brushstrokes, and the nod to Japonisme that is the hallmark of some of her best work.

Margaret's stuff has become very popular in the last twelve months and, as I expect, multiple bidders in the room, on four phones, and on the books, quickly push the price up. I throw in a few highly visible bids. It's already more than I'd spend so I don't really want to be the winning bidder, but the opposition is so fierce, I can cast a smoke screen safe in the knowledge I will not be the one stuck with a ridiculously overpriced – but sensational – still life of riotous Australian native flowers. Slowly, the bidders drop out. One by one they falter. By the time only two are left, the price is already $30,000 above the reserve and, to me, at least twenty-five grand above the current market for Margaret. They keep at it, leapfrogging each other in a slow race to the finish. The tension in the room rises with the price, compounded by the fact that one of the bidders is on the phone. Every time the room bidder makes a move, a frisson of anticipation ripples through the crowd as everyone waits to see if the girl murmuring so importantly into her phone will nod her head, wave her hand. It's like the crowd at Wimbledon: hushed, with heads flicking back and forth, back and forth.

She nods. The figures jump: $72,000. The crowd sighs and seems to lean collectively toward the place where the room bidder sits. Rob rests his forearms on the podium, focuses on his target and conjures up a sympathetic half-smile. The rest of us cease to exist as he locks in. 'Oh dear.' He is tweaking the line, making sure he has firmly hooked his catch. 'That was an awfully long time before they decided to bid. I thought you had it there. What do you think? One more? Just one thousand? Or maybe show 'em you mean business and go for a knock-out bid – seventy-five?' Rob seems to lean even further over the audience. 'You've come this far.' One hand curls up from the podium, each finger unfurling in turn until they point to the bidder, palm up. It is a subtle yet powerful gesture: come with me, I'll help you over the last hurdle. A

THE PORTRAIT OF MOLLY DEAN

paddle flicks. Rob straightens, all business. 'Seventy-five?' He gets confirmation. 'Seventy-five thousand, against you on the phone. Fair warning! Are you all finished? All done? Selling at seventy-five thousand in the room. Once, twice, three times.' He hovers his gavel hand above the podium for an extra few seconds, seconds that must feel like an eternity to the buyer. Cracks it down. 'Sold! Congratulations to buyer number … one-five-nine.'

A smattering of applause breaks out, part release of tension, part admiration. Whether the admiration is for the buyer and his fat chequebook, or for Rob and his ability to beguile, well, I know which performance I'm clapping. Then Margaret is whisked away and forgotten, and we all refocus our acquisitive eyes on the next lot.

We're only two lots away from Molly now and I scan the row of phone bid girls. How many are on a call? Usually the house calls a phone bidder a couple of lots before time, making sure they have the connection and the auction can keep its momentum up. Three girls are actively bidding on the current lot, one is shuffling paper, and one has her phone held slightly away from her ear. She is letting her party listen to the action, so whoever it is, they're hanging on for one of the next few lots.

One lot to go. This is the tail end of the auction, works by lesser artists (or utter crap by famous names), and the room has emptied out a bit. People scuttle or stride out, their gait depending both on their success and on their level of courtesy. The polite make an apologetic escape in the suspended moment between lots, the arrogant bulldoze a path whenever, careless of the bidding, of the auctioneer's sight lines. At the same time as this egress, many of those who had been standing move into the vacated seats, exposing the few of us still adhered to the perimeter, barnacles when the tide rushes out. A second staffer is now on the phone, whispering nothings. 'Can you hear the

37

auctioneer? I'll relay the bids to you. Yes, yes. I'll tell you when the bid is with you.'

Suddenly, Molly is here. The warmth of the spotlight flatters her, and there are a couple of soft sounds of surprise from the otherwise wearying crowd. Badly hung as this painting was at the viewing, some are only noticing her for the first time. In the catalogue, her anonymity remains. No last-minute salesroom notice to indicate that artist or sitter has been recognised.

I want this painting. I'm actually surprised how much. Normally, no matter how much an artist or subject hits my personal connoisseur's buttons, the pragmatic me breaks it down to minimum possible expenditure versus maximum possible gain.

'Lot 186, Australian School.' Rob's voice is as strong as it was hours ago at the start of the sale, but his enthusiasm has left for the evening. Why waste energy on a cheap painting by no one in particular? 'I have a bid on the books so I'll start at two hundred.'

Both girls' hands go up.

'Three hundred with Amy's bidder, four hundred with Sophie's'. The allocation is arbitrary, and both phone bidders are probably annoyed. One because he was immediately pipped, the other because he's suddenly bid more than he thought.

'Six hundred with me.' He glances at his papers as though to allay any suspicions the absentee bid might be manufactured. Eyeballs the girls. 'Thank you. Seven hundred with Amy. That knocks my absentee bidder out.'

Amy is looking perky and smug, beside her Sophie (presumably) is slouching, a sure sign her punter has pulled the plug. Suddenly one of the other Stepford girls, the paper shuffler, leans forward. She was hidden behind the others, but now I can see that she, like them, has a phone pressed to her ear. She nods frantically at Rob.

'Eight hundred, new bidder.' Rob is languid, care factor zero.

Amy talks, listens, half lifts her hand from the desk, talks again. 'Nine hundred.' It sounds more question that statement. Her client is flagging.

The other phone bidder snaps back, the girl's hand punching the air.

'One thousand,' Rob relays the obvious.

I raise a finger, just a little, as though I'm making a don't-want-to-impose request of a passing waiter. Rob's response is instant, an almost imperceptible straightening of the spine, a bloodhound when the first scent molecules hit those highly specialised receptors.

'One thousand two fifty.' Bidding increments change when you hit a thousand. 'Fifteen hundred.' Again the last-minute phone bidder has struck back. I can see the other two phone bidders are definitely out and without looking at Rob, I nod.

'One seven fifty.'

Chairs creak as the dregs of the crowd sense a stoush. Something interesting is happening, but they don't know why. A couple of people have made me, and the direction of their gaze is a signpost for others. From the corner of my eye I see Damien Savage and another dealer looking my way, but until I see another room bid, they cease to exist.

'Two thousand.' The remaining phone bidder has returned, but slower. Genuine hesitation, a gambit or slow response from the phone girl? I'm still well within my budget for this painting, and in the time it takes to inhale, I decide go on the attack. I look at Rob and hold three fingers in the air.

His eyes open a bit wider. 'Three thousand!'

It's a move that could come straight back and bite me, hard. Not only could the other bidder call my bluff, but I've just made it clear to the entire room, dealers included, that I really want this painting. Every single one of them is now asking themselves, 'What does she know?' and the dealers are also wondering if they trust my knowledge enough to buy it out from under me. But while they're all doing mental gymnastics, Rob is coming down the home straight.

'At three thousand, once.' He's going fast. 'Twice, and three times!' Pausing to look at the girl on the phone, one final moment for her bidder. She is talking, not making eye contact. A quick check of the room, but no one is going to challenge. 'Sold!' No doubt Rob will later claim he knocked it down quickly just for me. He is, after all, one of those men who is brilliant at taking credit where absolutely none is due.

I hang around for a couple more lots, just a bit of final window dressing to suggest I'm not particularly excited about anything, then ease out into the hallway, making my getaway.

Damien Savage is waiting for me. 'What *have* you bought, Alex?'

He doesn't mean the Badham. I keep walking; I hate being buttonholed like this. 'Nothing you'd be interested in. I have a client who likes attractive women.'

He throws back his head and laughs. Bonhomie 101. 'Oh I've got a couple of those sort of collectors, but your girl is wearing far too many clothes to tempt *them*.'

Eeew. File that under things I don't want to think about. I decide there's no harm in playing. The painting is mine, and he'll find out something soon enough. 'It's a Colahan. Like I said, not quite your thing.'

'Ah. Well bought at three thou.' He touches an imaginary hat brim.

'I saw you picked up a couple of impressive works. The early Brack could just about sell itself.'

'True, but I'll get a much, much higher price.'

I fix a smile on my face. We've reached the accounts desk and Damien makes a show of discreetly falling back as I collect my invoice. Given that we each know precisely what the other has bought and how much was paid, I have to wonder if he's taking the piss. My account is less than 10 per cent of the amount he's dropped this evening. It's definitely time to get out of here. I clap the dealer on his Ermenegildo Zegna-clad bicep and head for the door

'Well, I'm off. Good to see you, Damien.' Sketching a wave over my shoulder, I push out into the cool night.

The next morning, I'm back at Lane's first thing with a cheque for last night's purchases. Naturally, the bank will play with the money for a day or so before seeing fit to clear the funds and magic them across to Lane & Co.'s account, but as a trusted client I can collect the paintings immediately. It's only just gone 10 a.m. – basically pre-dawn for most of the art crowd – so there are few of yesterday's buyers here. I quickly sort out the account and move to the collection point. This is essentially the door to the back room where all the lots are kept. Given my marginally elevated status around here, I scorn the idea of hovering in the doorway and step into the cavernous space beyond. Various minions are scampering about between the shelves and racks and it takes a moment before I am spotted. A girl approaches, her blonde hair so laden with product it resists the laws of physics, immobile despite her hurried gait.

'Help you?' Spoken politely enough but accompanied by

a lack of personal space designed to propel me backwards through the door.

'Yes thanks.' I thrust my paperwork forward, forcing her to step back instead. Simple pleasures.

She turns and surveys the entire room from where we are, apparently expecting the location of my paintings to be illuminated by Jesus-like beams of light from above.

I sigh, point. 'I can see the Badham right there.'

Her shoulders quiver and she goes to retrieve the painting, her pointy shoes tapping larghetto across the scarred wooden floor. Handing me the Badham, she disappears in search of my other purchase. I expect she'll dawdle, so I take the opportunity to study the Badham again and figure out what sort of frame I'll put on it. It's currently housed in a hideous, cheap thing from the 1960s, and it's also under glass. Not only is glass unnecessary for most oil paintings, but unless you're prepared to spend a fortune on non-reflective stuff, it's hard to see much more than your own face. I'm picturing this painting in a recreation of a '30s Modernist frame: flat, wide and white. It will look amazing. I don't understand why some people can't appreciate how the right frame completes a painting, while even the most exquisite frame can't save a painting that is inherently crap. Sometimes I buy things just for their frames. When that happens, the painting gets something different (truly bad paintings, I burn) and the frame is added to my stack of spares, waiting for its perfect match.

My deliberations are cut short by the arrival of Molly, safe in the hands of the girl with the hair helmet. A quick look assures me no one has put their foot through the canvas or scratched their watch across the surface (seriously, it happens) and I scrawl my signature across the bottom of her copy of the docket.

'Thanks, hon. Good to see you again!' I have no idea who

she is, but now she'll spend the rest of the day wondering if she just dissed an important client. My work here is done.

Back home, I prop Molly on the mantelpiece and set to work taking the Badham out of its frame. It only takes a few minutes, but instantly the painting looks better, colours previously overwhelmed by the tawdry glitz of the frame now sing in unison with the tones around them.

Molly doesn't need a new frame. Hers is a simple moulding – just a little bit of adornment on the corners and exactly the right shade to enhance the portrait without intruding. As I look at Molly's portrait now, it is even more obvious that this is the frame placed on the painting when it was new. Nothing has changed since *circa* 1930, except for the slow discolouration of the varnish and an accumulation of dust and grime. At least, wherever Molly has been for the past seventy years, no one has been blowing smoke in her face. Paintings are affected by what amounts to passive smoking, and I've handled many works that have come from a smoker's home, the spot above the fireplace or, worse, a men's club. Their yellowed surfaces have to be seen to be believed, although the damage can be easily fixed. Molly needs a light clean, but it won't take John long and I'll confirm that hint of a signature then. Personally, I'm certain of the artist and subject, but I still need to gather the evidence, so when the time comes to sell Molly's portrait, the proof will make her far more attractive to prospective buyers. I flip the painting over.

From my pre-auction inspection, I already know there is nothing much for me here. The paper on the back of the painting is pasted firmly to the stretcher but torn in a couple of places. Papering the back is quite common, serving to keep dust away from the rear of the canvas. In this case, the framer's label still adheres to the lower right corner, but that's it. I'm hoping there might be some more information underneath the paper, but the label is still an important part of the painting's past, so I grab a Mylar sleeve and a craft knife, ready to carefully slice around it, before I'll tuck it away for safe keeping. My knife is poised over the paper when the phone rings, a loud, obnoxious trill. Sighing, I put the knife to one side.

'Alex Clayton.'

'Alex, Rob. Do you have a moment?'

'Sure, what can I do for you, Rob?' I can't think why he'd be calling me the day after the auction. Usually Rob would be busy rounding off a successful sale by continuing to schmooze the biggest spenders when they came to collect their purchases.

'Look, I hate to be even having this discussion, but ...'

I wait him out. Nothing good ever comes from being on the back foot in a conversation with Rob.

'The underbidder last night, the one on your Australian School work.'

'Colin Colahan, actually.'

'Really?' He pauses. 'Well, that's perhaps ... I had a call this morning from the bidder, and he felt – rather strongly, I must say – that he'd not had a proper chance to bid again, and he's a tad ... upset.'

When you're on the phone rather than in the auction room, you have to factor in that you can't see what's going on, and it's sometimes hard to hear the auctioneer. But at the same time, the person fielding your call is also relaying the current bid, telling you if it's with you or against you, and asking if you want to bid again. They also give you a bit of a nudge if things are wrapping up and you've gone quiet. There's a lot going on, but the auctioneer won't wait forever. So basically if you dip out, tough.

'Good thing all that's covered in your Ts and Cs then.' I inject an extra note of sparkle into my voice.

'The thing is, he wants the painting and I said I'd ask if the purchaser – you – if you'd consider allowing him ...' I hear the distinctive clink of ice on glass. This is early in the day for Rob, even for post-auction-celebration drinking. He's still talking, platitudes interspersed with flattery, but I'm wondering why he's so wound up over something that's virtually a weekly occurrence in the auction world.

'Huh?' It takes me a moment to realise the cascade of words has dried up.

'For somewhat more than you paid, of course.'

He wants me to sell the portrait to his other bidder.

'Fastest profit turnaround you've probably ever made!' The polish is slipping from his voice, a wheedling tone creeping in. My silence is making him edgy. 'He's prepared to offer nine thou.'

'Can't Rob, not this time.' Or any other time.

'You already have a buyer? A client?'

'Sorry.'

'Perhaps if you ask them? Or I could?'

'*If* I have a client, and I'm not saying I do, I would not be handing them to you on a platter.'

'Of course, of course. It's just this gentleman is really very keen.'

'Rob, what's really going on?'

'Nothing! You're a dealer, I have someone who wants to buy. I'm doing you a favour.'

'Bullshit. Tell me what this is all about. You and I both know that one of the staff would usually deal with this sort of problem. Why are you so involved? More to the point, why are you so concerned?'

Silence, then the sound of something (no doubt rare

45

and expensive) being generously poured. A heavy sigh, no, a controlled exhalation. Rob is steadying himself. 'This one was really aggressive, Alex, nasty, and not in an I'm-calling-my-lawyer way.'

'What kind of nasty are we talking about then?'

'The dark-alley-know-where-you-live kind.' Typical Rob. Even when he's scared shitless, he can't help injecting a few theatrics into proceedings.

'Come on. It was a phone call from a losing bidder who was pissed off. He was blowing off steam, that's all. And if you're really worried, you've got his name and address, so you can just send the police around.'

'That's the thing. I thought there was a chance it might come to that, but when I checked the buyer details the name was Julian Ashton.'

'I see your point. That does seem rather improbable.' Julian Ashton was an artist and art teacher who taught many famous Australian painters and was the first (officially) to paint en plein air in this country. He died in 1942.

'So I checked the address – 8 Wahroongaa Crescent, Murrumbeena.'

'Ah.' The location of the Boyd family's home and pottery studio between 1913 and 1964. A famous art family and a well-known address. 'No chance the mystery man genuinely lives there, I suppose?'

The hum of the open line is my only answer and, really, who am I kidding? This guy is obviously some kind of nutter and his liberal use of Australian art references in creating his buyer ID is a tribute to the oblivious idiots at Lane's. Someone happily punched those details into a computer without even blinking.

'What about the vendor? Was the sale above board? I mean, your underbidder isn't claiming the painting's a family heirloom sold without his knowledge, is he?' I ask. Sometimes things get nasty when families argue over how to divvy up an estate.

'No, I thought of that. But the painting was consigned for sale by the local Salvos op shop; someone left it outside their door with a bunch of other stuff. The op shop people thought it looked quite good and brought it to us for an opinion.'

'Well then your underbidder has no claim. He's out of luck.' So am I. There's no way I'll ever find out where Molly's portrait has been all these years.

'Alex, please. Can't you sell? Make this … this person go away?'

I consider it. A $6000 profit in less than twenty-four hours has a lot of appeal. Any other painting and I would've agreed ten minutes ago, no questions asked, but I've already done a lot of work here and for some reason I want to see it through with Molly. Besides, I still think Rob isn't giving me the full story. This person is trying to bully me into selling a painting and he's used a fake name and address. At the very least I'd expect to be ripped off.

'I don't want anything to do with this, Rob. It stinks. I know I don't have to remind you not to give out any of my details, dealer or not.' I wait. 'Do I?'

'Sure, no, of course not. You know I'd always get your approval before I told anyone anything, Alex.'

'Of course.' Yeah, right.

1930

MOLLY COULDN'T REMEMBER WHEN she'd first met Colin. Perhaps it was at an exhibition opening or a poetry reading, but more likely she had arrived at a gathering as a friend of a friend and there he was. It didn't really matter, because the moment Molly realised there was something special about Colin was the evening she noticed he wasn't there, and the room was duller without him.

By the time she was standing on the doorstep of Colin's Yarra Grove home, finger on the doorbell, Molly had put aside all the problems of her current life and was solely focused on the weekend ahead. She'd promised herself that tonight she would try to make herself more agreeable to the women, if only to show she was above their pettiness.

The door opened with a flourish.

As usual, Colin Colahan's lean frame seemed to vibrate with an intense energy. His blonde hair was pushed back as though he'd dragged his hands through it a dozen times, and reading glasses dangled drunkenly from the pocket of his jacket. Molly glanced at his hands, speckled with scarlet and green, as he reached out and drew her over the threshold.

'Molly darling, every time I see you wearing that scarf, I think you should wear it more often! The gold tones bring out the fiery flecks in your eyes.' Colin didn't mean to flirt, but what woman, Molly wondered, could resist a man who not only noticed her clothes, hair and perfume, but commented on them in a way that was always complimentary?

'Come in, come in! You're first to arrive, so you can help me get the drinks sorted.' He closed the door behind her. 'Now let me say hello properly.' He lent down and softly, his lips found hers. Colin smoothed his thumb across Molly's cheek and his hand came to rest gently cradling the nape of her neck. Molly breathed in his scent, an exotic mix of cologne and paint, and felt like she had come home.

After a few moments, they eased apart. Colin picked up her discarded case and bag and whisked them away to the bedroom before following Molly through to the lounge, a large room somewhat overfilled with an assortment of comfortable chairs, two sofas and a well-stocked cocktail cabinet and drinks trolley. Everything a group of artists needed. An eclectic mix of paintings adorned the maroon walls, some by Colin, some painted by other members of his circle. Currently the prime spot above the fireplace held a large landscape, a study in light and shade clearly the work of Colin's mentor, Max Meldrum.

'Who's coming tonight, Colin?' Molly fluffed up an already plump cushion and aligned an alabaster ashtray more precisely with the edge of the end table.

Colin stepped forward and folded his arms around her, pulling her in close. 'Just the usual crowd. I know a couple of the women bristle around you, but you mustn't let them upset you. Lena thinks you're lovely, Polly and Alma wouldn't hurt a fly and as for Betty, well ... Let's just say she has a rather large axe to grind and doesn't care who's in the line of fire!'

'You're mixing your metaphors,' she mumbled into his chest.

'Things can't be too worrisome if you're correcting my grammar.' Colin leaned back in the embrace and searched Molly's face. 'No frown lines, Molly darling. I haven't finished your portrait yet. Besides,' he moved his face closer to hers, 'this is just a few hours. We have the whole weekend to ourselves. And I don't plan on painting *all* the time.'

Molly was under no illusions about her relationship with Colin. She knew it was unlikely to lead to anything permanent, but it was certainly enjoyable. There was no doubt in Molly's mind that Colin loved her, it was just his idea of love and relationships was not exactly conventional; after all, he was still legally married to Vi. And as for Mireille Wilkinson, well, everyone except Mireille's husband knew the stories about Colin and Mireille were not just torrid rumours that could be ignored. But Molly was sure that particular dalliance would burn hot and fast. Colin and Molly were close friends and occasional lovers, and it suited her perfectly. Being a wife was not part of Molly Dean's plan; she had a career to build and fully intended to become famous. It was only a matter of time.

Tonight's dinner would likely be tense on occasion, but nothing she hadn't been through before. It never ceased to amaze Molly that, in a supposedly bohemian environment, the women frowned at her refusal to cook, clean and chatter. She felt their disapproving looks when she sat and talked with the men, loudly voicing her opinions, but she tried not to let it bother her. Among the men was where the power lay, so that was where she wanted to be, and her relationship with Colin meant she was accepted without question.

The others began arriving within the hour. Mervyn and

Lena Skipper were first as usual, with Percy Leason and his wife, Belle, pushing through the door behind them. Alma Figuerola and Betty Roland were next, with the artist couple John Farmer and Polly Hurry turning up a few minutes later. Fritz Hart and Norman Lewis were the last to arrive, already engaged in a passionate debate about the role of philosophic thought in operatic libretto. It looked like it was going to be a long but interesting night. Molly had briefly entertained the idea of taking coats and hats as people arrived, but then decided it might make her seem too much like lady of the manor. Instead, she positioned herself near the drinks trolley, gin and tonic in hand, ready to either pour cocktails or make small talk as Colin's friends filtered in.

As was usual, once everyone had a glass of something alcoholic in their hand, the artists sauntered into Colin's studio, keen to see what he was working on and to discuss their own current projects. Lena made a quick check in the kitchen to see what the woman who 'did' for Colin had prepared, then returned to the lounge, where Betty and Mervyn were arguing about whether the script of a stage play such as Betty's *The Touch of Silk* could be altered to suit the format of a talking movie, while Fritz railed against the demise of classical music. Molly, almost engulfed by the deep cushions on the chair she had chosen, sat back and watched as the conversations flew to and fro. It didn't escape her that Lena moved to sit between Mervyn and Betty on the sofa, leaning into her husband and placing a proprietorial hand on his knee. Molly turned her gaze to Norman, who was the recipient of Fritz's diatribe. She could almost see him cogitating, preparing a pithy response for the moment when Fritz must finally pause to sip his drink or, at the very least, breathe.

In this house, with its revolving cast of artists, writers and intellectuals, Molly felt like she belonged. It didn't matter if some of them – Betty in particular, if Molly was honest – didn't like her; in her heart, Molly knew these were her people, her real family. For the most part she had been welcomed into their circle, and she could always hold up her end of a conversation, no matter how esoteric or avant-garde the subject. But she realised that she was still perceived as Colin's friend, the teacher, or, worse still, the girl who wants to be a writer but had so far made only minimal headway. Lost in her own thoughts now, Molly paid scant attention to the people around her as groups formed, broke apart and reformed somewhere else in the Yarra Grove house.

'Molly dear.' Colin planted a casual kiss on the top of her head and Molly blinked as he stepped back and came into focus. They were the only ones in the lounge. 'Where were you? We're ready to eat and neither Lena nor Belle could get a response out of you. Come on.' He held out a hand and pulled her up and out of the chair, then wrapped an arm around her shoulder, steering her toward the dining room and the sound of conversational parry and thrust, interspersed with the clink of cutlery on china. A couple of steps before the door she stopped, forcing Colin to stop with her. 'What? Come on, before John and Merv eat our share.'

'I just ...' Molly hesitated. 'I've just decided something, that's all.'

Colin looked at her, waiting.

'I've always enjoyed teaching, but it's simply not the same anymore. It's not enough. I think the time is right for me to give up the classroom and really make a go of writing.'

Colin frowned and was about to reply when Fritz appeared in the doorway. 'For goodness sake you two! What are you doing out here? Whatever it is, there's plenty of time for it later. Now, we eat.' And he dragged them forward toward the brighter light and waiting diners. Molly wasn't sure if it was her imagination, but in the moment they passed through the door, she thought she caught an odd expression on the face of one of the people seated at the table. When she looked again it was gone, but for an instant she'd felt as though a wave of pure malice had washed over her. She laughed. It was definitely time to put her overactive imagination to better use and start writing. For the rest of the evening, Molly resolved to forget everything that was troubling her and focus on having a good time.

IT WAS WELL PAST noon the next day when Colin and Molly finally emerged from the bedroom. For her part, Molly was feeling rather under the weather, and she thought Colin didn't look much better. But he was keen to get on with painting her portrait, so after tea and toast Colin quickly herded her into the studio, setting her back in the pose she had occupied three or four times already over the past few weeks. His brushes were ready and it took him only a few moments to mix up the colours he'd need and adjust the blinds so the light was exactly as he wanted it. Colin gave Molly a smile.

'If you can hold the pose for half an hour or so, I should be far enough along that I can let you go and I'll just crack on.' With that he loaded up his brush, bent his head to the canvas and didn't speak a word for the next hour. Colin looked at her of course, but only with an eye to resolving an artistic conundrum. Molly was acutely aware that she may as well have been the proverbial Grecian urn.

'Tilt your chin a little more toward the right.'

Colin poked his head around the easel to study her again. It was only Molly's second stint as an artist's model, and she was still finding it hard to hold her pose. Focusing on the delicate cornices of the high ceiling, she tried to keep her brain busy.

'Don't look up! Just straight ahead. Hang on.' Dropping his palette with a clatter, Colin strode across to the wide north windows and adjusted the muslin, immediately softening the light. With a grunt of satisfaction, he got back to work.

'I rather thought, with all the women you paint, you'd be able to dash this off in no time at all.' Molly arched an eyebrow.

'Relax your face.' Colin added a minute dab of paint to the portrait. 'You my dear, are different from the usual sort of women who sit for me, and it is your otherness that I am determined to lay down in paint.' He paused to stare at the canvas. 'Tonalism is perfect to capture your energy. The soft blurring of line and colour suggest perpetual motion – and you're virtually never still. I've got your gorgeous eyes sparkling from the depths of the canvas, but what I really want to capture,' he made another gentle stroke, 'is what's in your heart. All that hunger and yearning and … and … drive. And I'm not there yet.'

Molly sat silent and still, staring at the back of the easel. 'Speaking of yearning, I've been thinking …' she began.

'Mmmm.' Colin had a spare paintbrush in his mouth.

'Teaching is all very well, and the children at the Opportunity School all try so very hard …'

Colin let the silence stretch. He stepped back from the canvas, squinted and then lunged forward again, his brush like a sword, attacking the subject.

'I know if I buckle back down to teaching, they'll offer me a promotion soon.'

'Mmmm.' He altered his inflection to convey enthusiasm.

'But as I was trying to tell you last night, I think now is the time for me to chuck teaching in and really push on with my writing and journalism.'

There was silence again, broken only by the soft whisk of bristles on canvas. Finally, Colin took the brush from his mouth.

'Molly darling, that's a huge step.'

'But I've had a few things published now!'

'I know, and they're brilliant. But a few articles and one poem in a tiny subscription pamphlet is still a long way from making headlines at *The Argus*.' He began to wipe his brushes. Molly had long since abandoned her pose, and it was clear they'd get no more done today. 'You should keep up the teaching while you work on the writing. It would be madness to throw away a solid career – and source of income – on a whim!'

Molly froze then slowly turned to stare at him. The temperature in the room seemed to drop a couple of degrees. Abandoning his defensive position behind the canvas, Colin opened his arms and strode across the room, enveloping Molly in a hug. She stood immobile and tense in his embrace.

'What I mean is,' he rubbed his hands across her back, 'we need a plan for you. Otherwise you'll only be offered kitchen tips or writing up society news for *Table Talk*.'

Molly's felt herself soften. 'All I want to do is write. Every day. Just like you get to paint every day.'

'And you will, darling girl, you will. But one step at a time, okay?'

They sat together on the chaise as the light slowly faded from the studio, the shadows lengthening across the paint-splattered floorboards and creeping into corners, forming pools of night.

Finally, Molly stirred and nodded toward the easel. 'Show me then.'

Colin pressed a hand to his high forehead and smoothed back his hair. It was a fairly innocuous gesture, but one that

Molly knew was a sign of anxiety. 'I haven't got the shape of your hands quite right yet,' he said.

'Don't worry! I know it's not finished!' She held out her hand and pulled him to his feet. 'Besides, after the last painting you did of me, what could possibly shock me?'

Colin laughed. 'Virtually no one knows you were the model for *Sleep*.'

'Good. It may be a highly praised and quite brilliant painting, but I can't flout the rules like one of your artist or actor friends. Why, I'm apparently already risking my reputation as a teacher by associating with the bohemian set! If anyone knew I'd posed nude ...'

Colin stood back as Molly moved behind the easel, and she knew he was watching to gauge her initial reaction to the portrait. Unsure of what she would see, Molly prepared to arrange her features into something conveying warm appreciation. But there was no need. What she beheld made her eyes widen and her lips slowly part, softening her entire face into an expression of both delight and admiration.

'I don't look like that.' Molly glanced quickly between Colin and the painting.

'I told you it's not finished yet.'

'No, I mean ... You made me look ... You've been rather kind, haven't you? Artistic licence?'

'Oh Molly, no. You're incredible! Beautiful and smart, and I've just tried to catch it all and put it there in your face, where I see it all the time.'

Molly pressed her lips together.

'I promise you, this is what the world sees.' Colin went and stood behind Molly and together they looked at her portrait. 'They see the amazing, stunning, clever, funny Molly Dean at the start of her career!'

Molly leaned back into him and he rested his chin on her

head. 'I hope the world is interested in Molly Dean and her career as an author and not as a boring school teacher who was lucky enough to sit for a famous artist.'

'You'll get there darling, you just need to be patient and keep slogging away.' Colin didn't bring up the subject of sticking with her teaching job, but it hung in the air between them. Instead he gave Molly a squeeze and forced a lighter note into his voice. 'I almost forgot, Molly dear. A letter arrived for you today. All very domestic, you receiving post here.'

Molly slapped his shoulder playfully with the back of her hand. 'You know that's only so that my mother doesn't get her clutches on things. Besides, I never realised you saw me as the domestic type.'

'Darling, I can't even begin to imagine you in command of a kitchen. And if you ever brandish a knife, it will be because you're posing as Judith. I'm sure you could think of a suitable candidate for Holofernes.' He gave her a wry smile. 'Letter's on the hall table.'

1999

I DROP THE PHONE into its cradle on the desk and stare at it. Rob's response to the irate underbidder is really worrying: I can't remember ever seeing him with a single hair of his silver quiff out of place over a pissed-off client. I'm sure fake IDs aren't uncommon, they just don't get noticed. After all, if the person on the phone had the winning bid and the account was settled – cash or bank transfer, so the buyer's identity remains hidden from the auction house – there'd be no questions asked. It's still a fair and square purchase. The problem this time is we have an aggressive personality hiding behind a false identity. And why use a fake name to try to buy a painting worth no more than ten grand? It doesn't make sense.

After a few more minutes trying to figure out this person's angle, I decide to give it a rest and focus on digging up more details about Molly Dean's life, other than the fact she was bludgeoned to death in an Elwood laneway. While the newspaper reports contain plenty of detail, I think it's time to go to the Public Records Office and request the coronial and police files relating to Molly's murder. I've never requested this sort of thing before, only old paper files relating to the National Gallery of Victoria's collection and the occasional birth, death, marriage or immigration record for an artist. I grab my bag, laptop and a notebook, but then have to spend five minutes looking for my keys. After locating them in my pocket, I give Hogarth a quick pat. 'I'll try not to be too long, buddy.'

He sighs heavily and fixes me with a sorrowful stare.

'Promise.'

With a groan, Hogarth flops over onto one side as I head out the front door.

The drive into town takes me past Albert Park Lake and around the edge of the city, and for once traffic is flowing smoothly. Twenty minutes later, I pull into a carpark not far from the Public Records reading room. When I shuffle through the revolving door, I find the place half empty, and my footsteps echo strangely on the lino as I make my way to the lift. Several storeys later, I head down an institutional corridor with worn synthetic carpet and fluorescent lights placed slightly too far apart for good illumination. Automatic doors hesitate before parting, and then I step into the reading room. I've missed the deadline for the day's first round of file retrievals, but it doesn't matter because I need to talk to the archivist about exactly which documents I should be requesting. I look around to see if there are any staff members I know and spot a familiar face at the information desk. I can't remember his name, but I do recall his thinning grey hair, RSL tie and bifocals. This guy is how I imagine librarians should be. None of your videos or audiobooks for him, just shelves, stacks and the heady smell of old paper and ink. I start over and once I'm close enough, I can see his name on the precisely aligned badge pinned to the pocket of his tweed jacket.

'Hello, Ian. I don't know if you remember me, it's been a while.' I tuck some stray bits of hair behind my ear.

'Miss Clayton. It has been some time since your last visit, I hope you've been well?' It's not a rhetorical question. He really is an old-fashioned gentleman.

'Oh, yes, fine thanks.' I smile. 'How have you been?'

'I can't complain, although these days the family historians are trying my patience. I hope you've brought me something more interesting than a desperate search for a convict ancestor. He gestures to a chair on my side of the desk and, as I sit down, squares up the notepad in front of him and clicks his pen, ready to go.

'I'm investigating a murder.' I lift a placatory hand before he can interrupt. 'But this one happened in 1930.'

'What documents are you after?' The pen is still hovering in midair and the crease between his eyebrows has deepened.

'Well, anything really. The coroner's report – medical examination and inquest – police files, any court documents, basically whatever we can find, please.'

Ian has been making notes while I talk, and studies his list for a moment. 'The police and coronial records will be here with us, but if there was a criminal trial the documents may be sealed as the case is less than seventy-five years old. There'll be no problem with any of the rest of it, though. What was the name and date of death?'

'Mary Winifred Dean, of Elwood. Date of death: 21 November 1930.' Saying her name out loud gives me a bit of a chill. I wonder if I'm getting too carried away.

'Hmmm.' Ian makes another note. 'Was it a long investigation and trial?'

'From what I've read in the newspapers, the coronial inquest concluded in late January 1931 and that was it. I've no idea if the investigation continued or not.'

Ian regards me across the desk, eyes made abnormally large and bright by the refraction of his lenses. 'No trial?' Eyebrows rise above the glasses.

'No trial.'

He stares at me a moment longer before turning back to his computer, the clatter of his typing loud over the soft background sounds of the reading room.

Despite the fact only a handful of people are here today, there is a constant thrum, the strange mix of muted voices, rustling paper and occasional electronic buzzes and beeps that is the anthem of libraries. From an open door, I can hear the hum-clack of a photocopier and the occasional distinctive accelerating whir of a microfiche spool.

As Ian is peering at his screen and noting down file numbers, I start to feel impatient. I want to know what's in those files. What wasn't reported in the papers? I sit up straighter. Why, after all the sensationalism of the murder, did the whole thing just fade away? Surely there should have been more of an outcry, more calls to find the violent offender and make the streets safe again? Given that the Jazz Age was taking Melbourne by storm, I'd even expect some sort of opinion piece on the falling standards of the Modern Woman, out alone at night. But I'd seen nothing in all the articles I'd read on the case. Once the coroner's verdict was in, the whole thing just dried up.

I realise I've balled my hands into tight fists and I force myself to slowly relax and uncurl my fingers. This was getting ridiculous. All I need to do is add a little colour to the Molly Dean story to give the painting a bit of extra cachet and bump the price. But it bothers me that all this poor girl's life amounted to was a scandalous footnote in an artist's biography. I want to know the *real* Molly Dean, as much as is possible from newspapers and the Public Records Office anyway. She deserves that much.

The sound of ripping breaks into my thoughts. Ian is tearing off a request form and I see he has listed several items for retrieval.

'Do you have your user ID number with you? I just need to fill that in and then you're set.'

I rummage in the side pocket of my bag, the place where I keep all the coupons, cards and random things I may need, but not so often I want to jam them into my purse. I flip through a borrower's card for the State Library, membership cards for the National Gallery of Victoria and National Trust, and a loyalty card for some shop I don't remember, before I find the right user card. I hand it over and Ian adds the details to the top of his sheet. A glance at the large clock over his shoulder tells me it's not quite 1 p.m., which means a long wait until the next file retrieval time at 2.30. I sigh. There's a cafe downstairs, but nowhere in this part of town that makes a decent coffee, and the thought of bad coffee is worse than no coffee at all.

Ian gives me a conspiratorial wink. 'It's highly irregular, but as I'm about to go on my lunch break, it's entirely feasible for me to just pop into the stacks and see what I can find for you right now. Of course,' he holds up an admonishing finger, 'I can see the inquest file is in cold storage, so that's a special request. I've logged it for you, but they won't pull those documents until tomorrow. However I can get you started with the rest. Strike while the iron's hot and all that.'

I can see he's rather fired up at the prospect of delving into the records of an unsolved murder. This is probably the most exciting thing that's happened for years.

'Would you really be able to do that, Ian? Thanks.'

'This is a one-off, mind. Can't buck the system for a mere whim.' He injects a note of authority into his tone.

'Of course, of course. I'd never dream of ignoring protocol.'

'Shan't be long then.' He flips a sign onto his desk that reads, *Currently unattended. Please see staff at main desk.* It seems an obvious statement, but I've no doubt some people would stand in front of an empty desk for ages and then complain because nobody helped them.

'Is it okay if I see if one of the private research rooms is free? I'll wait for you there.'

'You should be able to take your pick today.' List in hand, Ian heads off through the *Staff Only* door.

I find an empty room, empty being the operative word. Three of the walls are blank white while the fourth is glass, so the archivists can make sure you're not breaking any rules or stealing documents. The table is grey laminate and the chair is designed to prevent the user from settling in for a long stretch. A fluorescent light overhead bathes me in its unforgiving glare while it buzzes quietly to itself. Sitting down, I set my things up on the table, ready for action. It doesn't take long. I put out my notebook and pencil (no pens allowed), camera, for if I want to photograph documents, and laptop. I fire up the computer just in case I need to refer to any of the notes I've already made, then toy with the idea of playing solitaire while I wait. But I want to look professional when Ian returns.

What's taking so long, I wonder, then realise it's been only ten minutes since Ian left. I fiddle with my stuff a bit, realign my pencil and notebook, and have just decided to start ditching old files on the laptop when I see Ian crossing the main reading room. His wispy hair is no longer military-neat, but sticks out behind one ear. Even as I notice, he lifts a hand and smooths the strands back into place. With that gesture I realise his hands are empty; he hasn't been able to get the files after all. Perhaps he ran into his boss out the back and ended up having a discussion about the rules of the Dewey Decimal System.

Oh well, I have to come back tomorrow anyway. I plaster a quizzical yet encouraging expression on my face as he reaches the door of my room.

'No luck?'

'No ...'

'Never mind, I'll look at everything tomorrow.' I close the laptop and gather my things into a pile.

'Actually.' Ian pushes his glasses further up the bridge of his nose. 'I couldn't find the files. They weren't on the right shelves.' He is still holding the list he wrote and now he taps it repeatedly into the palm of his other hand. 'Someone must have misfiled them.'

'But you can find them, right? Maybe they're with the rest of the stuff in cold storage?'

'Perhaps. I'm sorry, this is quite disconcerting. We're very proud of our record keeping here at the Public Records Office. I've spoken to the retrieval team.'

I arch an eyebrow. Is there a SWAT team for lost files?

Ian sees my look. 'That is, the staff doing the collections today, and when they've done the afternoon pick-up they'll start checking surrounding shelves. Hopefully the items are not far away and we'll have everything for you tomorrow.' He tries a smile but it dies before it reaches the corners of his mouth.

'It's okay, really.' I can see how this has disrupted the smooth order of his archival world. 'What's a day? I've got some other errands to run, so I'll go and do that and be ready when the doors open tomorrow. You've already done so much, Ian.' I scoop my things up and step around the table. 'I'll see you in the morning.'

Ian takes a backward step to allow me to exit the private room, then walks me to the main door, still tightly clutching my request list. Just before we trigger the sensors, he stops.

'I really don't know what to say.'

'Nothing to say.' I pat his arm. 'Hard to get good help these days. Someone probably left the work experience kid alone for five minutes.'

Ian straightens up and his chin tenses. I figure I'm about to get a version of the 'In my day …' speech, so I step forward, triggering the doors to glide open. 'See you tomorrow then, all right?'

He nods and I head out toward the lift. The doors close but I can still see him there, list in hand, completely deflated, betrayed by the archival system.

Ten o'clock Wednesday and I am first though the doors of the reading room, beating out a silver-haired lady whose bulging folder screams family history and a teenager in school uniform who has spent the past ten minutes sucking on a strand of hair. I make a beeline for the information desk, but pull up short when I see it is staffed by a young, skinny guy with blonde hair and a tan so deep he looks out of place in an indoor setting. I do a slow pirouette, trying to spot Ian somewhere in the room. He knew I'd be here, so perhaps he's just sorting out my stuff. I cross to the private rooms in case he's set one aside for me, but they're all empty. I turn back just in time to see him emerge from the *Staff Only* door. Ian spots me straight away, squares his shoulders and heads over, his precise stride proclaiming his military past.

'Miss Clayton. Alex.'

'Good morning, Ian.' I realise he's never used my first name before and suddenly I'm worried. 'What have you got for me?'

He stares at me for a moment, minute twitches of his mouth suggest that he has something to say but doesn't know how.

Instead, he gestures back to the information desk. The skinny guy sees us approaching and swivels his chair around, ceding it to Ian. Ian takes a moment to pull the visitor chair around to his side of the desk, so when we sit our knees are almost touching. He leans forward, clasps his hands, then leans back and visibly straightens his spine.

'I'm not quite sure how to begin.'

'I gather there's a problem. Have I broken a rule or something?' It's the only reason I can think of for Ian's odd demeanour.

'No, no.' He holds up his hands in a double stop motion. 'It's nothing like that. Yes, there is a problem, a rather significant one at that, but you are entirely blameless. The fault lies squarely with us.'

I wait. Nod my head forward and raise my eyebrows.

'It seems that, ah, all the documents you're seeking, with the exception of the death certificate, have been misplaced.'

'All of them?'

'It would seem so, yes.'

'All of them.' I can't figure this out. The various bits and pieces should all be filed in different areas. One missing item I can understand, but five or six?

'Well, have they all just been stored somewhere together? Off-site? They are old files.'

'We've checked. I've checked. It's all gone. The only thing that turned up was an empty manila folder with the file number on it, and we only found that when we moved a shelf to check if anything had fallen behind it.'

I imagine how desperate a bunch of librarians must have been to even contemplate moving a shelf. Ian is probably just as put out about this as I am, maybe more so. It takes me a moment to come up with something to say. 'So not one single file or scrap of paper anywhere?'

He shakes his head.

'Do you even know when it went missing? I mean, are there records of when the material was last requested?'

Ian brightens and swivels toward the computer terminal. His fingers dart across the keyboard as he enters a file number. It seems he has memorised it now; there must have been a lot of frantic searching going on. He gives the return key an emphatic thwack, then leans forward, chin raised so he can use the bottom part of his bifocals. I see his face fall a moment before he throws himself back into the chair.

'It hasn't been requested since the electronic catalogue was established.'

'And of course there's no way to check before that.' I can't believe such a simple research exercise has blown up like this.

'Unless ...' Ian pulls open the bottom drawer of the desk and extracts a manila folder. He waves it at me. 'This is what we found. See? The file number is here.' He shows me the front of the folder, which carries two coloured tags and an alphanumeric string. 'But even though the catalogue is computerised, up until very recently users had to sign files in and out. Card system, that sort of thing, and they had to sign that they'd abide by the viewing and copying restrictions imposed on certain documents.'

He opened the folder. On the left-hand side, a lined sheet was stuck to the cardboard. From my upside-down perspective, I could see that two of the lines had been filled in.

Ian sighed. 'No joy. The only time this was signed out was in 1958.'

'But two lines are filled in,' I say.

'No, there was only ever a single request.' He grimaces and shakes his head. 'On the second line someone has simply made a note, stating that when it was signed out in 1958 there was no material in the folder.'

'So it was all lost as long ago as that?' My voice rises. 'Why on earth put the folder back then?'

'I assume so there was a place to put the documents if they turned up somewhere, and in the meantime it would act as a placeholder so a librarian didn't spend fruitless hours searching for the file. I should have checked the log sheet when we found this, but all I could think of was the empty folder and all the missing documents.'

Ian's words calm me down. I realise how much time and effort he has put into this search for me, and how much of a hit his professional pride has taken.

'Never mind, it's not the end of the world,' I say, although Ian's face tells me otherwise. 'I was only hoping to flesh out some facts but I'll just work with what I've got.'

Ian offers me a half-hearted smile. 'I'll endeavour to lift my game when you're in next, and I'll put out the word to the other archivists to keep an eye out for misfiled things. However, I suspect someone's made off with these items long ago. I'm really terribly sorry. I feel I've failed in my duty.'

'Don't be ridiculous, Ian. It's not your fault.'

'Thank you, Alex. I only hope Daphne Lambell was as understanding as you.'

I freeze, staring at him. My mouth is hanging open and I snap it shut, swallow. 'What did you say?'

'Just that I hope Daphne Lambell didn't get too upset over the missing files.' He frowns at me, then turns the empty manila folder in my direction, pointing to the neat pencilled writing on the first page. 'Daphne Lambell was the last person to be disappointed by the absence of files. In 1958.'

'Daphne Lambell.' I look where he's pointing and see it for myself. Lambell. It's an uncommon sort of name. It's also the name of the detective who investigated the murder of Molly Dean: Senior Detective Percy Lambell. Things had suddenly become very interesting.

A quick check of Ian's White Pages shows no listing for D. Lambell. I could be chasing another ghost; the odds are small that 1958's Daphne is still around, but you never know. I figure if I draw a blank with Daphne, I can always cold call the other Lambells in the phone book. There are only six listed.

Part of me wants to call it quits right now, but for some reason I can't let this go. Whether it's Rob's reaction to the mysterious underbidder, some noble idea of justice, sheer pigheadedness or the chance to increase my profit, I decide to push on. Ian is sitting there, patiently waiting for me presumably to either say something or get the hell away from his desk and let him do some work. I look up from the phone book and meet his questing gaze. 'Do you have the electoral roll here?'

'No.' His shoulders droop a little more. Another archival wish unfulfilled. 'That's State Library for historical records or any office of the Australian Electoral Commission for the latest version. I'm not sure what the most recent version at the State Library would be, although they do keep things fairly up to date, so I've heard.'

'Thanks.' I stand up, return my chair to its proper place and settle my bag on my shoulder.

'I hope you have better luck with the rest of your research, Alex.'

'I'll come and buy you a coffee and tell you how it went.' Ian has been great and this setback will make him even keener to help next time I need something.

'I'd be delighted. Especially if this avenue bears fruit!' There is a hint of the old vibrancy creeping back into his tone.

'Let's not get ahead of ourselves.' I knock on the laminate desktop. There must be wood in there somewhere. I raise my palm in a final goodbye and leave Ian at the centre of his kingdom. As I pass through the doors, I call directory assist for the address of the nearest Electoral Commission office. There's one in Lonsdale Street on the opposite side of the city, so I decide to move the car and hope I can find a meter.

I score a parking spot in Little Lonsdale Street. It's a few blocks away from my destination, but right in front of a coffee shop, so I grab a skinny latte and call it lunch. It's a beautiful autumn day, bright sun but with a winter crispness to the air. Cutting down Exhibition Street, I dawdle along, enjoying my coffee and the lovely play of light through the fluttering golden leaves of the plane trees. When I reach my destination I'm feeling pleasantly warm from the caffeine and sunshine. That feeling is instantly dispelled when I walk inside and am confronted by a decor that can only be described as public servant blah. Everything from the carpet to the workers looks washed out and careworn.

'Excuse me.' I approach the nearest desk.

'You have to take a number.' She doesn't even look up.

I look around and confirm that not only am I the only non-employee in the place, but all the lanyard wearers are studiously avoiding eye contact. Sighing, I walk back to the door and rip a paper ticket from the dispenser.

'Number eighty-eight.'

I look at my ticket – eighty-eight – and head back to the same desk. 'I'd like to see the electoral roll, please.'

'Are you wanting to check your enrolment status?'

'No.'

'Is there a change of address?'

'No, I just want to see the electoral roll.'

'For the division of Melbourne?'

'No, all of Victoria, please.'

'All of Victoria.' She regards me silently, looks at her pink acrylic nails. 'The entire roll or just A to E, F to K –'

'Isn't it all on computer anyway?' I cut her off.

She purses her lips, then pushes back from her desk. 'Over here.'

There is a computer tucked away in the corner. The public servant stomps over to the terminal and jiggles the mouse, bringing the screen to life. 'No copying, recording or photographing.' She returns to her desk but keeps her eyes fastened on me.

The chair turns out to be way too low for comfortable typing. I feel for a lever or wheel to raise it, stand up and take a look, then resign myself to looking like a begging dog. I can almost feel the smirks behind me. It takes me a moment to work out how to navigate the roll, but then I'm staring at *Lambe, W.,* followed by a short list of Lambells. Right at the top is Daphne Elizabeth Lambell and an address in East Brighton, barely a suburb away from where Molly Dean lived and died. This might be the daughter of Detective Lambell; a sister or wife would most likely be dead by now and even this woman could be quite elderly. I jot down the address, half expecting a sharp rebuke at any moment, but when I get up to leave I realise the public servants have erased me from their collective memory and I've ceased to exist. I return the favour and depart without a backward glance.

Back home, I type Daphne's address into Yahoo to see if anything comes up. It's always nice to know what you're dealing with, and I'm hoping I don't find anything about a derelict house with a rubbish-filled garden. It would be just my luck to track down Daphne Lambell only to find she's a batty old cat lady. What appears on the screen gives me a glimmer of hope. It's a link to the website of a place called Hillview.

Clicking on the link, I navigate to the site. I'm greeted by an image of a high brick fence, crowns of riotous pink rhododendrons peeking over the top, and a wrought-iron gate bearing a discreet brass sign, *Hillview. Five-Star Aged Care.* I click through to the Contact Us page where the phone number is displayed in large, vision-friendly format. Pushing the laptop away, I pick up the desk phone and dial. The call is picked up on the third ring.

'Good afternoon, Hillview. This is Sandra, how may I help?' She sounds like Julie Andrews on happy pills.

'Hello Sandra, my name is Alex. I was hoping to speak to Daphne Lambell, please.'

'May I ask what this is in reference to, please?'

I hesitate. I can't exactly mention murder. 'I'm researching family history and I was delighted to find a Lambell descendant. I don't know Daphne Lambell, but I'm hoping she might agree to speak with me.' It's not all that far from the truth. I really was delighted to find a Lambell descendant, I just don't happen to be related.

'Could you repeat your name for me?'

'Alex Clayton.'

'One moment, please.' There is a click and I am left with an orchestral version of Henry Mancini's 'Moon River'. We're just becoming Huckleberry friends when Sandra comes back on the line.

'Miss Lambell will speak with you. I'm putting you through now.'

Before I can thank her there is another click and the burr of an internal line ringing.

'Hello?' The voice has a thinness that speaks of the years, but the tone is warm with no hint of tremor.

'Miss Lambell?'

'Yes. I presume you're Alex Clayton. Sandra tells me you want to talk to me about family history. I'm not aware of any Lambell relatives. How do you think I can help you?'

Clearly Daphne Lambell is in full possession of all her faculties.

'To be perfectly honest, I'm not sure Miss Lambell. May I just double check ... you are related to Lambell, the police detective?'

'He was an inspector when he retired, but yes, Percy Lambell was my father.'

'Well, it's his history I'm really interested in. I'm not a genealogist or family historian. I was just hoping you might be able to help me with some details about Det ... I mean Inspector Lambell's working life, please.'

'Can you be more specific, Miss Clayton?'

I swallow. I don't want her to think I'm some sort of ghoul or that I'm going to criticise her father. 'I'm hoping you might be able to tell me more about his investigation of a particular case from 1930.' I swallow again but before I can say another word, Daphne Lambell beats me to it.

'Molly Dean.'

'How did you know?'

'It's not hard to guess. It was such a sensational case at the time and Dad could never stop thinking about it. He hated the fact someone got away with it and he carried it with him for the rest of his life. But tell me, why are you interested?'

And so, leaning back in my office chair, I tell this elderly woman about the portrait of Molly and my decision to find out more about her story, although I leave out the bit about hoping to make a huge profit. Finally, in response to another question, I explain how I managed to track her down to Hillview. There is a moment's silence when I finish speaking, then I ask a couple of questions of my own. 'Why did you request the files in 1958? And what did you find?' A deep sigh echoes down the line.

'Dad retired in 1950. He talked about the Dean case for most of my life, but after he retired it became almost an obsession. I thought if I could see the documents – the evidence – for myself, perhaps I could help him somehow. I don't quite know what I thought I'd do. Suddenly solve the case?' She sniffs, sighs again. 'Anyway, to answer your second question, the only thing I found was a folder with a single sheet of paper in it.'

'The folder's completely empty now. What was on the paper?'

'Essentially nothing. It was simply a requisition slip with the Dean file number written on it. Someone's idea of a joke, I suppose.'

'Oh.'

'Quite. But you've gone to so much trouble already, I think you'd best come and visit me, Alex Clayton.'

'Really? I mean, thanks, I'd like that.'

'I'll tell you what I can about my father and the Molly Dean case, but don't expect any sort of grand revelation.'

'Miss Lambell, I'll just be pleased to meet you and grateful for any thoughts you have.'

We organise a time for me to visit Hillview the next day and Miss Lambell promises to put my name on the visitors' register. After I terminate the call I just sit there, gazing sightlessly at my filing cabinets and bookshelves. Several times today I've told myself I'd stop, let the Molly Dean thing go. But now as thoughts of murder and missing files chase each other around my head, I realise something: I'm completely hooked.

1930

IT HAD BEEN AN effort for Sarah to convince Molly, but finally here they were, walking through the gaping mouth of Mister Moon into Luna Park. Saturday evening and the air was rich with the scent of fairy floss and toffee, while 50,000 lights twinkled. Faces around them were glowing with delight and wonder.

'I can't understand why you were so keen to come,' Molly said, but as the colours washed over them, she felt herself begin to relax. She pulled off her red beret and tucked it in her bag. Her saxe blue crêpe-de-Chine coat, with its rucked collar and shirred belt, was just heavy enough to protect her from the light breeze without being too warm, so she left the buckle firmly fastened.

'It'll be the bee's knees, Molly!' Sarah executed a little skip. 'We can have our fortunes told, there's the carousel and the River Caves, I'm dying to go on The Whip, and it's been simply an age since I was on the Scenic Railway.'

As if in response there was a loud rattle overhead, followed by the extended scream of passengers as they plunged down one slope and up the next. Both girls turned to stare. The brakeman, standing like a warrior between the two carriages, gave them a jaunty salute as he swept past.

Molly didn't see herself as an amusement park sort of girl. This type of entertainment was for the masses. She had loftier ideals, still … she felt herself being swept up by the sugar-laden night, the crowd, and Sarah's infectious enthusiasm. Molly resolved to put aside her qualms for the moment. Perhaps she could write an article about the experience, she mused, or better still, a poem, using Luna Park as a metaphor for the ills of modern society. One hand crept into her handbag and felt for her notebook and pencil.

'Come on then.' She grinned at Sarah. 'If we're going to do this we'd better get our skates on.'

Molly and Sarah decided to start with the Big Dipper, and Molly's plan to document the experience came unstuck the moment their carriage inched over the crest of the first incline. As her stomach flew up into her chest, all Molly's pent-up frustrations and anxiety about the future collided with the excitement and fright of the ride, and she screamed until her throat was raw.

'The Whip now.' Sarah grabbed Molly's arm and began pulling her through the crowd toward an amazing octopus-like machine. 'Let's do all the really wild rides before we eat.'

For once, Molly was happy to let someone else take charge. 'But I want to do the River Caves later.'

After a couple of hours of dips and spins and the secret childish delight of the largest carousel in the southern hemisphere, the girls emerged, giggling uncontrollably, from the House of Follies.

'I'm famished, what's the time?' Molly said. It was impossible to tell. The night was hidden beyond the walls of the funfair, the sky dimmed by the glittering fantasy of the Luna Park world.

'Food, fortune, then River Caves.' Sarah turned toward the *Refreshments* sign and the friends joined the short queue in front of the kiosk.

'Hot dog, fairy floss or do you fancy something else?' Molly stared at the menu.

'In for a penny! Hot dog and then ice cream.'

Hot dogs in hand, Molly and Sarah found an empty bench and settled in for their late snack.

'How's things with you anyway, Molly?'

Molly glanced at Sarah, who was studiously examining her food.

'I don't know why I ever moved back home.' Molly paused to take a bite. 'It's been worse than ever.'

'Your mum or your brother?'

'Her. It's only ever her. Ralph is just a great lump of a thing.'

Sarah paused a moment. 'Last time I called around, your mother asked me all sorts of questions about you. Who your other friends are, men, where you go. I thought she was going to shake me when I didn't give her any answers!'

'She probably was. I've started getting my most important letters sent to Colin's house so she can't intercept them. Did I tell you about how she dragged me into the house by my hair a few weeks ago?'

Molly generally told Sarah most of what went on at Milton Street, and she'd shown her some of the bruises too, visible despite Molly's best efforts with make-up.

'Has your mother followed you again?'

'Not since that time she sent Adam after me as well. But she hides – or burns! – my best clothes instead, to stop me going out in the first place. And then flies off the handle when I spend the night somewhere else.' Molly crumpled the paper serviette in her hand. She'd consumed the hot dog in a few savage bites.

'Is she still trying to make you go out with him?'

Molly's face twisted and she laughed bitterly. 'Oh she keeps pushing it all right. That's when she's not taking him into her bed.'

'But she's … I mean, he's …'

'Yes, exactly.'

Sarah hesitated. 'She sent me a letter.'

'Who?'

'Your mother. She told me to leave you alone. Said I was leading you into a bohemian life.'

'Oh this is madness! I'm sorry she's dragging you into her spiteful, vitriolic little world. If she sends you anything else, tear it up. Please? I'll be out of there just as soon as I can, and then she'll have to leave me alone.'

'I'd share a place with you, Molly, only I just can't afford it.'

Molly smiled and placed a hand on Sarah's knee. 'It's okay, Sarah. I've saved up a bit – and she won't find it – but I think Colin might ask me to move in with him.'

'Molly Dean! Aren't you a dark horse? Just like Janet Gaynor in *Sunny Side Up*. Will he look after you?'

'He'll let me be me and that's what matters. I'll be free to write, all day if I want to, and talk about important things to all sorts of people all night.'

'Well, I know you can't stay in Milton Street for much longer, but don't do anything rash. You don't have to turn your entire life upside-down all at once. You're a marvellous teacher and the children love you. Why not just worry about finding new digs for now, and surely the rest will follow once you're more settled.' Sarah paused as Molly slowly shook her head. 'So! How about ice cream and River Caves?'

'What, no one-penny fortunes?' Molly said, and dusting herself off, she stood and offered her hand, pulling Sarah up and back toward the Penny Arcade. 'What do you think? Wealth or a tall dark stranger?'

'Definitely tall dark stranger. Or maybe something unexpected.'

They began strolling in the general direction of Noah's Ark, letting themselves be carried by the surge and flow of the crowd.

'I don't need something unexpected, I just need a chance,' Molly murmured.

In that moment, for anyone watching, the flashing lights made the two girls look like a flickering image on a cinema screen. Then the crowd shifted and they were gone.

1999

THE DOOR IS OPEN and I can see through into the bright room. An elderly woman is ensconced in a large, very comfy-looking recliner, the sun spilling over her shoulder and turning her fine white hair into a fragile corona. Her eyes are closed so I take a moment to study her, trying to figure out my best approach. She has a long frame, lean in the way that only the elderly can be, but with traces of an active, possibly athletic life still in evidence. Her legs – what I can see below the hem of her dress – show no signs of swollen ankles, arthritic joints or any other infirmities, but a walker tucked discreetly in the corner tells a different story.

I tap on the doorframe and instantly her eyelids snap open. Green eyes appraise me for a long moment before the rest of her body stirs. 'You must be Alex.'

'Yes, Miss Lambell. Sorry if I disturbed you.' I walk in and immediately the institutional smell of the hallway, a soul-destroying potpourri of disinfectant, decay and a hint of urine, is replaced by Jean Patou's Joy. The scent of rose and jasmine is not heavy; Daphne Lambell hasn't doused herself for my

85

benefit. Rather, the fragrance is ingrained in every corner of the room. I suspect she's been wearing this perfume her entire life.

'Don't be ridiculous. I've been waiting for you. Besides, anyone who gets to my age needs to be disturbed on a regular basis. Sometimes this place makes me feel like I've already slipped into a coma. Sit down, sit down.'

I have the choice of perching on her bed or taking an old wooden chair with a kangaroo-carved back rail. It looks original, so I give it a little shake to check for sturdiness before sitting down. Aware that I am being closely scrutinised, I straighten my spine against the chair's wooden slats and make sure I don't slump. 'Thank you for seeing me, Miss Lambell.'

'Oh call me Daphne. I'm far too old to be a miss. Now, they come around with tea and coffee at about ten, but if you'd like something now?'

Shaking my head I get straight to it. 'I want to talk to you about Molly Dean.'

'So you said.' Her eyes narrow a fraction. 'May I ask why?'

I frown. Maybe Daphne isn't as on the ball as she seems. Dutifully, I repeat everything I told her yesterday.

'I'd wondered, when you first called me, if you were some sensation-seeker, perhaps looking for a way to make money from the story.' Daphne glances at her hands, the knobbly fingers steepled in her lap. 'But hearing you now, and watching you as you say it, I think you genuinely want to know what happened.' She both turns and tilts her head, fixing me with a keen gaze.

'There's something about the whole story that's reeled me in. It's bothering me and I can't let it go.' It's true, but I feel a bit guilty not mentioning the money angle.

'Dad couldn't let it go, either.' Daphne leans forward a little. 'Molly Dean's killer was the one who got away.'

'Did he keep a notebook or diary? Do you have any of his papers?'

'Oh no dear, he wasn't a diary sort of man. There were the official case notes of course, property of Victoria Police and, as you've found out, "unable to be located".' She emphasises the last words.

I feel myself deflate. Daphne is just another little old lady on for a chat. Then I realise she's been toying with me.

'But he talked about it all the time. All the details, over and over. One of my strongest childhood memories is Mother shushing him so I wouldn't hear. But of course, when it happened, the whole neighbourhood was talking and I was certainly old enough to understand the details. Several years later, he told me the full story. I don't think a week went by that he didn't mention her in some way. It used to drive Mother up the wall, but I thought it was fascinating. It was the only bit of work he ever brought home.' She pauses, lost in the memory of her policeman father.

I try to steer her back to Molly. 'So what did he talk about? Do you remember much?'

'It's all here.' Daphne taps her temple. 'But you might need to take notes.'

I decide to record Daphne on the voice recorder I always carry; I've found it's much easier than deciphering my handwriting. While I fiddle about with that, the tea lady arrives to deal out insipid caffeinated beverages, which I cautiously accept, and shortbread biscuits. I've been fishing around for a way to get Daphne to tell me what she knows, and as we settle in with our cups of tea, I realise how to begin. 'Did your dad tell you how he first heard about the murder?'

A moment as she sips, sighs and with a genteel rattle sets her cup and saucer aside. Then she tells me her father's story: the story of Percy Lambell and the murder of Molly Dean.

❧

'Dad – Senior Detective Percy Lambell – was quickly on the scene. He was there within ten minutes of the alarm being raised, right after the local constable. His colleagues said he always had a knack for being hot on the heels of Melbourne's criminal element. He crash-tackled pickpockets, led raids on Squizzy Taylor's Barkly Street address … Dad was always in the thick of it.'

'What sort of a man was he?'

'He wasn't averse to putting his fists to use when it was warranted, if that's what you're asking.' She smiles. 'He had the sharp suits and Gary Cooper looks, but he was clever too. Most people tended to underestimate Percy Lambell. They didn't expect such a tall, debonair man to be quite so handy when things got physical.'

Daphne takes a deep breath before continuing. 'Dad told me every minute detail of the case, always replaying his actions, asking himself what more he could have done.

'The Owens were the people who'd telephoned for the police, and they were huddled by their gate when Dad stepped into the gloomy laneway where Molly lay. There was little to be done until more officers and the medical people arrived, but Dad liked having time alone at the scene.' Her voice has taken on a storyteller's cadence.

'He snapped on his torch and played the beam up the girl's body, taking in the torn clothing, bruises, splayed legs and undergarments. There was blood everywhere. Her knickers were gone and her petticoat was tied around her arm, and it stopped him cold. Instinct told him there was something particularly foul about this crime. The stocking around the neck, tied so tightly that it puckered the flesh, at least made sense. Then the beam of his light found Molly's face.

'He swore to himself, flicking the light back to her chest, and sure enough she was still breathing, just the tiniest bit. He stormed back to Addison Street, yelling at the boys in the wireless car to radio for the damn ambulance to hurry. Just like Dad, the ambulance driver thought he was attending a fatality, so when the Dodge wagon finally rumbled around the corner from Dickens Street, it was with all the urgency of a country vicar heading out to afternoon tea with the CWA. But one look at Percy's face and his wildly waving arms had the crew snatching up their gear and hustling toward the poor, broken girl.

'He yelled at them to be careful of evidence, but the lead medic ignored him, focusing on the patient and keeping his wide-eyed junior on track. I gather it was rather a gruesome scene.

'The younger medic was sent back for the stretcher and he half stumbled, half ran back to the ambulance, brushing through the small gathering of morbid locals. Then he got to work, the familiarity of routine and practice taking over from the horror of a girl lying like a crushed lily in a pool of her own blood.

'In a matter of minutes, Molly had been loaded onto the stretcher, bumped over the cobbles and was on her way to the Alfred Hospital. This time, the siren was screaming.'

Daphne is back in that Elwood lane with her father, and as her well-remembered words flow around me, I am there too. I recall one of the worrying details I'd come across in the paper.

'Daphne.' Her eyes refocus on me. 'I have to ask. The stocking around her neck... Why didn't your dad take it off? She was still breathing.'

Her face fills with pain and when she answers, for the first time, her voice sounds like every one of her seventy-something years. 'He never forgave himself for that. The moment he saw she was alive he ran to hurry the ambulance, and then he simply left it up to the medics. After all, they had the instruments and – he assumed – the knowledge to take the stocking off without doing any more damage. But when he got to the hospital and found out they'd done nothing, that the stocking was only cut off in the emergency room … He said the doctor was livid.'

I reach out and place my hands over hers, which are now twisting into her skirt.

'I'd have put my faith in the ambos too.'

We sit a moment, both trying and failing to dispel the horror of the last hours of Molly Dean. I give her hands a final squeeze. 'What happened once the ambulance left?'

'Just as the ambulance was speeding away, a divisional car swung into Addison Street, coming to a stop with its lights angled on the scene. Three uniforms piled out and, with a nod from my dad, began to ease the locals back and form a rough perimeter around the scene. Then another figure unfolded itself from the front seat.'

She takes a sip of tea. I lift my cup but quickly put it down again. The tea is stone cold.

'Detective Jerry O'Keeffe had arrived. Physically, Jerry was the opposite of Dad, looking exactly like the brawler he'd once been. He was short, but a solid block of a man, and his physique seemed to incite every ruffian to have a go, but Jerry's thousand-yard stare changed their minds just as quickly.

'Jerry came and stood a few steps short of Dad, hands in pockets, and took a slow survey.

'Dad gave him a moment to take in the sights – the clear signs of a struggle and dragging, and the copious amount of blood. He waited with his face turned to the faint breeze that chased through the streets, whisking the last of the day's sultry heat from the air. It carried a hint of the ocean, he said, and he took a deep breath before turning back to his partner and the slaughterhouse reek of the narrow lane.

'Jerry was already lighting up a cigarette to mask the smell, and of course his first question was, "Who was she?"

'"At the moment, the question is still, who *is* she," Dad said. "But I reckon that'll be a different story by morning. I'll talk to those people." He pointed to the Owens, a middle-aged couple, still standing at the nearby gate in their dressing gowns. "You have a look and get her bag, books and the rest." He and Jerry were partnered, but Dad was the senior officer.

'My father picked his way across Addison Street toward the gate, set back from the footpath a few feet and flanked by a tall, sharply trimmed hedge. He turned to look back at where the trail of blood began, and realised this shadowy alcove would hide a man completely. The perfect spot to lie in wait for an innocent girl to come along. But he was always careful not to jump to conclusions, was Dad. Who would expect a lone woman to walk past at this time of night? It was just as likely she'd been followed, he thought.

'He turned back to the man and woman, safe behind the pickets. Dad told them who he was and they introduced themselves as Beatrice and Frank Owen, brother and sister.

'Dad asked them if they knew the girl, and the brother, Frank, jumped in and said he hadn't let his sister see, once he'd realised what it was. The story they told was that she – Beatrice – had heard something and roused her brother. She made him go out, and as soon as he saw the blood he went to call the police. That's all they knew.'

Clouds have been building while Daphne talks, smothering the sun and making the room seem suddenly cold. She reaches out and pulls the cord of a standard lamp, casting a pool of light around her chair. I shift in my wooden seat. 'And then?'

'Dad went back to see what Jerry had come up with and found him bagging up all Molly's bits and pieces, all the things that had been scattered across the street.' Daphne shakes her head, still feeling sadness at a crime committed sixty-nine years ago. I feel the same, even though I haven't lived with it like she has.

'The last thing he picked up was her wallet. All she had was threepence, but there were also letters and each one was addressed to Mary or Molly Dean, 86 Milton Street, Elwood. That's when they found out her name, and that's when they realised she was only two minutes from home. So Dad called for a car and they went to tell the family. Then things really got interesting.'

Daphne is ready to forge ahead with the story, but her voice is starting to sound a little strained. 'Would you like to take a break for a while? I don't want to wear out my welcome.'

'I could keep going until lunchtime, perhaps. They serve quite early here.'

As she says it, I realise my nasal passages are being assaulted by the smell of boiled cabbage and the unmistakable oleaginous signature of frying. The scent of Daphne's perfume has been leeched from the room. 'Perhaps I could take you out for lunch? I thought I noticed a little cafe just down the road.'

Her wrinkles deepen, every one a testament to a life filled with smiles. 'It's been some time since I had a decent outing.' She slaps her hands on her thighs. 'I broke my hip badly, so when there's a bit of distance involved, these things don't work like they used to.'

I point to the walker. 'I don't mind if you don't.'

'It's been a hard thing to get used to,' she says. 'But with such lovely company I'm quite prepared to swallow my pride.'

I pull the walker out and get Daphne organised, then we cruise slowly out past reception, making sure they know

Daphne's okay and when we should be back. As the receptionist buzzes us out, an old guy makes a determined dash for the door. He's snagged at the last second by a nurse who steers him gently back into the bowels of Hillview.

'Poor Herb,' says Daphne. 'Bad dementia. Thinks he's in a POW camp again.'

I usher Daphne out into the fresh air and we trundle through the gate.

By tacit mutual agreement, we avoid the topic of Molly Dean over lunch. Instead, I explain how I make money and Daphne talks about her father's rise from lowly constable to police inspector.

'You and your dad were obviously quite close,' I say.

She eyes me over her water glass. 'He was my hero and I was his only child.'

It's the rationale for her whole life, in a simple sentence.

I nod gently. 'You want this solved too, don't you?'

'For Dad just as much as for Molly.' She puts her glass back on the table, watching herself do it, and when her eyes meet mine again they are all business. 'So enough of this lollygagging about. I've got things to tell you, and you've got work to do.'

Back at Hillview, Daphne talks me through Percy's first meeting with Molly Dean's mother. What I'd read in the papers had painted Ethel Dean as a fairly hard woman, but that was nothing compared to what Percy Lambell revealed to his daughter.

When the detectives arrived on her doorstep at 2.30 in the morning, not only were they surprised to find Mrs Dean seemingly wide awake, but they were gobsmacked at her apparent lack of concern for Molly. She berated them, insinuating that whatever had happened, Molly had brought it on herself, then left the detectives standing on the doormat while she went to rouse her son, Ralph.

'What did she say when they asked her if she knew where Molly had been?' I ask.

'Oh she claimed she hadn't seen her for days. Molly was too busy living a bohemian life. Then she pointed her finger squarely at the artist Percy Leason and also that music chappy, Fritz Hart. Dad said her voice was full of venom when she spat out the names … Made it sound as if her daughter was carrying on affairs with both men.'

The two men were part of Melbourne's artistic circle, but both were happily married with children in 1930. I shake my head and gesture for Daphne to continue.

'Ethel Dean's behaviour didn't get any better. Jerry O'Keeffe was carrying the bag of Molly's belongings, and as soon as Ethel found out what he had, she started shouting for him to hand over her daughter's handbag. When he refused, she tried to wrestle the parcel away from him, and it took both Percy and Jerry to calm her down. They couldn't decide whether she was just after money or if she thought there might be something else in her daughter's bag, something damning. Apparently it was a very icy ride to the hospital.

'When they all got to the Alfred Hospital, Molly was in surgery but not expected to live. Her mother didn't ask about her daughter's injuries or condition. She had no interest in what had happened to Molly, although she did ask one nurse if Molly's face had been "marked much". Of course Dad wondered why she'd specifically asked that question. The more the detectives saw of Molly Dean's mother, the more suspicious they became. There was something very wrong between mother and daughter.

'The detectives left Mrs Dean and her son at the Alfred, keen to follow what clues they had while the trail was still fresh. There had been another girl, Mena Griffiths, murdered in Ormond just a couple of weeks earlier, and although she hadn't been bashed like Molly, she had been throttled. Dad thought the same man might be responsible, so he didn't want to waste a moment.'

Once again, the hypnotic lilt of Daphne's words have drawn me back to Elwood, 1930. I lived the dash through dark streets, the hostile atmosphere in the police car and pictured Percy Lambell bursting from the brightly lit front doors of the Alfred into the comparative darkness of Commercial Road.

'After he'd left the Alfred, Dad headed straight back to Addison Street for another look. A couple of uniforms were standing around, but everyone else had gone back to bed, or to meet a deadline at the *Truth* or *The Argus*. What struck him was the darkness. The newish moon was hidden behind a blanket of cloud and in that particular place there was no street lighting to chase away the shadows. Molly's attacker had chosen his spot well, but had he been waiting for her or following? And was it Molly he was after or just any girl?

'Dad had a lot of strings to follow and he started by walking the path Molly would've taken to her home in Milton Street. It was still early and there was no one to question but the milk-o. He matched his pace to the man as the horse walked on, it was so accustomed to its route that it'd stop by itself at every delivery before heading back to the dairy. The man's answers were what Dad had expected. Saw nothing and no one. Dad reckoned the bloke was on the level and left him to finish his round.

'When he got to the Deans' home there was no one about, so it was a good chance for a look around. Dad let himself into the garden, but there was nothing to be seen. It was just after five o'clock and there was a shift in the sky, a promise of sunrise. Time to go home for a shower, shave and coffee. Dad had to be ready to face Mrs Dean.

'Molly died before the sun came up. They'd known she wasn't going to make it, but all the same … After, when Dad had a chance to talk to the hospital staff again, he found out that as soon as she was told Molly had died, Mrs Dean was out the door without a backward glance or a word for the doctor. No tears, no emotion, nothing.

'Later that morning when the detectives went round to Milton Street, there was still nothing of the grieving mother about Mrs Dean. She grudgingly showed them into the "good room" but beat them to the punch with a question of her own, "How soon can I get the death certificate?" Apparently Molly was insured for £200. They fobbed her off.

'Ethel Dean settled herself in the most comfortable-looking chair, leaving the men to sort themselves out. Jerry lowered himself onto the overstuffed couch, murmuring condolences to no discernible effect, while Dad stood near the mantelpiece, careful not to jostle the array of candlesticks and china ladies.

'After the insurance question, Mrs Dean had a go at the detectives, asking if they'd questioned the men she'd mentioned the night before, then telling them to chase up Mervyn Skipper.'

I interrupt Daphne. 'You mean *The Bulletin*'s man in Melbourne?'

She nods. 'According to Mrs Dean, Molly carried on about Skipper so much "you'd think he made the sun rise and set". And Mrs Dean was quite comfortable referring to her daughter in the past tense. That really bothered Dad.

'The interview went on,' Daphne continues. 'Dad asked question after question about Molly. Waiting for a crack in the facade, anything that would show him this bitter woman felt something for the violent death of her only daughter. Nothing.

No pride in Molly's work as a teacher, only suspicion about some of the male teachers at the school and the teachers' college. No admiration for her daughter, only scorn for her ambition and another tirade about bohemians.

'Dad ascertained that a year or so back, Molly had moved out for a few weeks, taking a flat in the city with the intention of devoting herself to writing. But she soon found the financial burden too great and had to return to the house at Milton Street. Ethel had plenty to say about that.

'Up until then, Jerry had been quiet, taking notes and leaving Dad to bear the brunt of Mrs Dean's verbal onslaught. But now he suddenly jumped in, catching the woman off guard, causing her to swing in her chair, redirect her focus. It was a technique the two detectives used often.

'Jerry asked, "Where were you last night, Mrs Dean?" Ethel Dean was adamant: she'd been home all night. Jerry pushed, "Didn't leave the house?" Dad was quiet, waiting by the mantel.'

Daphne tells me Ethel Dean then admitted to getting up at around quarter past one, thinking she heard Molly coming in the gate. She wasn't getting up to let her in, rather to chastise her for her wanton ways. Of course, Molly wasn't coming in the gate and Mrs Dean claimed she went back to bed.

Daphne stops and takes a breath. 'Then just as Dad and Jerry thought they'd heard it all, this vitriolic woman smoothed her skirt, looked Dad square in the eye and said, "I wish you'd make no inquiries into the matter. So far as I am concerned, I would sooner you let the matter drop."'

'She didn't want them to investigate her daughter's brutal murder?' I'm gobsmacked.

'Not a bit. She told them they'd never catch the man who did it and everyone should just move on.'

'Why would she think they'd never make an arrest?'

Daphne nods sagely. 'Of course that's exactly what Dad and

Jerry thought and they instantly became even more suspicious, if that was possible. When pushed, Ethel Dean said *of course* she hoped they'd arrest someone if there was a fiend preying on young women, but otherwise it would be better if things were just left alone.'

It's getting late in the afternoon now, and in the lamp's warm glow I can see Daphne is tired. 'I've taken up your whole day. How about we pick this up in a few days' time?'

'You may be surprised to know my diary is remarkably free.' Her smile wavers. 'I've been waiting an awfully long time for this, Alex. Do you know, my father questioned more than 300 people over the Molly Dean affair? You and I having a chat is nothing.'

I try another approach. I want the story but I like this lady too much to push. 'I have to deal with a couple of work things tomorrow. Still have to earn a buck!' I try to sound light and breezy. Daphne isn't fooled.

'What if I write some things down then? For when you next have a moment to pop in.' She shoots me a sharp look. 'You can read the salient points then ask questions, or I could go over another part of the investigation.'

I give her a wry smile. 'That sounds perfect. Shall I call you later tomorrow and we can make a date?'

She waves me off. 'I'm not going anywhere. Come when you can – I'll be here.'

I smile again and stand, the smile becoming a grimace as I discover the wooden chair had not been kind to my backside. Daphne arches one eyebrow. 'I'll dig out a cushion for your next visit.'

In the doorway, at the olfactory threshold, I turn. 'Thank you.'

'Thank you, dear.'

IT'S SUNDAY BEFORE I make it back to Hillview. Daphne is waiting for me, a yellow legal pad covered with the elegant cursives of a bygone era resting on the table beside her.

I stoop and peck the proffered cheek. It seems a day of talking murder has created something of a bond. 'I'm sorry I didn't make it yesterday.'

'I wasn't expecting you. I'm sure you had plenty to think about after our time on Thursday.'

I nod. 'I do have a couple of questions about the murder scene, but perhaps ...' I gesture to the legal pad.

'Ask your questions, then we'll get to that.'

'Okay. First, since the official reports are missing, I'm still trying to figure out exactly what the injuries were. I know Molly was beaten with some sort of metal bar or club, and probably assaulted with the same thing, but what were the external injuries like? What did your dad and the doctors see? Do you know?'

She is silent for a moment. 'Dad wouldn't say for such a long time. Not until I was in my twenties. Finally I got up the courage to ask … She was mutilated, beaten and scratched all over. There was blood on the fence – they thought she'd hit her head going down – Dad remembered the head injuries vividly. It turned out most of the blood was from her head. There were six deep gashes on her scalp and her skull was fractured in two places. The injuries were so bad, at first they thought someone had put a gun to her head and shot her, just like that. And until Molly started groaning in the lane, no one heard a thing. She never saw it coming.'

'Were there any clues? Any fingerprints?' I frown. 'Sorry, did they do fingerprints then?'

'Oh yes, it was very specialised work and of course not nearly as sophisticated. Detective Martin, the print expert, and the photographer Constable Hobley both spent a long time at the scene. They did get some prints from the gateway at the Owens' house, but nothing ever came of it. Any number of people would have been in and out that gate. There was no weapon found, of course.'

'Did they look very hard? I read the police decided not to search the canal. The reason sounded a bit weak.' I don't want to get Daphne offside by besmirching her father, but it is an important detail.

'Dad was furious. They just wouldn't allocate the money or resources. And they told the press there was no point searching the canal because there'd be so much rubbish in there, it wouldn't be possible to identify the murder weapon if they found it!' She shakes her head. 'No reward for information either.'

'Why?'

'The order came directly from the Chief Commissioner, Thomas Blamey. He told the press it was because the detectives had a theory, knew the motive and believed the murderer was someone well known to Molly.'

'But even if the detectives had a good theory, surely they needed evidence?'

'Apparently not enough to warrant a reward.'

Daphne seems agitated, picking fretfully at her skirt, and I wonder what she isn't telling me. I refer to my notebook, giving her a moment to regroup.

'Were the Owens somehow related to the Deans? I thought I saw something in one of the papers about a relative.'

'No dear, not the Owens. But Molly's uncle, a Mr Blyth and his family, lived right on the corner of the lane where she was found.'

'And no one thought that a strange coincidence?'

Daphne regards me approvingly. 'Hard to believe, isn't it?' She sighs. 'But Blyth — I think he was a real estate agent — said he and his family didn't wake up until they heard the ambulance and then he thought it was an accident. Shocked to hear his niece had been attacked, etcetera, etcetera. Completely innocent.'

'Speaking of coincidences, what about those rumours of attacks on other women?'

'Oh they weren't rumours.'

'I don't mean Hazel Wilson or Mena Griffiths.'

Daphne nods. 'I don't mean them either. No, there was a rash of other attacks. Mostly after midnight, and the man went for the girls' throats every time. He also tore the stockings off some of them. No beating though.'

'How many were there?'

She looks at the ceiling and her fingers twitch, mentally ticking through a monstrous checklist. 'Six. Three in St Kilda: Canterbury Road, Brighton Road and Foster Street. Two in Addison Street, a few yards from where Molly Dean was attacked.'

I rock back in my chair, my mouth falling open in surprise.

But before I can say anything, Daphne delivers the coup de grâce.

'And on 31 July 1930, one girl was attacked and dragged into the front yard of the house opposite the Dean's home in Milton Street.'

We look at each other. None of this was in any of the newspaper accounts of Molly Dean's murder. There was a vague mention of a couple of girls being followed, written in a way that made the reader think they were scared and imagining the whole thing, or making it up, presumably to grab a spot in the limelight. Six other women attacked and not a whisper. I draw a mental map of the streets Daphne listed. She must see the realisation dawn on my face because she is nodding as I say, 'All of them between St Kilda Station, where Molly Dean got off her train, and the Dean's home.'

We stare at each other some more, and I am suddenly hyperaware of the ticking of Daphne's clock (French, ormolu, late eighteenth century).

She reaches for the legal pad. 'I think, Alex, that now would be a good time for you to read my notes on Adam Graham. What they printed in the papers doesn't even begin to scratch the surface.'

I leave Hillview in a bit of a fog. Daphne wouldn't say a word about Adam Graham, only insisting I read her notes thoroughly before visiting again. I already know a bit about Graham from the newspaper reports, and none of it is flattering. It could be the way the articles were written, but this man had *prime suspect* virtually tattooed on his forehead.

The Citroën may as well be on autopilot for all the attention I pay to the roads as I head home. The only things that register are the gracious swags of the brick fence encircling Brighton General Cemetery. It flashes past, the occasional madonna or ostentatious cross like a macabre jack-in-the-box, popping above the red and grey. I wonder if Molly is buried here, or perhaps in St Kilda Cemetery. She lived and died roughly halfway between the two. That edifying deliberation lasts until I reach home.

I force myself to put Daphne's notes aside for an hour while I deal with some neglected business matters. The chequebook takes a hammering as I attend to a small stack of bills, and I soon have a neat pile of envelopes ready to send out on Monday. Now I know exactly how much money I have to play with, I turn to my current auction catalogues. I have a long-time client who collects works by Napier Waller, and one of Waller's paintings, *The Hunt*, has just been listed for auction at Deutscher-Menzies. Because this company is a newcomer to the Melbourne auction scene, I think there's a very good chance I'll be able to pick up the painting for my client at a good price. Waller's stuff rarely appears on the open market, but he's also responsible for a lot of public works around Melbourne. My favourite is the mosaic on the first floor of Newspaper House in Collins Street, but I also love the Myer Mural Hall and the triumphant *Peace After Victory* in the State Library. Few people know about Napier Waller, despite the fact that in his day, he was just as successful as the most significant of his artistic contemporaries, like Arthur Streeton. Perhaps the most impressive thing about Waller, though, is that some of his best work was done after the Great War. Waller fought for his country and was so seriously injured he lost his right arm. But he was a determined man, so he simply taught himself to draw and paint with his left hand instead. I always enjoy handling his work.

Once I've confirmed the viewing times and made a note

in my diary, I figure I've done enough work-related things to justify sitting down with Daphne's notes. In the lounge, Hogarth is already installed on the couch. I settle into a burgundy velvet wing-backed chair in the corner of the room, switch on the floor lamp and unfold Daphne's papers.

My plan is to skim through once and see if anything jumps out, then go back for a closer read. Two lines in I realise this stuff is too interesting to skip over. I start reading again.

The newspaper accounts of the murder investigation and inquest had mentioned Adam Graham, a family friend of the Deans, but Daphne's notes give much more detail. Adam and his family – mother, brother and sister – had boarded with the Deans in 1921, when they'd first emigrated from Scotland. The Grahams moved out after two years and the two families had remained close until there was a falling out. But somehow, Adam had re-established a place for himself in the Dean household. He spent time talking cars and machines with Molly's brother, Ralph, but his relationship with Molly and her mother Ethel was rather more complex. According to Ralph, his mother had hoped to set Molly and Adam up as a couple, despite the fact Adam was quite a bit older. Ralph said Molly had laughed in Adam's face when he'd invited her out, but oddly claimed that afterwards it was all perfectly amicable and the two were quite happy to sit at the table together whenever Adam came round for dinner.

Adam Graham claimed he'd never been interested in Molly and had only asked her out to please Molly's mother. A strange claim to make when Ethel Dean confessed she and Graham had a sexual relationship that had been going on for a number of years leading up to the time of Molly's death. Graham, for his part, first admitted to, then later denied, the relationship with Ethel, a woman at least twenty years his senior. He claimed police had tricked him into admitting to the affair using questions laden with innuendo and veiled references, which he took to mean a close friendship. Unfortunately for him, other people also knew what he and Ethel Dean were up to, including Molly. It was when Molly confronted her mother about the relationship that Ethel Dean pulled a knife on her daughter.

I realise I'm leaning forward on the edge of the chair and sit back. Just one page in and the whole Molly Dean story is even more screwed up than I'd imagined. This family makes a *Days of Our Lives* saga look positively tame by comparison.

I keep reading as the shadows grow longer and the pool of light around my chair becomes more defined. At 5.40 Hogarth yawns, rolls himself over the edge of the couch so he ends up in a standing position, then saunters over and shoves his head in front of my face, obscuring the pages with his shaggy noggin. Canine dinner time is generally 5.45 and Hogarth has the best tummy alarm in the business. I stand up, feeling my stiff joints pop and creak. The notes are temporarily abandoned as I head to the kitchen, Hogarth close on my heels.

I turn on the lights over the island bench and pull Hogarth's meat and veg from the fridge. As I mix things together in his bowl, I think over what I've read so far about Adam Graham. Anyone prepared to try to date the daughter while sleeping with the mother is clearly a creep of the first order, but that doesn't make him a murderer. Perhaps if I make a list of the key points about Graham that were reported in the news, I can cross reference with Daphne's notes and see if that tells me anything more about this man. I put Hogarth's dish down and open the fridge again, trying and failing to get excited about cooking something for myself. Molly is calling; I want to get back to work.

In the study, I sift through the heap of articles I printed off at the library, searching for Graham's name among the fuzzy print. This whittles my pile down considerably, and I discard a couple more pages when I realise they are syndicated articles; the one I printed from *The Argus* is the same as the one in the *Ballarat Advertiser*.

The coroner's inquest was held in late January 1931, about two months after Molly's murder. Technically it was an open court, but there were so many witnesses and media that the general public were turned away. The murder of Molly Dean enthralled the populace because of the violence of her death and a wider concern a maniac might be on the loose. The press were happy to pander to this thirst for knowledge, and the testimonies of the key witnesses were reported virtually word for word in the major metropolitan newspapers. I open my notebook and start a list of information relating to Adam Graham as told to the court by Ethel Dean, Ralph Dean, Percy Lambell, Graham's sister and mother, and the man himself.

Other than the relationship with Ethel Dean, there were a lot of odd things about Adam Graham and his story. I flip from article to article, noting down the other key points that count against him. I'm so engrossed in the task, it takes a moment before I realise the phone is ringing. At this time in the evening that means only one thing.

'Hi, Mum.'

'Alex dear, I thought you were going to call me today.'

'Ummm, was I supposed to?'

'No, but it's always nice to phone your mother from time to time – or even take her out for lunch – and I haven't spoken to you for a few days, so I just felt that today must be the day.'

'Oh. Well thanks for taking the initiative. I've kind of gotten caught up with work. I bought this painting and –'

'Alex, you don't have deadlines or office hours.'

'Mum, before we launch into a lively yet at the same time enervating discussion about the detour on my career path to professorial tenure at Melbourne Uni, I want to tell you about this painting.'

'I wasn't going to –'

'Of course you were. It's a mother's job to harangue her daughter about these things. But just listen, tell me what you think, and you can berate me to your heart's content when I take you to lunch next week.'

She laughs. 'Tell me about this painting then.'

I give Mum a full account, from when I first spotted the portrait at Lane's through the whole research thing to Daphne and her story. She is silent the entire time, so I know I've piqued her interest. 'It's great that you called because, given how your mind works, I could use your opinion on some of the details about Adam Graham's story.'

'Are you implying I have a nefarious bent?'

'Of course not, Mummy dearest.'

'Watch it, kid.'

'I just meant you read a lot of crime books, so I thought if I told you some of the odd things about Adam Graham, you could tell me if you think they really are screwy or conversely, if I'm just off in my own little fantasy land.'

'Well, I'm definitely good at the latter. Okay, let's have it.'

'First, Adam Graham had no solid alibi for the time of Molly's murder. In fact, his mother and sister told conflicting stories about the time he returned home and where he slept. His mother said he was home and tucked up in bed in his room by midnight. The sister said that first thing in the morning she took him a cup of tea in bed, only this was the camp bed in the sleep-out, a place where he often dossed when he came home late, as no one could hear him come in. Under questioning on the stand, the sister changed her story and said she'd just been confused, what with the shock of it all. The trouble was, she'd told the police the same story several times.'

Mum butts in. 'Well the mother lied to protect Adam and no one thought to tell the poor honest sister before she was questioned. Now mother's instinct aside, if her darling boy had nothing to hide, why lie? Makes me far more suspicious than if she's just said she had no idea when he got home or where he slept.'

'Oh and they lived in Gordon Avenue, just one block from Molly's home.'

'I have my eyebrows raised here, Alex. What else?'

'There were a few blood stains on his suit, but they sound like fairly small marks.'

'Hmm. I'm not sure what to make of that. You said there was a lot of blood at the crime scene, which makes me think a couple of little spots would be unlikely. You'd expect great big splatters. Unless he was wearing overalls of course.'

'Hey! That makes a lot of sense, given he was a mechanic.'

'Of course, in 1930 there was no blood type or DNA testing, so maybe he'd just cut himself shaving.'

'Right, so inconclusive on the blood. Well, then there were the witnesses who saw Molly Dean walking home and reported a man with a distinctive gait following her. After they'd seen Graham outside court, each witness independently confirmed that not only did Graham have the same height and build as the mystery man, but he moved in the same way.'

'Walks like a duck – literally in this case – has to be him then.'

'And Graham admitted to following Molly on other occasions, but claimed it was only because Ethel Dean asked him to.'

'Refer previous comment. The man had form as a stalker. Everyone knows the next step up from common-or-garden stalking is a violent attack.'

'I actually did not know that, Mum.'

'It's a logical progression when you stop to think about it.'

'See, this is why I needed your input.'

'Is there more?'

'Just one last thing. Molly's mother refused to give the police Adam Graham's details, telling them, "He knows nothing. You do not want to go bothering him."'

'Uh-huh. Nothing suspicious there. The bastard did it.'

'I made a few more notes, but it looks as if those were the main points to come out at the inquest. There are a couple of reports that Adam Graham said police treated him badly, but he didn't cry police brutality. Anyway, even if the police were a bit rough, nothing he said to them was particularly incriminating by itself. It was his statement combined with the evidence of other witnesses that put him in the spotlight as a key suspect. The only problem is, even though the coroner committed Adam Graham for trial, he was never prosecuted. All the charges were dropped on the day the trial was due to start.'

'What? That's crazy! So the poor girl never got any justice?' Mum stops and sighs. 'Alex, much as I'd like to take this opportunity to fulfil my maternal duty and tell you to get a proper job, I have to admit you're on to something. Not only is it interesting, but it seems like a story that should be told.'

'Thanks Mum. And thanks for hearing me out.'

'I still reserve the right to nag you if I think it's warranted.'

'I wouldn't expect anything else.'

We talk a bit more before hanging up and I decide to go and grab Daphne's notes and finish reading while everything is fresh in my head. I push the chair back from the desk and hear a crunch. A wheel is caught on a piece of paper; one of the printed articles had fallen from the stack and I hadn't noticed. Picking it up, I see it's from the *Adelaide News* and dated 30 January, the last day of the inquest. I scan the first few lines and realise this is not syndicated from a Melbourne daily. Molly's murder was so sensational, the interstate newspapers had sent their own pressmen. A couple of paragraphs in there's a new piece of information, something I hadn't seen in any of the other articles. A young Elwood woman named Gladys Healey had spoken to police about Adam Graham. She'd known him for over a year because he looked after her car and had been working on it the week before Molly's murder. All well and good, Graham was a mechanic after all and he probably did the same sort of thing for a few people. The thing is, Gladys kept her car garaged and naturally enough, Graham worked on the car in Gladys's garage. A garage that happened to be located in the very same lane where Molly Dean was found.

I grab Daphne's notes again, wondering what else there is to learn about Adam Graham, although I'm starting to think it doesn't really matter: the cops clearly liked him as the murderer. There's only another half page to read and it seems to confirm Adam Graham was in a relationship with Ethel Dean. Apparently, he was in the habit of parking his car under the streetlight in front of the Dean's house, claiming it was safer there. But why leave your car a block away from your own home, unless you were spending time in a different bed?

Then I read Daphne's final paragraph and now I'm even more certain of Adam Graham's guilt. On the night of Molly's murder, when detectives Lambell and O'Keeffe first went to tell Ethel Dean what had happened, Graham's car was parked under the streetlight tightly covered. But when Lambell returned several hours later, the cover was gone. Either Adam Graham's mother lied and he wasn't asleep in bed at midnight, or he went out again. As Molly Dean lay in hospital, dying, the man with a history of following her was out in his car.

Of course, that still leaves me with a pressing question: why did the trial never happen?

1930

IT WAS LATE BY the time Molly swung back in the direction of Milton Street, but Saturday night meant the streets of St Kilda and Elwood were anything but quiet. A fitful wind had started blowing in from the west, whipping up whitecaps on the bay and snatching at the hats of unsuspecting pleasure-seekers. When she and Sarah left Luna Park, they linked arms to forge a path through the crowd streaming out of the Palais Pictures. A full house had spent the evening transfixed by two full-length films, and now nearly 3000 movie-goers swept across the St Kilda triangle. Some charted a course for home but others, determined to extract every last ounce of pleasure from the night, made their way toward the Palais de Dance or toward the coffee shops and soda fountains of Acland Street. Along the Esplanade, men still wrapped in distinctive red, white and black scarves, high on the combined effects of a win at the footy and a celebratory evening of sly grog, stumbled among the more smartly dressed Saturday night crowd.

Molly saw Sarah onto the South Yarra tram before turning for home, still smiling, even though her tired legs were telling her it was time for bed. She watched people as they passed, measuring their clothes and voices, picturing their lives, seeing some of them as characters in her soon-to-be-written novel. The crowds fell away as she moved into the residential streets, but the lights behind numerous curtains signalled that Molly was not the only one unwilling to surrender to sleep. Somewhere, a gramophone played, jazz spilling through the night. Molly kicked a heel up behind her as she recognised Paul Whiteman and his Orchestra playing 'Happy Feet', quickly glancing about to see if anyone had witnessed her impromptu Charleston step. The song carried her around the corner into Milton Street.

Her hand was on the gate, when from the other side of the road came the distinctive scrape and hiss of a match. She turned. A man stood in the shadowed gateway of the house across the street. His hands were cupped around the flame, the glowing tip of a cigarette flaring as he inhaled, briefly illuminating his face. Molly's hand flew to her chest.

'Adam Graham! You gave me the fright of my life. What on earth are you doing out here?'

'Evenin' Mary. Been visiting your ma and she sent me out to see if you were coming. Thought I'd have a fag and wait awhile, but here you are, large as life.' Adam stepped from the darkness and walked slowly across the road toward Molly, a slight swagger in his step. As he passed through the sulphurous light of the street lamp, Adam's stocky frame was thrown into stark relief, his shadow stretching away behind him, as though reluctant to leave the gloom. He veered away from her at the last moment and leaned against the fence, a few feet between them.

Molly's eyes narrowed as she looked at him, at his large hand dwarfing the glowing cigarette. She realised he was wearing his homburg. 'You haven't been following me again, have you?'

Adam spread his arms wide. 'I was just standing here and you came along.' The cigarette tip bobbed and dipped like a firefly as he spoke, but his features were cast in shadow.

'Why should I believe you? After last time? Besides, who wears a jacket and hat to step out for a smoko?'

There was silence except for the harsh rasp as Adam drew deep on his cigarette, then a sigh as he exhaled a steady stream of smoke that coiled up, thinned and dissipated into the night.

'You were following me.' Molly reached back and grabbed the iron spike of the fence, gripping it hard.

'Your mother worries about you.'

'That's rubbish and you know it. What I don't understand is what you get out of it. Or is her bed part of the bargain?' Molly's voice was harsh.

Adam came up off the fence, fast, his hand raised.

'You wouldn't dare.' She lifted her chin. 'Not unless she asked you to, anyway.'

Adam lowered his hand and seemed to relax, slouching back against the fence and bending one leg to brace his foot on the railing. 'Does it matter if I followed you? I didn't bother you, just making sure you were safe.'

'Stop it. I know you report back to her, tell her who I'm seeing and where I go.'

'Look Mary, I like you.' He paused as Molly sniffed derisively. 'You know I like you and I thought we had a chance, but you're for better things, aren't you? Doesn't mean we can't be friends. Your brother doesn't have a problem with me and your ma certainly don't.' Adam's lips pursed around the cigarette.

'Don't.' Molly's eyes filled with tears. All the energy and joy of the evening were gone. 'Don't talk to me, don't come near me, and don't ever, ever follow me, no matter what she says. Lie to her if you have to but leave me alone. Once I'm gone, you can marry her and move in, or go back to Scotland and take her with you – I don't care – but I want nothing to do with you. Ever.' Molly half turned and unlatched the gate but stopped when she heard the sound of low laughter.

'You ought to be thanking me, Mary Dean. Thanking me for looking out for you, because you know what happens when yer ma decides to follow you herself. Remember what happened that time at the university? Be a shame for your arty pals to hear Ethel carrying on like that now, wouldn't it?' Adam pushed himself off the fence and in two bounding steps was looming over her, hand on the gate, stopping Molly from opening it. He drew hard on the remains of his cigarette then flicked the butt away into the gutter where it glowed bright for a moment before it spluttered and died. 'Just remember who your real friends are Mary, that's all I'm sayin'.'

Molly shook her head vigorously and shoved hard against the gate, struggling for a moment before Adam suddenly let it go, sending her spinning into the front yard, almost losing her footing. The sound of his laughter followed her all the way up the path and into the house, and kept ringing in her ears deep into the night until sleep finally claimed her.

1999

IT'S LATE NOW AND my eyes feel like I've dipped my face in vinegar, so I decide to take Hogarth for a quick walk around the block before bed. We go out the gate and take a left, away from the main road. I love walking through residential streets. In the daytime I can admire gardens and architecture, but a night-time neighbourhood is a different thing entirely. At this time of year, there is a hint of wood smoke in the air from those enjoying the comfort of an early season open fire, the mulch smell of wet leaves, and occasionally a late-blooming gardenia lends its exotic flavour to the mix. But what I really love about night walks is the chance to spy on other people's lives. Safely anonymous in the dark of the street, I take every open-curtained opportunity to gaze through the windows we pass; it's amazing how much you can see in a well-lit room as you dawdle by. It's not the people I care about, it's the decor. Most important of all, it's what they have hanging on their walls. I keep hoping I'll spot an undiscovered masterpiece hanging over a dusty mantel and make a fortune, but no luck so far.

As Hogarth and I amble along, my brain is a jumble of thoughts about Molly, Adam and the various other people in her world. I wish I could find out more about Molly's relationship with Colin Colahan, but I might as well be chasing shadows. In the days immediately after Molly's murder, before Adam Graham came to the attention of the police and public, Colin was briefly the main suspect for the killing. He was, after all, a bohemian, Molly's lover and the last person seen in her company. Fortunately for Colin, Molly had phoned him after getting off her train, and the operator who connected the call had logged it in his register and remembered putting Molly through. The police theorised Colin could have taken the call at his Hawthorn home, jumped in a taxi and raced to Elwood in time to intercept and kill Molly. But that was wild speculation and quickly dismissed, particularly when no obliging cab drivers came forward to tell of a mad ride through the midnight streets. Colin's testimony at the inquest also showed how much he cared for Molly Dean. He spoke of her with love and happiness, even stating that they were 'betrothed'. Given his Don Juan ways, I wonder if this was true or simply a gallant attempt to protect Molly's reputation when she was no longer able to defend herself.

By the time we arrive back home, I've decided I need to hash this out with someone. And the best person I know for bouncing ideas around with is John. I'll catch him first thing. Inside, I change into my PJ bottoms and wander through the house as I brush my teeth, checking all the door and window locks. Finding everything as it should be, I wash my face and slip into bed, cranking on my electric blanket for a few minutes. Hogarth scratches up the cover on his bedroom dog bed before folding himself up with a grunt of contentment. I pick up my book, but my brain is already occupied with

Molly's story and I toss it back on the cedar chest I use as a bedside table. Snapping off the light I close my eyes, but sleep is slow to come.

I'M AWAKE AT FIVE as usual and Hogarth and I get out for an hour of real exercise. It's still dark, but as we head home there's a hint of the new day trying to assert itself in the east, and objects like cars and rubbish bins have become more than just looming shapes. I take a quick shower, throw on some jeans and a better class of t-shirt (solid colour, no writing), then head into the kitchen where Hogarth has the fridge staked out. I realise for the first time in days I haven't been obsessing about Molly Dean.

Our breakfast doesn't take long and once I've tidied up, I grab my laptop, printouts and Daphne's notes. I'll be at John's studio by eight, but he should be there getting organised for the day. A crap marriage is a great motivator for getting to work bright and early, and John's wife, well... I did try to warn him: now I'm just waiting to pick up the pieces.

Sure enough, when I swing the Citroën into the small church car park, John's nondescript white van is already there. It looks like every other disreputable, beaten-up van on the road, and occasionally it causes his clients to flare their nostrils when he pulls into their Toorak and Brighton driveways. But why advertise the fact you may be carrying millions of dollars' worth of art? The van's only distinguishing feature is a plastic figurine stuck to the dash. It's Buddy Jesus – a small statue of Jesus winking and giving the thumbs up – that I gave John after he'd had a particularly gruelling time restoring some religious paintings for a certain Melbourne church. It wasn't the paintings he'd had trouble with but the priest's attitude, and things got a bit heated. Now John tells his woes to Buddy Jesus and it's all cool. The fact that he charged the diocese a fortune for his work also helped.

John's door is open and the sound of a lush piano and Latin strings pours out into the morning sun. I bounce up the four steps and knock on the door frame.

'John.'

'Shhh. He's just getting to the good bit.' John waves a laden brush in the direction of his sound system. I wander over and squint at the artist information on the CD case. Enrique Chia. The music soars and swoons its way to a flourishing finale and I tap the pause button before John can get lost in the next track. John dabs delicately at the canvas on his easel, a Dutch still life that has clearly had a long, hard couple of centuries.

'To what do I owe the pleasure?'

'It's about Molly Dean.'

John glances in my direction. 'And yet I see no painting. I was expecting you the day after the auction.'

'Yeah, I got sidetracked and now ... Well, I think she's probably safer under Hogarth's watchful eye for the moment.'

John applies a final stroke of deep vermilion to the edge of a tulip petal, then places his brush in a jar of mineral spirits and sets his palette down before turning to stare at me. 'Speak English. You are making absolutely no sense.'

So I tell John about the dodgy underbidder, Rob's weird

reaction, the missing files and Daphne Lambell. While I've been talking, we've gravitated toward the two '60s wicker bucket chairs near the fridge. John has sprawled into the red and white one, while I'm perched on the edge of the yellow chair, forearms resting on my knees. I pull out the stuff on Adam Graham and hand it across to John. As he flips through, I give him a rundown of what it says and also what it doesn't say. I finally wind to a stop and sit there watching as John continues to eyeball the material, flicking between pages, arranging articles around his feet, and occasionally grunting in response to what he's reading. He taps the papers he's holding against his chin and frowns.

'You've lost the fucking plot.'

'Aren't you even the tiniest bit intrigued?'

'Look, it's one thing to do a bit of provenance research or dig up a juicy backstory on a painting – that's money in the bank – but this is nuts. Next thing you'll be in here saying, "Oh by the way, John, I've been digging around and I have a theory on what Leonardo said to Mona Lisa that was so bloody hilarious."'

I cross my arms over my chest and flop back in the chair. 'I'm not trying to go all Holmes and Watson here.'

John snorts.

'When I started it was like you said, a bit of backstory to boost a sale. But when I read about how she was killed, yeah, I wanted to know more. Then with all the stuff with Rob and the archives, it just sort of snowballed.'

'You think?'

'Forget about the fact you think I'm an idiot.' I jerk my chin toward John and the papers. 'What do you make of all that?'

'The man was clearly a bastard of the first order, but I can't decide if the mother was an above average cold-hearted bitch or an absolute psycho. I'm leaning toward the latter.'

'Adam Graham was the main suspect and the coroner committed him for trial.'

'Well, case solved then.' John drops the remaining papers to the floor. 'Was the mother in on it?'

I spread my arms wide, palms up and give an exaggerated shrug. 'She did ask the police to let the matter drop *and* told them they'd never catch the man who did it.'

'Not exactly the response you'd expect from a grieving parent. Sounds like she knew something.'

'I think so too. There are a couple of problems with Graham, though.'

'Of course there are. Man's a murderer. Or was. Your Miss Lambell's notes say he carked it in 1980.'

'Not that, problems with what happened after the coroner's findings.'

'What? The brother confessed? Molly had an evil twin who burst into court?'

I roll my eyes. 'Despite the fact Adam Graham's bail was set at £1000 – about four times the average annual income in 1930, remember – he was out forty-five minutes after the coroner remanded him in custody.' I tick off a finger. 'Bail was posted by a St Kilda resident, a retired farmer called Carter. I have no idea who the hell he is or what relationship he has to the whole thing.' I tick off another finger. 'Graham was completely calm through the whole inquest, even when the coroner fingered him as the murderer. In fact, he was so bloody calm that when bail was posted and a copper went to let him out, Adam Graham was fast asleep on the wooden pallet they had in the cell and had to be shaken awake so they could cut him loose.' Now I hold up my thumb. 'And most importantly, when Graham actually came to trial only four weeks later, the prosecution dropped the entire case before a jury was even sworn in.'

John leans forward. 'But all that stuff in the articles and notes. Following Molly, dodgy alibi, blood on his suit, the garage ... How could they not go to trial? And since when do farmers retire to St Kilda?'

I nod. 'Oh yeah and one other thing. After they dropped the charges, I can't find any further mention of the Molly Dean murder in the papers. Nothing to suggest the case was being pursued, and no cries of outrage from the media that there was still a brutal killer on the loose. The whole thing just disappeared.'

John stares at me for a couple of beats then jumps up and starts fiddling with his Atomic coffee maker and the hotplate. 'We'll need coffee while we figure out what to do next.'

While John messes with Arabica beans, I duck out and jog-trot around the corner to a trendy little shopping strip. In the bakery I order two croissants and a couple of pains au chocolat for variety, then double-time it back to the studio.

We sit on the steps outside John's studio, the morning sun warm on our faces, and enjoy the first few sips of coffee in comfortable silence. The crumble of flaky pastry as we begin on the croissants acts as a signal to the local pigeon population and they start appearing from all corners, flapping in to land at a distance before bobbing toward the steps. I'm not a fan of pigeons and I wave my arms and stamp my feet in a feeble attempt to move them away, but these feathered deros are a hardy lot and barely take a step back.

John puts his coffee down. 'Watch this.'

He disappears inside and I hear the fridge open and close. Then he's back with a small piece of minced meat. Standing on the top step, he looks up toward the top branches of a eucalyptus, a massive grey gum that must have been here since the church was built late last century. John holds out his hand and whistles, a strange, single tone that starts on a low note, swings up through an octave and then dips back down. Instantly, there's a response from the tree canopy and a black shape appears, heading toward us like a missile. As the bird gets close, John tosses the meat out and up. I see a flash of white among the black feathers as the meat is caught with an audible clack of beak and the bird describes a tight curve and heads back to the tree. I'd been so transfixed by the display I'd hardly registered the panicked fluttering that was going on at ground level, but now I look down and see all the pigeons have decamped.

I nod my head at John. 'Impressive. Was that a currawong? He came and went so fast I couldn't tell.'

'Yeah. Pest control. Nothing more frightening than a dark shadow looming over you.'

'How much real work do you do around here anyway?'

'Speaking of not working, let's consider this Molly Dean thing.'

'Right. I guess the big question is, do you think it was Adam Graham? I mean, the cops had him pegged as the killer and the coroner thought so too. Everything we've read and talked about points that way, but I guess we're only getting a certain perspective.'

'Sure, but your Daphne woman's notes seem fairly straightforward.'

'Yes, but her dad was the cop trying to nail Adam Graham.' I think about it for a moment. 'Percy Lambell might never have told his daughter things that didn't fit the case. Daphne believes in him 100 per cent, and even at her age you can tell she loved her dad to bits.'

'Okay, so we're Mulder and Scully. Trust no one.'

'And you had the temerity to tell me I'm nuts.' I raise an eyebrow at John. 'But I get what you're saying.'

John nods enthusiastically, his eyes bright. 'Oh and I've been meaning to ask: what happened to the murder weapon?'

'Oh they never found it. Probably thrown into the Elwood canal – it's just around the corner – but the police didn't bother to look. They figured there'd be lots of things in the canal that could be the murder weapon, so it'd only be more confusing.'

Now it's John's turn to arch his eyebrows at me. 'So, no weapon, no other real suspects, no reward for information?' He looks at me and I nod in confirmation. 'Any other theories?'

'A few. Colin Colahan was quickly ruled out, so that leaves random attack by crazed sex maniac, who may or may not be the same guy who killed Hazel Wilson and Mena Griffiths around that time. It could also be an escalation of the attacks on those six women; one of them happened opposite Molly's house, and they all involved strangling and stockings. Then there was a suggestion of some other unidentified jealous lover Molly had supposedly hooked up with while Colin was out of town on a painting trip ... Oh yes, and there was one idea the killer was a woman, based on the fact Molly was dragged not carried into the lane.'

'A mystery woman? Motivated by the fact Molly stole her man?' John puts a country twang on the last words.

'Pretty much.'

'But we're ignoring the oestrogen-crazed rival theory, right?'

'Well ...' I tip my head from side to side.

'What?'

'I think there were two women in the Meldrum circle who had the hots for Colin: Betty Rowland and Sue Vanderkelen.'

'Oh, come on. Given Colin was a well-known Casanova, it's a real stretch to believe one of those women decided to take out her rival so violently. A bit of slapping and scratching I could see, but not such a grisly murder.'

'How very sexist of you, John.'

'That's not what I –'

'Although you might be half right.' I cut across him. 'I checked out some crime stats and women don't tend to beat people to death. They prefer to kill by poisoning or stabbing, but more importantly when they do kill, the victim is likely to be a man – husband or boyfriend. Plus in 90 per cent of cases the murder happens at home. Men are the outdoor lurkers and bashers.'

'You need a different hobby. But does this mean we agree about the gender of Molly's killer?'

'I'm not sure, but let's put the women aside for now. Which means we're back to Adam Graham or unknown assailant, be he jealous lover or mad fiend.'

'You're enjoying this, aren't you?'

I think about the cast of characters for a moment. 'I don't see the jealous lover theory. Molly was trying to get out of her life and into something better, so she wouldn't have had a fling with anyone except someone else in Colin Colahan's group.'

John nods and waves at me to continue.

'We know Colin had a string of lovelies and probably wouldn't have been too upset if Molly, er … cast a wider net shall we say, but at the same time, anyone in that group would know she'd hooked up with Colin first. They'd know the score and I doubt any of them would care, not enough to bludgeon the girl to death anyway.'

'I could maybe see a heated exchange but that's about it. And from everything we know about her, I think Molly was too smart to risk being frozen out of that group. At least, not until she was far more established, until she'd well and truly left the old life behind.'

'So no jealous lover and no women.' I stop. 'What about the mother?'

'Nup. If she put Graham up to it, well that's still Graham,' John says, 'but I reckon Ethel wouldn't lie in wait. She's a nasty piece of work, and I could imagine her stabbing Molly in a fit of anger in the kitchen or bashing her with the copper stick on laundry day, but she doesn't strike me as a lurker and I can't see a mother doing all that stuff with a stocking and underwear.'

We sit with our own thoughts for a moment. I don't know if John's are as dark as mine, but from the bleak look on his face I guess they're not far off. I sigh and drag a hand across one eye. 'So why didn't Percy Lambell look for someone else? Okay maybe at the start he was all gung-ho for Graham, but after that? Or why didn't he try to get more evidence or something so they could reinstate the charges? It doesn't make sense.'

John has been leaning back on his elbows, head thrown back and eyes closed, but now his eyes snap open and he lurches upright. 'Holy crap.' He stares at me, mouth slightly open. I can almost hear the squeak of tiny cogs and wheels as his brain grinds toward an incredible thought. 'Holy crap.'

'You said that. What is it?'

He holds up his hand in a stop gesture and I obligingly shut up.

'There were other attacks, right? One in the garden opposite Molly's house? And others?'

I nod, wondering where he's going. We've been over this.

'And no investigation that we know of after Adam Graham was let off? And no outcry from the press? And all the files have vanished?'

He's clearly on a roll with the rhetorical questions, so I just wait it out.

'It's a fucking cover-up!'

I open my mouth to speak but get the hand again.

'Maybe Adam Graham killed her on someone's orders, or the killer was someone else and Graham was the convenient fall guy. Either way, if Graham was in on it, that would explain why he was so cool through the whole thing, especially if he was being paid. I wonder if they'd have let him swing for Molly's murder if the chips had fallen that way?'

'Seriously?'

'Don't forget, this was 1930 when Thomas Blamey was chief of Police. His whole term of office was tainted by allegations of corruption and misbehaviour, both by him and by the police force in general.'

'What?'

'Oh yeah. There was an enquiry. Allegations the police were trafficking cocaine, running an insurance scam, taking bribes ... Blamey had to resign a few years later when a Royal Commission found he'd covered up the truth about a shooting in Royal Park.'

I stare at John. 'Blamey was the one who said a reward for information about Molly's murder was unnecessary.'

'See? And all those other crimes were used as a distraction.' He pauses to dramatically slap the back of one hand into the palm of the other. 'And Adam Graham was being manipulated – whether he actually killed Molly or not – by someone important with the power or money to first misdirect and then shut down the investigation. Connections high up in the police force.'

I'm still staring at John and have no idea what to say. Somehow he's rolled at least four possible scenarios into one giant conspiracy theory starring Adam Graham working with a malevolent Mr X, who may even be a senior police officer. It sounds completely ludicrous and yet it makes a weird kind of sense. John is looking at me expectantly.

'You really are Mulder.'

1930

IT WAS THE END of another school day and after checking to see that the ink monitor had done his job, Molly decided to stay back and catch up on some of her marking and administrative work. The headmaster, always an intimidating figure in his starched collars and flapping black robe, had spoken with her earlier in the day. It seemed Molly's recent distraction had not gone unnoticed and although it wasn't an official reprimand, she had been told – in no uncertain terms – things had better improve quickly or there would be consequences. Seeing the look on Molly's face, the headmaster had softened.

'Miss Dean. Up until the last month or so, your work has been exemplary. The children like you and more importantly they all seem to be progressing well, regardless of the challenges they face. You have the potential for advancement and a satisfying career in the field of education. Indeed, prior to this recent lapse, I had put your name forward to the Education Board for promotion. Please don't give me cause to regret that decision.'

Molly had made all the right appeasing sounds, expressing

dismay that she had allowed her work to suffer and promising a return to her previous standards. But all the time she was acutely aware she had lost heart. Through college, and the first two years of teaching at the Queensberry Street School, Molly had convinced herself she was content, that making a difference in the lives of these children was enough. But in recent weeks her thoughts had been turning more and more to a career as a writer. Dabbling in her spare time was no longer enough and Molly knew she had to make a decision: put writing to one side and concentrate on being a good teacher, or give up teaching and the security of a regular wage to chase her dream. Every time she thought about leaving the classroom for good it made her feel a bit sick, but it wasn't as though she had nothing waiting for her outside. Molly had sent proposals for articles to a number of Australian publications and so far one of those had already borne fruit. Together with her poem and a handful of other published pieces, it felt like a good start.

The hush of her classroom at four o'clock was in sharp contrast to the constant hum and murmur of children trying to be quiet for hours on end, and she found the deep silence almost more intrusive. While she did not have a large number of students, their challenges and special learning requirements meant that during school hours the room was seldom quiet, and Molly was never still. But now afternoon sunlight streamed through the tall Gothic windows, and as Molly watched chalk dust drift in its warm rays she acknowledged that this room, at this time of day, was one of the few moments she could claim as her own, undisturbed and uninterrupted.

After an hour of correcting spelling and writing reports, Molly locked the schoolwork in the desk and reached down into her satchel, pulling out her notebook. There was still time for writing, a good half hour before the custodian would come through to lock up, and Molly had plenty to do. She flipped through the first dozen pages of the notebook, past ideas and musings, poems half penned and snatches of prose. Then a few blank pages, a pause before the opening chapter of her yet-to-be-named novel announced itself with a flourish of ink. She stopped to read a couple of phrases, then moved on. Suddenly impatient, she picked the book up by its spine and held it over the desk, fanning the pages and shaking it at the same time. Molly was rewarded when a single sheet detached itself and fluttered free, sliding onto the desktop as though it had meant to be there all along. She put the notebook aside and ran her hand across the letter, smoothing invisible creases, her fingers lingering on the embossed *Table Talk* letterhead. The letter had only arrived a few days before, and she could still hardly believe they had not only liked her work, but were willing to at least consider taking her on as a freelance columnist.

'We await your submission.' She read the sentence out loud and frowned. 'Who can I write about?'

Molly sat back in her chair and absently brought her thumb to her mouth, chewing the already short nail. Writing for *Table Talk* meant a society piece: gossipy descriptions of parties or concerts, or a profile of one of Melbourne's beautiful people, be they actress, singer, playboy or simply someone wealthy and enviable. She knew it would be easy to write about Colin or one of the other artists in their group, like John Farmer, but she wanted more of a challenge. The women artists she knew led lives too quiet to be of interest to the public and, besides, she wanted to make a splash. Molly needed a name, a big name. A person everyone would want to read about.

Absently, she scanned the walls of the classroom, but there was no inspiration to be had in a portrait of the King or a map of the British Empire.

She pulled her notebook in front of her and flipped to a blank page where she started a list of names, a who's who of Melbourne. She left a couple of lines empty in case any interstate – or even international – theatrical or musical types flitted into town to indulge in the social whirl of Melbourne Cup week. Not one name leapt out at her. Molly sat in the gathering gloom, tapping a pencil against her lower lip. 'There must be someone.'

Suddenly she sat up straight with a gasp of realisation, the pencil falling to the floor with a clatter. He had been right in front of her the whole time. A local boy made good, someone who had made the transition from humble beginnings to the rarefied atmosphere of Toorak and the mansions of St Kilda Road. He'd always been loath to reveal much about his private life, and his attendance at society events was sporadic and always cause for sensation. The upper classes were suspicious of his bona fides, the man on the street wanted to know the secrets of his success, and women just wanted to know if he was available. Donald Raeburn's story would pull readers in like moths to a flame – he was perfect.

Molly slapped her palms down on the desk and pushed her chair back hard, causing it to scrape loudly across the wooden teaching platform. All she had to do now was track the man down and persuade him to talk to her.

ONCE MOLLY HAD DECIDED Donald Raeburn was her target, she felt it best to begin with some background research. She started in the Public Library, checking the latest *Sands and McDougall Directory*.

'How much does this book weigh?' Molly muttered to herself as she hefted it to a reading desk. It looked impressive with its red binding and gilt text, and she turned to the last page to check exactly how long it was. 'Nearly 3000 pages, good heavens.'

A studious-looking young man at the next table gave her a sharp glance and Molly quickly sat down and bent her head over the book. Starting with the A to Z listings, it didn't take her long to find Raeburn, D, but there was no occupation listed next to his name. She had been hoping for something descriptive, but it seemed listing a profession was beneath those with large amounts of money. The only detail that suggested D Raeburn was perhaps a cut above the average citizen was the fact the entry also included a telephone number, which Molly noted. The listing naturally gave an address, so Molly turned to the street directory and then the maps, confirming her own impressions about the topography of the city's premier suburbs. It would be an easy trip from Elwood to Raeburn's St Kilda Road residence.

Sands and McDougall had no more useful information to impart, so she thumped the book down on the returns shelf and threaded her way through to the periodicals. Molly decided *The Home* magazine was unlikely to yield any information as it was published in Sydney, and instead started with the social pages of *Table Talk*. Given it was only printed as a weekly, she thought it would be relatively quick to skim through looking for any mention of Raeburn. She wasn't sure how to tackle the daily newspapers. Raeburn would certainly appear in their society pages, but she'd also need to try to find out anything she could about his business dealings. It was a frustratingly slow process and Molly had to frequently pull her attention back from digressions into unrelated articles or serialised stories that caught her eye as she flicked through the pages. Telling herself a journalist was nothing without diligent research, she stuck at it, reading and making notes, and only emerged with a jolt from the accumulated pile of newsprint when the librarian announced, 'Closing in ten minutes!'

Dutifully, she stacked the papers at the end of the table and made her way from the reading room, joining the shuffling parade of fellow readers and researchers as they made their way through the foyer and down the front steps to Swanston Street. Molly decided a good walk would clear her head, so rather than catching a tram she struck out toward Flinders Street Station, stepping out at a fair clip but soon finding her pace reduced to the start-stop of a crowded footpath. She set her gaze on the gabardine-clad shoulders in front of her, adjusted her stride to match their owner, and puzzled over Donald Raeburn. It didn't take her long to sift through what she had learned; details of the life of Donald Raeburn were even more scant than she had realised. He seemed to frequent the races but not the hunt, his name appeared in the same sentences as those of some of the city's most powerful people, but he had not yet been invited to join their ranks at the Melbourne Club. Donald Raeburn also attended a selection of parties and openings, but did not seem to do so with one particular woman.

As Molly veered down Collins Street and made her way through the arcades and lanes that would take her to Flinders Street, she realised just how well she had chosen her subject, provided she could pull together an article. Should she phone and make an appointment, or just present herself on the doorstep and request an audience; perhaps try to attend an event and simply introduce herself to Raeburn? Various ideas and scenarios occurred to her as she ducked through a sudden gap in the press of people and dived down Degraves Street. The surge of the crowd carried her past the barber and the tobacconist, each person in the throng convinced the distorted echo of squealing brakes and train horns must signal the imminent departure of their service. Molly clattered down the ramp to her platform to find the train just pulling in, and she moved a short distance along before shouldering her way into a carriage. She found a strap to cling to and swayed lightly as the train jolted across the Sandridge Bridge and away. The one thing she knew for certain was this was her chance to start making a name for herself as a writer. Molly Dean wanted all of Melbourne – Australia – to know who she was. Donald Raeburn was only the beginning.

1999

I LEAVE JOHN TO his Dutch painting and head off to East Melbourne. I have an appointment at eleven to catalogue and value a private collection, which I'm hoping the owners may want to sell. The traffic down Punt Road is not too bad for mid-morning, but the slow speed still gives me plenty of time to think about Molly Dean and John's theory. It would explain a lot of things, especially the dropping of all charges against Adam Graham. But I'm not sure about John's idea that the murders of Mena Griffiths and Hazel Wilson were used as a distraction, masking the real story behind Molly's death. The next time cars in front of me grind to a halt, I grab my voice recorder from the passenger seat. The traffic immediately starts to move and it's a moment before we stop again and I press record.

'If Adam Graham isn't guilty, did the killer target Molly specifically or was it just a random thing? Is Molly's murder related to the other attacks in the area and why did those attacks stop not long after Molly's death? Check similarities between Molly, Mena and Hazel's deaths. Was Mena and/

or Hazel's killer identified? Who knew Molly was going to the theatre that night? Why didn't Detective Lambell keep pursuing Adam Graham after the initial trial was abandoned?'

I drop the recorder again so I can make the turn into Hotham Street. I pass the Johnston Collection, a lovely little house museum, and pull up in front of my client's home, a Gothic Revival fully restored to show off the beauty of its bluestone and the whimsy of the gingerbread trim. I put all thoughts of Molly out of my head as I grab my phone, camera, measuring tape and laptop, and lock the car. The client, or at least one half of the client couple, meets me at the door.

'I saw you pull up. Here. You'd better put this on your dash; the inspectors are like vampires around here.' He hands me a residential parking permit and I see a flash of French cuff and delicate double cufflinks. Good taste which hopefully extends to the art collection.

'Thank you. I won't be a moment.' I hurry back to the car and place the permit prominently on the passenger side of the dashboard before turning back to the house. 'Hello?' The guy has disappeared so I step through the open door and close it behind me. I hear a skittering of paws and claws on marble and a whippet slaloms round the far corner of the hall and heads toward me.

'Jade, sweetie! Sorry hope you don't mind dogs!' My host is hot on the dog's heels, but by the time he appears, she's already jumping all over me.

'Love dogs, especially a divine hound like Miss Jade.' I crouch down to give her a proper pat, running my hands over her lean white and tan flanks. She squirms with delight.

'Oh well, if Jade likes you, you've passed all the necessary character tests! Geoffrey told me I should ask you some questions before I let you loose on the art, but I said, she already comes highly recommended and it would be a little gauche to wait until she's in the house, then start calling her qualifications into question. And now that you've got the paw of approval, I don't have to.' He pauses to take a breath. 'But listen to me rabbiting on! I'm Tony, which I'm sure you've guessed and Geoffrey will probably be back from his appointment in an hour or so.' He taps his forehead meaningfully. 'Collagen injections.'

'Great. Alex Clayton.' I straighten up and belatedly remember to stick out my hand. 'Pleasure to meet you both.' Jade is coiling around my legs. 'Would you like to give me a tour of your collection first? Then I can get started with the cataloguing.'

After taking me through the entire house pointing out paintings and keeping up a running commentary on the decor overall, Tony leads me back to the entrance hall and leaves me to my own devices. Jade hesitates for a moment over whether to follow him and decides to stick with me for the moment. I imagine she's attracted to the promise of a quiet few hours.

I get to work photographing each painting, taking measurements and noting the details down in a spreadsheet I've customised for this sort of work. I have to look at the back of the paintings as well, in case there are any notes or labels giving additional information, so it's a slow job to do an entire collection like this. Happily for me, Tony and Geoffrey have wonderful art and the time passes quickly as I work my way through the rooms on the ground floor.

At some point I hear the front door open and close and a moment later a man walks into the dining room where I'm currently running my tape measure over a very nice little Nora Heysen floral still life.

'Hello, I'm Geoffrey. Shan't disturb, just wanted to say hello.'

'Hi, I'm Alex.' I have to make a conscious effort to look him in the eye and not stare at his forehead. After a brief exchange of pleasantries, he disappears and I get back to work and finish up with the Heysen. This is the last of the ground floor art, so I head upstairs to start working through the rooms Tony showed me. The banister is one of the most fantastic things I've ever seen and, now I'm alone, I take my time to look at it properly and run my hand across its surface as I slowly ascend. The newel post at the lowest stair is shaped like the head of a fantastical dragon, mouth agape, each tooth and scale carved to perfection from richly hued mahogany. Some detail on the top of his skull has been lost under generations of caressing hands, but that only enhances the patina. Intricate newel posts are not uncommon, but what makes this special is the fact that it's not just about the post. Instead the handrail extending out from the dragon's head forms his body. The entire rail is carved with scales and it undulates like a writhing serpent, while at the very top, a pointed tail lashes the air. It's glorious, Gothic and probably far older than the house it currently inhabits.

I drag myself away reluctantly; there's a lot of work still to be done. The master bedroom, guest bedroom, study, second guest room, even the powder room, all have small paintings that need to be added to my growing list. It's just after five when I finish and I realise I'm starving. It was easy to ignore the hunger pangs while I was concentrating on the job, but all I've eaten since breakfast is a Mars Bar and a couple of Tic Tacs. Looking out the window, I see the weather is closing in and rapidly darkening the sky. Cars sweep past with their headlights already on and I grimace at the thought of battling peak-hour traffic. I double-check that I've saved the list properly in the laptop, then grab my things and head for the ground floor. There's a small table facing the bottom of the stairs, weighed down by a large and elaborate bunch of flowers in a Worcester vase, and as I step onto the parquetry of the entrance hall, I catch a glint of light from behind the dense foliage. There is a painting there, something under glass that Tony failed to mention and I failed to notice because, hey, dragon staircase. Tony appears from the back of the house. He must've heard me come down and no doubt he and Geoffrey are ready for me to leave.

'What's this?' I move toward the table.

Tony's eyes widen. 'Oh my God! I totally forgot about that!' Suddenly he looks a bit embarrassed. 'To be honest, the painting gives me the creeps so I do that with the flowers. Geoffrey likes it though. He got it from an old lady years ago and I think it was probably the first painting he bought, which is why he has a soft spot for it, because otherwise … Anyway, neither of us has any idea who the artist is, although apparently the woman who sold it to Geoffrey said he was German.'

I pick up the vase of flowers and lower it carefully to the floor, exposing the painting.

'Oh.' I can see why Tony finds this a bit creepy. It shows the ruins of a church, the shattered steeple bathed in moonlight. A few gravestones, tilted at crazy angles, can be seen to one side of the ruin. The sky is filled with leaden clouds, indicative of a fast-approaching storm. In the foreground, the black outline of a horse and rider gallop across the canvas, desperate to be somewhere else. Almost behind the edge of the church, deep in the shadows, a tall figure is just visible, dressed head-to-toe in white, a large cowl obscuring the face. 'Oh!' My brain has just made its connection on the thought train. 'This looks like an Arnold Böcklin.'

'A what now?'

I lean in close to the painting, but it's no good – the reflections from the glass plus a bit of bloom on the canvas mean I can't see any details, let alone a signature. I step back and turn to Tony. 'Arnold Böcklin, Swiss painter, late nineteenth century, best known for his mythological scenes and his heavy use of symbolism. His most famous painting is *Isle of the Dead*, but most people have never heard of him. Your painting has a very similar style and feel. I'd need to get the glass off to be sure, though.'

'How important is he?' He is staring at the painting with the hint of a smile on his face.

'Well, he's represented in most major galleries: New York's Met, the Musée d'Orsay, National Gallery in London, all of those. But I'd have to make sure the work is his. In any case, as you already know, this sort of work isn't to everyone's taste, so auction prices can be difficult to pin down.'

'Off the top of your head?' Tony sees my hesitation. 'Let's assume it is by Böcklin. For the sake of argument.'

'Assuming that, probably around $100,000 plus in a European sale. Böcklin's more of an academic's artist than a collector's artist, and you have several far more valuable paintings in your collection.'

'Yes, but that sort of price should still be enough for Geoffrey to part with it. Shall I call him?'

'I'd rather you let me confirm the details before we get too carried away.' I glance at my watch. 'I can either come back with some tools and take it out from under glass or, if you'd like me to, I can take the painting with me, have a proper look at it and return it to you when I come back with the catalogue and valuation of the collection in about a week's time.'

'Take it away. I'll explain to Geoffrey so hopefully the moment you bring it back, we can get you to crate it up and ship it off to an auction in Switzerland.' As he's talking Tony is lifting the painting from its hook and heading for the door.

'Are you sure? Would you like to check with Geoffrey first?' I don't want to get caught in the middle of a row. I've valued collections for divorcing couples before and it can get very awkward very quickly. 'I'd hate him to be upset.'

'Upset about what?' Geoffrey has appeared while Tony is trying to hustle me out the door with the painting.

'Alex needs to have a closer look at your spooky painting so she's going to take it with her.' Tony's voice is bright.

'Entirely up to you,' I jump in. 'I can come back and look at it properly another time.'

Geoffrey looks hard at Tony, then shakes his head and sighs. 'Take it with you. Otherwise I'll never hear the end of it.'

Tony is beaming. 'I'll tell you everything Alex said about it. It's really quite exciting.'

'Well, I should go and let you get on with your evening.' I gently take the painting from Tony. 'I'll be in touch next week so we can organise a time to discuss your collection and the valuation, and of course get this back to you.' I heft the painting to emphasise my point.

After a flurry of goodbyes and polite-ese, I make it out the front gate and – safely stowing the painting – make my getaway.

I crawl along in heavy traffic, radio off so I can at least use the time to go over the Molly Dean thing again. The problem with John's conspiracy theory is there is absolutely no way to prove or disprove it. Then again, I reason, after seventy years I doubt there's a way to prove or disprove anything. I debate whether it's worth trawling through the social pages of 1931 to see if anyone important suddenly left the country, but I'd have no way of connecting an abrupt departure with Molly's death, particularly if she was just a random victim.

'Dead end,' I mutter, as the car in front of me abruptly flashes its tail-lights and I jerk to a stop. But what if it wasn't random? What if Molly was targeted? But if I discount the jealous lover theory and put Adam Graham aside, why would someone specifically go after Molly? I picture my lists in my head. All the accumulated facts and information about Molly's life and death. The driver behind me toots his horn and I snap back to the present to see the car in front of me has moved ahead a few metres. Dutifully I roll forward and close the gap.

'Happy now, dickhead?' I direct the question to my rear-view mirror. Once again, I decide I have to let the whole thing go. Daphne will be disappointed, John will be content with his fantasies of cover-ups, and if I sell the painting I won't have a constant reminder of the fact Molly's killer got away with it. I still have a good story and can make a tidy profit. Perhaps I should give Rob a call and see if his pushy underbidder is still keen.

As I try to convince myself I'm happy with my decision, I stare idly at the cars either side of me. The girl on my left is bopping her head from side to side, singing along to a tune I can't hear. On my right, a guy has pulled out his newspaper and propped it against the steering wheel. I tilt my head sideways to try to read the headline, but the light isn't good enough. Naturally, at that moment, with me twisted forward over the wheel and bugging my eyes in the dark, he looks up from the paper and meets my eye. I smile weakly and thump back into my seat, eyes straight ahead. And then it hits me. What if Molly Dean, aspiring writer slash journalist, actually dug up some dirt on someone? What if she was going to write an exposé? I hum a few bars of the *X-Files* theme.

'Who's Mulder now?' I slide my eyes to the right and, sure enough, newspaper driver is watching me talk to myself. If this really was the *X-Files*, he'd be a G-man and I'd be in deep, deep trouble. Craning my neck, I stretch tall in the seat and shift from left to right, trying to see if the traffic is moving at all, but my view is blocked by the mammoth four-wheel drive in front of me.

I decide to phone John in the morning and tell him my idea, knowing how delighted he'll be with the new twist. Not that it matters; it still doesn't bring us any closer to identifying Molly's murderer. I've got to stop messing around and get on with things. Get the portrait cleaned, sort out the frame so the signature is visible and sell. I've become so distracted by the story, I haven't even taken Molly out of her frame to confirm Colin's signature is there. More evidence I've let this thing go too far.

I'm about to rest my head on the steering wheel and re-examine my life choices when the lights in front of me flicker and cars begin to move. It's slow but at least it's progress, and it continues without any more major hold-ups all the way home. The day has well and truly gone by the time I pull into the drive, and my house is dark except for the glow from the hall light on its timer switch. I sit in the car for a moment, completely exhausted, and listen to the pop and ping of cooling metal. A night in front of the television is called for. I gather my bits and pieces, and haul myself out of the car, slamming the door behind me. I can hear Hogarth whining basso profundo in the front hall. Two steps up the path I remember the painting on the back seat and with a sigh and dragging feet, turn back, fiddle with the keys and open the door. Then I perform a little dance as I juggle the painting and my other stuff while I lock the car and jam the keys into my front pocket. Hogarth seems to be working himself up to a crescendo.

'All right, buddy. I know I'm late but I'm coming now.'

As I start up the path for a second time, I hear the slap of leather shoes coming up fast behind me, but before I can fully process the sound I'm shoved hard in the middle of the back. My feet paddle in a cartoonish fashion as I stumble forward on the path, trying to stop myself from face planting while also preventing my client's painting from becoming a pile of matchsticks and canvas. At the point where a subconscious part of my brain registers that gravity is overcoming equilibrium, preservation instinct kicks in. Not self-preservation, but the preservation of valuable art, triggering muscles to act rather than react. Somehow I fling the painting toward the grass, and a softer landing, just before I hit the path in a twisted heap, one hand bent underneath me and the side of my head making a decidedly coconut-like sound as it bounces none too gently on the concrete.

Hogarth is barking furiously now and there is also a pounding sound coming from the house – or is that my head? My vision is blurred and filled with flashing colour and my right wrist, momentarily stunned, has now begun sending screaming neurological alerts up my arm.

'Shit, shit, shit, ow, shit.' It takes a moment for the fog to clear a little and I'm suddenly aware there could be more to come. I roll onto my back and curl my legs, expecting my attacker to be right there, ready to kick what I can. But there is no one standing over me. Instead, a few steps away, a tall figure in a dark hoodie is picking up the painting from my lawn where it has landed facedown. I scrabble to my feet and back up toward the house, where the pounding has resolved itself into the sound of Hogarth throwing himself frantically against the door. I keep one eye on the yard as I fumble for my keys which are miraculously still half in, half out of the front pocket of my jeans.

'Fuck! Son of a bitch,' my attacker yells. He has turned the painting around and is staring at the image. 'Fuck.'

I'm trying to keep one eye on him – the voice confirms the gender – and fumbling for the lock at the same time. Hogarth has a much better chance of dealing with this than I do.

'Fuck!' He turns toward me. The hood is pulled well forward, so I catch only a glimpse of chin, but at that moment I feel the lock turn and shove the door open.

'Hogarth!' I don't need to say anything. My hound launches himself through the door, across the verandah and over the two front steps in a single bound.

'Holy shit.' Throwing the painting in Hogarth's direction, the man turns tail and sprints for the street. Hogarth's momentum slows as he swerves to avoid the flying canvas, which catches him a glancing blow on the shoulder. It gives the escaping figure an extra moment and he gains the street, turning left with Hogarth closing in rapidly. I hear a car engine start and feel sudden fear for Hogarth. If there is a second person waiting in a car they may try to run him down. The engine guns and at the same time I hear a terrified yell.

'Hogarth!' I'm frantic. 'Close to me, Hogarth!' This is Hogarth's emergency recall signal. There is casual, everyday recall and then there is this rarely used phrase. It means, stop immediately, no matter what, and come here now. He doesn't let me down. Within seconds he is here, standing crossways in front of me, pushing me back toward the house. I grab his collar to be sure and we move together. He is staring intently into the darkness pooled between two streetlights and I follow his gaze toward where I can still hear the rev of a car engine. Its lights are off, but at that moment, the door is opened and in the weak glow of the interior light, I see what must be the person who attacked me, left arm at a weird angle, tumble into the passenger seat. The car races off, ignoring the speed humps lining the street.

Hogarth and I make our way inside, stopping to pick up the painting. The glass is a web of cracks but I can't tell if the canvas itself is damaged. Right now I don't care. We go inside and I lock the door and dump the painting in the study, propping it against the wall. As we walk through the house, I snap the lights on and off in each room we pass. I know Hogarth would not be calmly trailing behind me if there was anyone in here, but the empty gesture offers a modicum of reassurance. In the kitchen I turn on all the lights and pull the blinds. My wrist is swelling up and I'd like to burst into tears, but I ignore my own crap while I make sure Hogarth is okay.

'Drop, buddy.'

Hogarth folds himself into a sphinx-like posture with no complaint. With my good hand I signal him to roll on his side and he obliges, flopping onto the flank that did not come into contact with the painting.

Kneeling, I run my palm over his shoulder, parting the fur and checking with my fingertips for any trace of blood, but there is no break in the skin. Next I take his leg through a range of motion, gently stretching it forward and out to the side, folding it back and flexing each joint. He doesn't even lift his head from the floor. Finally, I carefully flex his neck around to the shoulder. There is no stiffness or soreness and all Hogarth does is sigh heavily as I let him go. I lean forward and rest my head on his chest.

'Thank you little man, thank you.'

When I was under attack, all I could think was that Hogarth would help me, but then the moment that arsehole threw the painting at him I was horrified; I'd exposed my best friend to danger and possible injury. I'd never forgive myself if anything happened to Hogarth because of me. Now I know he's okay, I can feel the tears threatening again and I'm rather pissed off when a couple squeeze their way out and track down my face. Not my style at all.

I haul myself up and over to the fridge where I pull a flexible ice pack out of the freezer. I keep it on the off-chance Hogarth ever strains something. I fold it carefully around my right wrist and even more carefully waggle the fingers. All seem to be moving with only a slight increase in the pain level, so I work on the assumption nothing is broken, torn or requiring the services of a medical professional. Holding the ice pack in place by keeping the arm against my body, I move across to the medicine cupboard where I briefly debate the merits of various painkillers. I rarely take codeine because I get loopy on the smallest amount, but this is definitely one of those times when a bit of a buzz is called for. I dry swallow two tablets then lean back against the kitchen bench. I need to feed Hogarth, have a really, really hot shower and go to bed with the electric blanket on high. At least, that's what the organised part of my brain is chanting in endless rote. Another part of my brain is telling me to just stand there because it's all too hard right now. And way off in some very small but intelligent part of my cerebral cortex is a very insistent voice clamouring for attention.

What the fuck was that all about? Who was that? Why didn't he take the painting? Oh yes, and what the hell am I going to do now?

After a night spent waking up suddenly every time I roll onto my right side, I greet the dawn with relief. This morning there are a few additional aches in my back and hip, but at least the wrist hasn't swollen much more, although it is an interesting shade of puce. I take Hogarth for a long walk to make up for yesterday and even though I'm feeling a bit delicate, the exercise seems to loosen things up nicely. Later, when I emerge from the shower, I rub the mist off a corner of the mirror so I can see how my head wound looks. The blow caught me behind the hairline so the rather impressive lump is hidden, but there's still a bruise extending out to my temple. I press the lump carefully then flex my right hand. All in all I think I've been very lucky. I consider whether to report the episode to the police, but nothing was stolen. Besides, I don't need it getting back to my clients that their paintings might not be safe in my care.

I pull on some leggings and a jumper, then cap off the outfit with a pair of Ugg boots. I'm in no mood to see anyone today and at the moment I'm not feeling particularly well disposed to polite phone conversation either. I start to pull my hair back into a ponytail, but the tension exacerbates the pain of the lump so I opt for scruffing it up a bit with my left hand. It doesn't look windswept so much as cyclone-blasted. The overall effect of my clothes and hair is probably a guarantee that my mother will drop around unexpectedly.

'Stuff it.' I need something to eat.

In the kitchen, I put the kettle on and prise two pieces of sourdough rye from the loaf in the freezer. Hogarth shambles through the door, then slowly stretches himself into a literal downward-facing dog, rounded off with a simultaneous yawn and vigorous shake. Welcome to Tuesday.

I'm trying not to think about the potential damage to the canvas I was carrying last night, and I keep flashing to a vision of me trying to explain to Geoffrey what happened to his favourite painting. Of course, if I'd been an employee at a major auction house, I'd simply get John around to repair any damage and not say a word to the client. But I have morals, so that sort of thing is not an option. I enter the study, steeling myself for the worst.

First I grab some old newspaper and spread it across the top of my desk. Picking the painting up, I'm careful to keep it angled forward so if any of the glass slivers dislodge they will fall away from the canvas. I lay the frame facedown and set to work with fine pliers, carefully easing out the old nails holding the canvas in the frame. When I have them all in a neat pile, I lift the painting straight up and out, putting it gently to one side while I deal with the glass. At least I can see there are no tears in the canvas, but I'll have to do a close examination for scratches and paint loss on the surface before I can relax. Now I lift the frame by one edge and flip it onto the newspaper, letting the broken glass fall out. I carefully fold up the edges of the paper and place the whole lot in a plastic bag, then turn my attention to the canvas itself.

It has come through completely unscathed; not so much as the tiniest chip of paint missing. I let out a breath I didn't know I'd been holding. I've already told the clients the glass had to go, so I just won't tell them the circumstances surrounding its ultimate removal.

Without the glass, the Böcklin signature is evident and the surface is clean. All the bloom I'd noticed originally seems to have been on the inside surface of the glass. The canvas must have been well stretched before Böcklin set to work, because it's still relatively taut with no signs of restretching or lining. I give the frame the once-over to make sure it wasn't damaged and, after a quick wipe to remove a bit of grass and dirt, I replace the canvas in its nineteenth-century home. For my money, I'd have the frame rather than the painting. The latter is slightly unsettling, but the former is a divine hand-carved affair. The fact the original gilding only survives in traces here and there simply adds to the beauty of it.

I spend the next two hours looking through books for examples of Böcklin's work, making sure the signature is right even though he's not the sort of artist anyone would fake. More importantly, I check to see if I can find a similar scene among his other recorded paintings. As it happens, there are a number of works featuring moonlit ruins with varying casts of sinister figures, so I'm feeling quite confident. But just to be sure, I track down the name of a curator in Basel who knows far more about Böcklin and shoot off an email. Then I check various lists of auction prices so I can put a reasonable value on the painting. Feeling virtuous, I tidy up my notes from the East Melbourne valuation and collate the whole lot into a coherent catalogue of the collection. Actual, billable hours, I tell myself as I back up the file. To round off the morning, I send the clients an email informing them that preliminary examination strongly suggests the painting in my possession is indeed by

Böcklin and confirmation is pending. I also suggest a couple of days next week when we could meet to discuss the collection as a whole and whether they'd like me to handle the sale of any pieces. By the time the clock in the lounge chimes eleven, my desk is clear again and, apart from the dull ache in my wrist, I'm pretty damn happy with the way the morning's gone.

Of course, just as I'm congratulating myself, the thoughts I've studiously avoided all morning come crowding back in. I'm on the verge of believing it was just a random lout, some scumbag who saw me with the frame and took a chance, probably hoping it was a signed Richmond football jumper or something, then dropping it when he saw it was actual art. But as I stare vacantly at the Böcklin, something clicks. I retrieve the portrait of Molly Dean and prop the two paintings against the wall, side by side. Colin Colahan travelled extensively in Europe in the 1920s and was particularly taken with France. After that, he often prepared canvases to French or European dimensions, the sizes slightly different to those mainly used in England and Australia. The Böcklin and the Colahan are both exactly the same size, both in quite decorative frames, even if with vastly different subjects. Of course, no one else would know that, but what if my attacker just saw me with a painting and *assumed* it was the portrait of Molly Dean?

'Bullshit.'

From his place on the dog bed, Hogarth quirks an eyebrow at my tone.

I decide to call John, tell him the whole story and see what he thinks. I pick up the phone and start to dial, then put it down again.

'Don't be so stupid. No, no, no.' I may be talking to myself, but I'm not listening. No one knew I had the Böcklin and, frankly, even if they did no one would care very much. This isn't Monet or Picasso we're talking about. But people do know I have Colin Colahan's portrait of Molly Dean. It would explain why the guy hurt me only enough to get the painting, then swore and dumped it once he was able to see it properly.

I pick up the phone again and this time I follow through. I listen to it ring, once, twice, three times before there is a click.

'Hello, John Porter speaking.'

'Hey Mulder. Things have taken a somewhat unexpected turn.'

I tell John everything that happened. For his part, he alternates between expressions of shock and worry, threats to kill the bastard (when we figure out exactly who the bastard is), and wild speculation about secret societies dating back over a century. I wait for him to go all *Manchurian Candidate* on me, but luckily he has some standards. Finally he has all the crazy out of his system.

'Do you want me to come over?'

'What for? I mean, thanks, but it's okay. My wrist aches and I'm a bit shaken, actually no, I'm just pissed off now. Hogarth's here and no matter what it was all about, I doubt it's going to happen again. I told you the guy's arm looked funny when he got into the car? Well I reckon Hogarth broke it or dislocated his shoulder. I know that'd make me think twice.'

'But if Hogarth hurt the creep, what if ...'

'Don't say it.'

The silence on the line stretches. In my kitchen, I hear a click-hum as the refrigerator motor kicks in. From the dog bed in the corner come some rhythmic scuffing sounds followed by a few throaty growls and yips. I look over at my wonderful hound. His feet are jerking and his lips and eyelids are twitching as he dreams, probably taking down bad guys.

'You should have brought me Molly Dean days ago.'

'There was no rush,' I reply. 'All it needs is a light clean, and how was I to know this sort of thing would happen? Or even if it's anything to do with the portrait?'

'Is the wrist okay for you to drive?' John's voice sounds taut and over-loud.

'As long as I don't have to perform a handbrake turn, I think I can manage.'

'Shit Alex. This is serious.'

'Sorry. I was just picking up on your whole conspiracy-theory-evil-forces-at-work vibe.'

'Look, like you said, it doesn't matter what the whole thing was about, but just in case, grab Molly Dean, buckle Hogarth into his car harness and come to the studio. You can do your work from here or hang out if you want. We can hash over the whole Molly thing again or I can clean the bloody painting so you can move it the fuck on. Whatever. Just for once, please stop being Ms Independence. I'm worried, okay? I'm a temperamental artist, remember. Even if you don't give a stuff, please come and placate my sensitive soul.'

'Well why didn't you say it was all about you? I'll have to spruce myself up a bit so I don't look quite so much like a bag lady. It'd be my luck to be sitting there looking crap when the head of the National Gallery pops in.'

'Wouldn't be the first time, mate.'

'Bastard.'

We exchange a couple more insults and I get the feeling John is as relieved as I am that we are back to having a normal conversation.

After ending the call, I grab a couple of biscuits and then

change into jeans, a fresh black t-shirt from my vast pile of black t-shirts and some cosy boots. I briefly contemplate a white t-shirt, but the black makes me feel tougher. People write PhDs about clothing and colour in paintings, the way viewers respond to different things. If anyone sees me in my denim and black with my huge dog, I hope they feel suitably cowed. Then I add a pair of Chanel sunglasses and any impression of toughness is immediately negated by the Swarovski crystal double Cs adorning my temples.

I decide that as well as Molly Dean's portrait, I'll also take the Böcklin, the Jane Sutherland and my recently purchased Herbert Badham. If anyone decides to break in, the most valuable paintings shouldn't be sitting around. I can't really do any lifting with my right hand, so I'm going to have to make a couple of trips ferrying the paintings out to the car and the thought makes me anxious all over again. I loosely wrap the paintings in some old blankets and line them up in the hall, ready to go. Then I put Hogarth's car harness on so he's all set, pick up my mobile phone and sling my bag over my shoulder. I feel stupid and angry with myself, but at the same time I can't squash the last insidious tendrils of apprehension that are twining their way out of my brain and wrapping themselves around my heart.

'Right, let's get this show on the road.'

Hogarth trots to the front door and stands there with his head millimetres from the frame. Easing him back, I open the door and we step out into brilliant sunshine that instantly makes me feel even more ridiculous. How could anything bad happen on a beautiful day like this? Still, I'm not taking any chances and I put Hogarth in a sit-stay on the verandah, ready for action should it prove necessary. It's not, and I trot between house and car, moving the paintings into the boot before locking the front door.

'Get in.' I wave toward the open back door of the car. Hogarth doesn't need to be asked twice. If he spoke human, I'm sure he'd be yelling 'Road trip!' right now. He jumps onto the seat and I lean in to connect his harness. It's a moment where I feel exposed and my shoulders tense, but I click the buckle home and straighten up, suffering nothing worse than a big slobbery lick from Hogarth.

By the time we arrive at the studio, my wrist is throbbing but I'm feeling much brighter. I talked it out with Hogarth during the drive, and have decided that the sooner Molly is out of my life, the better. I'll type up what I have of the provenance and Molly's story – emphasising her relationship with Colin and the poignancy of the portrait given her untimely death – then I'll make some calls to a few of my collectors. If that doesn't work, I'll put Molly in an auction and feed the gruesome details to a stringer I know who does stuff for the *Herald Sun*. I figure that should whip up plenty of interest outside the regular art-buying fraternity.

John must have been listening for the car because he appears before I even pull the key out of the ignition.

'Hogarth!' John opens the back door and tries to unbuckle the harness, but his efforts are hampered by Hogarth's excited squirming. After a few attempts he manages it and the two of them explode from the car like some sort of clown act.

'You're both nuts.' I shake my head.

Hogarth rears up on his hind legs and thumps his paws onto John's shoulders. John lets out an audible 'umpf' and staggers slightly, but manfully manages to keep it together. Then Hogarth sticks his nose in John's eye socket and I can see it's all about to go south.

'Four on the floor, buddy.' Hogarth reluctantly drops his front feet to the ground. John's face is red.

'When will you learn not to razz him up if you haven't seen him for a while?'

John has the grace to look sheepish. 'Subject change!' He scrutinises me closely from large sunnies to particolour wrist to my boot tips. 'You look like a mob wife with domestic issues.'

'Thank you so very much. Perhaps you'd like to shut up and bring the paintings inside now?'

John moves to the boot of my car then hesitates and turns back. 'I'm glad you're okay, Alex.' He steps forward and gives me a hug. 'I'd be bored witless if I didn't have you around.'

'Yeah well.' I squeeze back. 'Good job I only hit my head or I might have damaged something.'

'I wasn't going to go there, but now that you mention it …' He steps back out of reach as I make to slap him and we grin at each other for a moment, then he gives me a salute and pivots back to the car, grabs all four paintings in one go and leads Hogarth and me into his studio.

Once his harness is off, Hogarth pokes around for a few minutes before finding a clear area of floor to settle. John unfolds the blankets from each of my paintings, just enough to see what the bundles contain before he puts them to one side. The third one is the portrait of Molly Dean and he drops her shroud to the floor then turns and places her on his easel. He slides the top clamp down and twists the wing nut gently, holding the painting in place. Molly looks a little lost against the frame of John's studio easel. It's not designed to be portable, but is built to safely support larger canvases weighing up to fifty or sixty kilos. Molly is a waif by comparison.

John steps back and folds an arm across his chest, cradling the opposite elbow. His chin dips into his free hand and he stands there, regarding Molly, taking in every inch of the canvas and each nuance of her face. 'She's much prettier than I'd realised. I've seen the dumpy photo that was in all the newspapers, and of course her face is hidden in the nude, but she's really quite stunning.' He comes in close and drops his glasses from his forehead to the bridge of his nose. 'Varnish is discoloured and the whole thing has dried into the canvas quite a bit, but should come up well.' He grabs a jumbo cotton bud and sucks it for a moment, then rolls the wet tip gently across Molly's cheek. Immediately her skin glows a delicate pink, the spot standing out so dramatically against the rest of the painting that it seems as though she is blushing.

'It always amazes me that spit is a legitimate restoration tool.' I step forward so John and I are shoulder to shoulder in front of the painting.

'Just the right balance of enzymes, and if I work on a big canvas it has the added advantage of keeping me off coffee and alcohol! Too hard to use it all the time, though, and not strong enough if a painting is really filthy or flyspecked or something like that.'

'Well Hogarth has an abundance of saliva. I'm sure he'd be happy to drool in your general vicinity.'

'I suspect the properties of dog drool may be different, but if you'd like to volunteer the painting as well as the dog, I'll give it a whirl.'

'Maybe another time. How about we take the frame off and confirm the signature?'

John looks at the painting again, bending down to touch the place where the writing disappears under the frame. Then he shifts his gaze to the top of the canvas, where a faint line is visible running left to right, about a centimetre from the frame. 'The canvas has slipped. But you noticed the line, right?'

'Sure. The signature would have been clear when it was

originally framed and the canvas has just worked a bit loose and dropped, which is good, because I want to put her back in this frame when she's all cleaned up.'

'Right, let's get on with it then.' John unclamps the painting and carries it to his workbench where he lies it facedown. 'Geez, you didn't even make a start and take the paper off?'

'Started to, got sidetracked.' I shrug.

John grabs a Mylar sleeve and his knife and I turn away. I figure I'll have a browse among the paintings John's working on right now and then put the kettle on. As I edge my way toward the back of the studio, I hear the crinkle of old paper and the whisper of the knife separating it from the back of the frame. I reach a pile of canvases leaning against the wall and start to look through them, leafing them apart and tilting them forward like a giant set of files.

'Alex.'

'Mmmmm?'

'Alex.'

'What?' I carefully replace the paintings and turn toward John, craning to see him around the easel.

'There's an envelope here.'

'What are you on about now?'

'Tucked in the back of the painting, wedged between the stretcher and the canvas. There's an envelope.' He's hunched over his workbench, staring at the back of the painting.

'Are you having me on with more of your conspiracy bullshit? Because I'm seriously over the whole thing.'

John turns to look at me.

'Really?'

He jerks his head in the direction of the painting. 'Get over here and see for yourself.'

My head feels strange and light as I pick my way across the studio. For a moment I wonder if I'm concussed after yesterday, but then I focus on the sensation and realise I'm slightly freaked out by this.

'It's probably nothing.' I'm not sure if I'm saying it for John's benefit or mine.

'Sure. I come across this sort of thing all the time. Envelopes stuffed with cash, the family jewels, last will and testament. Just another day in the office for me,' John says.

I reach the workbench and lean over John's shoulder as he scooches to one side. It's a largish envelope, about A5 size and a rich cream colour. It looks like quite a heavy sort of bonded paper and the flap, which is facing us, has been stuck down. The envelope bulges slightly, hinting at a secret larger than a single page could bear. The lower edge of the envelope has been tucked between the canvas and the stretcher. Not shoved down so far that the bulk of the envelope would push into the canvas, but enough to hold it in place, although without the paper covering the back of the painting, it would have flopped around. I pick up the piece of paper John has just removed and look at the framer's label again. The work was done by a venerable Melbourne firm, popular with the leading artists of the late nineteenth and early twentieth centuries. I give the label a tap.

'That address and phone number puts it pre-1933, so the envelope must have gone in when the painting was first framed.'

'Unless that's what someone *wants* you to think. You could get an old label from somewhere and just paste it on ...' John trails off as I give him a dirty look. 'Maybe I am getting a bit carried away.'

'You reckon?'

'So shall we see?'

'It's probably just a bunch of exhibition reviews or I don't know, a copy of the catalogue?'

'Okay, I may be getting carried away, but you're just pissing in the wind now. What artist ever stuffed their reviews in the back of a painting? C'mon Alex.'

'So open it.' I bat my good hand irritably between John's face and the envelope.

He gives it a gentle tug and the canvas releases it with a sigh.

John holds the envelope for a moment, rubbing the paper between his thumb and index finger. 'High gsm. Personal stationery maybe? If it's office letterhead it's got to be from somewhere important, government or maybe an upmarket hotel.' He flips the envelope over, but the front is blank, the smoothness marred only by a faint brown line where the paper had been trapped.

'For God's sake, now we're a forensics team? Are we going to trace the pack of paper and hope the stationer has a record of purchases for the 1930s? Perhaps we should check the flap for a saliva sample or even dust for prints?'

John's eyes glint and I'm sure he's considering the possibility.

'Just so we're clear, I was being facetious,' I say. 'If we're really lucky it might be some letters or notes relating to Colahan. A packet of previously unknown source documents would be nice, but we both know that whatever is in the envelope, it will not contain the phrase, "If you are reading this, it means that I've been murdered."'

'Stranger things.' John's words hang in the air as he turns the envelope again, exposing the flap. 'You want to do the honours?'

I shake my head. John gently wiggles a finger under the top edge of the flap, then applies a bit of experimental pressure. The gum must have deteriorated with age, because the corner yields instantly, leaving a streak of yellow on the underlying paper. As he continues to ease his way along the stuck edge with conservatorial care, I pick up Molly's portrait and return it to the easel, leaving the workbench clear for whatever the envelope may contain.

Now the flap is completely free and John uses both hands to part the sides of the envelope and extract the contents, which he passes to me. It's a sheaf of onion-skin papers. They're folded in on themselves, but I can see through the translucent cockled surface of the outer sheet that they're covered with closely written text.

'Looks like someone had a lot to say.'

I unfold the papers. The creases are sharp and the pages crackle underneath my fumbling hands. I look at the top sheet but my eyes aren't taking it in. Or my brain isn't processing what my eyes are seeing. I'm not sure but there's a glitch in the circuitry somewhere. Instead, I start to lay the papers out on the workbench, starting with page one in the top left corner and moving across three before starting a new row. There is no reason for this to be anything momentous, but that's how it feels: like the beginning of something huge, or the ending. I finish a third line and John shuffles everything a bit so I can fit pages ten and eleven on the near edge of the desk. I scan my eyes across them, working in the same sequence, left to right, row by row. It's all one document. There are a few dates breaking up the bulk of the text, but that's all. No signatures grace the bottom of any of the pages, except for the last.

John reaches out two fingers and angles the final page to face him directly, then sits for a moment, hunched forward, hand sort of hanging off the edge of the table, as though he might suddenly drag that paper away and cast it to the floor. Instead, he carefully realigns it with the other pages and leans back leaving his hand caught in midair, a pianist about to strike the opening note. Suddenly he pulls his hand back and clasps it around the opposite fist.

We look at each other.

'She was a writer. It's probably a story outline or a draft chapter.' It sounds thin even as I say it.

'Which she hid in the back of her portrait, painted by her lover.'

'Something she didn't want her mother to find?'

'Why not just leave that with Colin or one of her friends?'

'You're not helping.'

'If it's nothing important, no problem. If it's juicy details of her relationship with Colahan, no problem, in fact, art history gold. If it's what got her killed, then fantastic! You will have found the missing piece of Molly's story.'

'Do you think that's it? The answer? Is that why I got attacked and Rob was threatened?'

John spread his hands wide and shrugged. 'Could be, but I don't see how anyone could know about this. We agree that whatever this is, it's been there since the painting was framed – since before Molly was killed.'

I nod. 'You've freaked me out with all your conspiracy theories. And then last night ...'

'Read it. Then you'll know. I'll bung the kettle on and dig out the Iced VoVos.'

'Not the Iced VoVos!' It's a lame running joke of ours, but it breaks the tension.

John gets up and I take his place at the bench, stretching forward to pick up the first page. I start to read. Behind me, I am vaguely aware of him moving about, a murmur as he talks to Hogarth, the clink of cups, then after a few moments the smell of coffee, fruity and chocolatey, washes over me. I glance up as John places a mug next to my elbow.

'All out of Iced VoVos, but there's shortbread if you want it.'

I shake my head.

'I'll start cleaning her up then.' He turns toward the easel.

Soon the coffee smell is replaced by the petroleum tang of mineral spirits, and after a while I hear faint music. John has put on some jazz and I fleetingly register the opening bars of 'Song for My Father' before the pages grab me again. I take a sip of coffee but it's already cold. I pick up another page and keep reading. When I get to the end, I stare at Molly's signature for a few moments, then pick up the first page and start reading again.

'Alex?'

I'm staring out the window with the pages stacked neatly in front of me, but at the soft sound of John's voice I blink and turn.

'You've been sitting like that forever and I'm dying to know what it says.'

'It's notes for a story, but not the sort of story we were thinking about.'

John rubs his hands on a piece of rag, then grabs a chair, dragging it over to me and sitting close. Hogarth pads across to see what we're doing and lays his head in my lap. I reach out a hand and start absently stroking his fur, comforted by the touch as much as I am by John's presence.

'Do you remember me telling you about her last phone calls to Colin? What she wanted to talk about?'

'She wanted to ditch her teaching job and get into journalism,' John nods. 'There was talk she'd been offered a trial, but I don't recall who'd made the offer or what the publication was.'

'Well, these seem to be the notes for an article. It's an exposé, and all the details are here.'

'An exposé of what?'

'Actually, of whom. A man, but Molly doesn't identify him. It sounds as though it started out as a sort of society piece, a bio. I think she took her research to extremes and came up with the story of a lifetime. There's sly grog, gambling, standover men and dodgy shipments, although she seems a bit unsure about that.' I take a deep breath. 'She also mentions police bribes.'

'And then she ended up dead.'

'And then she ended up dead.'

1930

BEFORE TELEPHONING DONALD RAEBURN, Molly decided to take a walk along St Kilda Road one afternoon and have a look at his house. Many of the old mansions that lined the leafy boulevard were now being subdivided into bijoux apartments and she thought if Donald lived in one of those buildings it would be a relatively easy matter to catch him coming or going, or even leave a message with the concierge, making her whole approach seem much more relaxed. If she could keep him from putting his guard up, Molly reasoned, he'd be far more loquacious and forthcoming with the sort of information she needed. She mentally ticked off the house numbers as she walked, planning her approach so her first sight of his home would be from the opposite side of the street. The last thing she wanted was to come face to face with Donald before she was ready.

Now she stared across St Kilda Road at the white facade of a mansion built in the Classical style. Slender fluted columns capped with scrolls and acanthus leaves flanked the glossy black front door and were mirrored by smaller faux columns on the two upper floors. The symmetry of the windows and the intricate egg-and-dart design of the cornice crowning the building combined to give an impression of elegant good taste and considerable wealth. A brass plaque affixed to the rather forbidding wrought-iron gate announced that the building – an edifice too grand to be considered merely a house, Molly thought – was called Conniston. Molly felt a momentary flutter of anxiety, which she quickly suppressed. That Conniston was a far cry from the chic bachelor's residence she had been hoping for was no reason for alarm, in fact it said something quite definite about the man who chose to live there. As if to prove this notion to herself, Molly took out her notebook and jotted down her impressions of the mansion. It made her even more determined to find out who Donald Raeburn really was. Despite all the little snippets she had so carefully collated from the papers, Molly realised the face Raeburn presented to the world was just as smooth and impregnable as the exterior of his home. One was left with the feeling that on the other side of the wall there was an entirely different and unexpected story, and without the right key, you would be forever on the outside, trying and failing to get in.

Molly crossed the wide road, moving quickly from the dappled light of one elm-leafed canopy into full sun, then under the spreading branches of the trees on the opposite side that stretched toward their counterparts. Traffic was relatively light, but she still had to dodge between cars and carts, narrowly avoiding a disastrous fall when one of her Louis heels caught in the tram tracks. She arrived in front of Conniston's fence like a shipwreck survivor washed up on an exotic shore and had to take a moment to catch her breath and straighten her hat.

Now that she was here, it seemed silly not to knock and see if Mr Raeburn was at home and receiving visitors. Molly squared her shoulders and lifted the latch on the gate, marvelling at how such a heavy-looking barricade could swing so smoothly at the lightest touch. She mounted the six steps to the front door, which seemed far larger now she was standing right in front of it. There was both a bell press and a heavy bronze knocker, fashioned in the form of a heroic-looking Neptune flanked by two chimeric seahorses, their equine heads and forelimbs tapering off into exotic, scaled fish tails. Deciding the knocker looked too valuable to hammer with any authority, Molly settled for pushing her finger firmly on the bell. She was rewarded with a loud trilling sound that seemed to reverberate inside for several seconds after she'd pulled her hand away.

Then there was silence. Molly thought she heard a door close somewhere deep within the house, but silence settled once more. Just as she was about to turn away, the door swung open revealing an older, dark-haired man in a sober black suit. His appearance didn't tally with what she'd gleaned of Donald Raeburn's looks, so Molly assumed this man must be some sort of assistant or even a valet. Molly glanced at his shoes, wondering why she hadn't heard his approach, then swiftly refocused on her goal.

'Good afternoon. I wonder if Mr Raeburn might be at home please.' She tried to keep her voice calm and even, not sound as though she was pleading.

'Whom shall I say wishes to see him and in what regard, madam?'

Molly thought she detected an almost imperceptible pause before he uttered the word 'madam', and immediately felt more determined than ever to get over the threshold.

'Miss Mary Dean.' It was her turn to pause. 'I wish to speak with Mr Raeburn on a private matter.' It wasn't strictly true, but she thought it might have the desired response.

'One moment, madam.'

Molly suddenly found herself staring at King Neptune

again, cast adrift in a sea of gloss enamel paint, as the door was shut quietly but firmly in her face. She felt her cheeks start to burn but willed herself to calm down. It seemed incredibly rude to leave her standing on the front mat but then again, she reasoned, the man had no idea who she was and even though she was attired quite smartly, her voile dress was more Foy & Gibson than Block Arcade boutique. She adjusted her low belt so the buckle sat neatly on her left hip, directly under the jabot that fell from the collarless neck. She'd particularly chosen to wear it today because of the fashionable cut and shade, but now wondered if it somehow betrayed its off-the-rack origins. Molly made a conscious effort not to look at her watch, in case she was under observation from within the house, but she felt very aware of the passage of time. After a few minutes that seemed like half an hour, she was beginning to wonder whether she should ring again or cut her losses and leave.

Caught up in her own thoughts, Molly began to pace up and down the length of porch, giving herself a pep talk that began as a murmur but was rapidly rising in volume. 'You can do this. Do not give up, you *can* do this!' She spun around at one extreme of her march to find the door had reopened and a different man was regarding her with some amusement.

She pulled up abruptly with a gasp of surprise. This man was taller than the first, with sandy brown hair smoothed back from a wide forehead. One lock of hair refused to be tamed and fell boyishly across green-brown eyes, as deep and impenetrable as a silent billabong. He lounged in the doorway with a loose-limbed insouciance that spoke of confidence and entitlement. As she looked at him, one eyebrow lazily elevated itself, mirrored by the opposite corner of his mouth.

'Miss Dean, I gather.' The voice was as languid as the rest of him. 'Apologies for Dickie. He's very protective of me and, alas, that doesn't always translate into good manners. I shall have words with him about leaving pretty girls standing on my doorstep.' He pushed himself off the doorframe and extended a hand. 'I'm Donald Raeburn. Perhaps if you come in and tell me how I can help you.'

Molly shook the proffered hand, which was smooth and dry, and was drawn gently but firmly into Conniston's cool interior.

Raeburn closed the door behind her, shutting out the sun and forcing Molly to blink rapidly as her eyes adjusted to the dimmer light. She was standing on a polished marble floor in a rounded vestibule. In front of her, a wide staircase led up to a landing, then branched left and right, continuing on to the higher levels. Tilting her head back, she could see a gallery running around the perimeter of the first floor, with marble pillars echoing those on the front of the house. High above, a domed ceiling with a small central glass panel was decorated as though it belonged inside a chapel, a host of winged cherubs gambolling among fluffy white clouds and cupid pointing his bow and arrow toward the oblivious humans far below. Molly brought her attention back down to earth, to find a pair of eyes watching her intently.

'It's a bit overly sweet for my taste, but too much of a bore to send a chap up there to paint over it.' He shrugged. 'Now, Dickie mentioned a personal matter, but,' Donald's gaze travelled from Molly's face to her toes and back up again, 'I'd remember if we'd met before and you don't look angry, so I assume you're not here on behalf of a friend.' He laughed at the expression on her face. 'Sorry, it's just that a man in my position, well, you'd be surprised at how many women there are whom I've never met but have supposedly wronged in some way!'

Molly forced herself to smile. She'd met men like Donald Raeburn before and normally had a smart comeback at the ready, but she knew she needed to play this differently. She couldn't afford to get him offside. 'Oh goodness, it's nothing like that at all, Mr Raeburn!' Molly put a suggestion of girlish giggle into her voice and mentally thanked all the coquettish little actresses she'd met and dismissed at Colin's parties.

'Don, please! Well now you have me intrigued. We'd best go through to the drawing room and you can reveal all.' One side of his mouth curled into a cocky grin. He held out an arm, inviting her to precede him across the vestibule. 'Second on the left. Just go on in.' He tucked his hands in his trouser pockets and strolled after her.

The drawing room made Molly stop short when she entered. Unlike the elegant front and entrance to the house, it was decorated along the latest Modernist lines. The fireplace and plaster mouldings were still original, but the colour scheme and low-slung furniture looked as though they'd been dropped into place from another world. The floor was covered in wall-to-wall moss-green marbled carpet and the pale gold walls were relatively bare, except for a large silver-edged mirror opposite the windows and a wildly modern painting over the mantel. A canary-yellow couch, all sharp angles and open at one end, dominated the centre of the room. It faced a dark green club chair, while between the two sat a round coffee table in royal blue, a book and some sort of plant arranged artfully on its surface. The colour of the table was picked up by blue scatter cushions on the couch and chair, and by the L-shaped sofa table that wrapped around the back and one end of the couch, providing the surface for a chrome lamp and a few books that looked as though their spines had never been cracked. A blue telephone table looking more like a giant shadow box squatted in the far corner.

Molly moved across to the painting, knowing Colin would be interested to hear what hung on the walls of a St Kilda Road mansion. It was the complete antithesis of Colin's style of art. Swirls of red, blue and yellow seemed to wrap around each other, sometimes converging into comet-tails of orange or violet before re-emerging to curve off in another direction.

'It's called *Rhythmic Composition in Red Orange Major*, one of Roy de Maistre's early colour music pieces. Apparently they're not so popular these days, but I like it.'

'It's quite dramatic, isn't it? But at the same time sort of mesmerising. The colours almost seem to dip and change as you look at it.' Molly turned from the painting to find Donald ensconced in the deep chair, legs stretched out in front of him, crossed ankles revealing a glimpse of argyle sock. She moved over to the couch and carefully lowered herself toward its cushioned expanse, only to find it was still a good couple of inches lower than it looked, causing her to thump down awkwardly.

'Traps for the unwary traveller.' Donald laughed, then sat back and steepled his fingers over his chest. 'You have the floor, Miss Dean.'

Molly rearranged herself on the couch, sitting up straight and bending both legs to one side. She hoped she wouldn't be out on her ear when he heard the reason for her visit.

'I'm a writer and I'm doing a piece on Melbourne identities.' She paused, expecting to be cut off there, but Donald was just staring at her, his fingertips gently tapping together. 'I see your name again and again in the society pages, and what I know of your story is quite inspirational.' All she knew was that he was a working-class boy who'd somehow done very, very well, but a bit of flattery never hurt. 'So I was hoping you'd consent to an interview, please. You're really quite an enigma, but I'm sure the rest of Melbourne would love to know more about you.'

Donald continued to regard her over the tops of his fingers.

'Of course, you could say as much or as little as you like.' Molly realised his silence was unnerving her and she was starting to babble. She snapped her mouth shut then widened her eyes and gently bit her lower lip. It was a technique she'd used with some success in the past.

The silence lengthened as they continued to regard one another across the sea of Feltex. Finally Donald brought his hands down onto the arms of the chair.

'I don't really give interviews.'

'I'd noticed that you hadn't in the past.' Molly bit her lip again. 'But I thought perhaps people have stopped asking, and now you might have changed your mind. It *is* almost a rite of passage for anyone who's remotely important in Melbourne society to share their thoughts and tastes with the wider population.'

'And how many other identities are you planning on writing about?' Donald emphasised the word identities.

'Well, you'd be the first, but I believe the profile on you will set the tone and everyone will be dying to follow suit.'

Donald suddenly sprang to his feet in a way that suggested plenty of practice with Modernist furniture and began prowling the room. 'If I agree to this – and right now that's a very big if – what would you want to know? About my business? My poor but happy childhood?' He exhaled sharply and shook his head. 'Or about my charming home?' Donald spread his arms wide and turned a slow circle, taking in the entire room.

'All of that really, but you wouldn't necessarily have to go into great detail. Readers also like to learn a few trivial things; the sort of things that make them feel as though they know you, although it doesn't really tell them anything. How you love the Melbourne Cup, for instance, or that growing up you wanted to be a fireman.' Molly was twisting around on the couch, trying to follow Donald's movement about the room.

Suddenly he stopped pacing and vaulted the open end of the couch, sitting down beside her so their knees were almost touching. Molly gasped with surprise.

'My dear Miss Dean – may I call you Mary? My dear Mary, it's an interesting proposition but one I'm not sure I can accept.' Donald shot his cuff to reveal a gold wristwatch with a distinctive hexagonal case and made a show of checking the time. 'I'm afraid I have another appointment. Perhaps if you leave me your contact details I'll let you know my decision. I'm just not sure Melbourne is ready to hear all about Donald Raeburn and where he buys his shoes.' He stood and helped Molly to her feet, then paused, her hand still in his. 'Even if I don't do your interview, I think I should tell you that I've never met a more delightful journalist.' He pivoted smoothly and without knowing how it happened, Molly found her arm was now linked with his and they were heading for the door. Realising how deftly she was being handled, it took all her fortitude not to pull away. Instead, she looked up at him and smiled.

'Thank you for taking the time to speak with me after I arrived unannounced on your doorstep. You've been more than kind.' She waited a beat. 'I do hope you'll seriously consider a more formal interview.' Molly handed him a piece of paper with her name and Colin's address and phone number, which he quickly tucked into his pocket.

'I shall consider it, Mary, and rest assured you're the only writer on my list.' They were across the vestibule and he disengaged her arm while opening the door with his other hand. 'Now, I have your details and I really must dash. It's been a pleasure, Mary.'

Molly found herself back on the porch staring at the glossy door without quite knowing how she'd got there. She took a deep breath before turning back toward the gate and the bustle of St Kilda Road beyond. Donald Raeburn had been curiously unsettling; she hadn't been able to figure him out and usually she could read men like they were penny dreadfuls. As she let herself out the gate and started off toward the tram stop, Molly was convinced she'd never hear from Donald Raeburn again, but equally certain she would see the story through. And she knew just how to get started.

1999

THE RING OF MY mobile cuts through our silence. I really
should change that ringtone to something less obnoxious – it
seems wholly inappropriate right now. The screen advises me
it's Damien Savage, and I contemplate letting it ring out. I'm
not really in the mood for his brand of forced ebullience, but
I don't want him giving any business to the competition, and
dollars trump emotion almost every time in my book.

'Damien! How are you? To what do I owe the pleasure?' I
lay it on so thick, John mimes throwing up. I half turn in my
chair to block him from my line of sight.

'Alex, glad I got hold of you. Sold that Badham yet? Let
me know if you can't find a buyer. Anyway, not the reason I'm
calling.' His voice becomes distant for a moment and I figure
he's moved the phone away while he speaks to someone else
at his end. I hear a sharp exclamation and what sounds like
a string of expletives before he's back, all silken tones and
amiability. 'Sorry, it's like a madhouse here. We're just about to
launch a new Angry Penguins selling exhibition and suddenly
my staff have turned into a bunch of butter-fingered imbeciles

with an apparent inability to read a simple hanging chart. Should I be surprised? Probably not. But I digress.'

I sigh. John has repositioned himself so I can see him. He's gesturing with his left hand, making circular motions next to his ear. I'm not sure if he means Damien is loony or if he wants me to wind up the conversation. Then he puffs his chest out and starts strutting around the room, so I figure it's the former. I turn my chair again before I start giggling. 'Sounds like a good exhibition. How can I help you, Damien?' I realise that came out a bit too abruptly. 'I'm just heading into a meeting with a client.'

'Shan't keep you then, my dear.' Damien would drop anything for a client, except a richer client. 'Just wanted to let you know that I passed your number on to a chap who came into the gallery asking about Colahan portraits.'

My stomach does that thing it does on roller-coasters. 'Oh.' I turn back to John and bug my eyes at him. 'Do you have a name for me?'

'No, but he seemed very keen. Quite disappointed that I didn't have anything and completely uninterested in every portrait I tried to show him. Insisted it had to be a Colahan. So I told him I knew of someone who had a charming Colahan of a young woman and I'd put him in touch. You can thank me later. For fuck's sake! Sorry, not you Alex. Look I really have to go before one of these halfwits ends up with their head rammed through a canvas.'

'Thanks Damien. And thanks for letting me know.' My voice comes out dry and scratchy.

'You know I like to do favours when I can.'

I don't respond to that. Damien's favours always involve paying it forward – to Damien. There's probably a ledger or a spreadsheet, because he always collects. 'Well, thanks again. Must dash and let you get back to it at your end.'

'Ciao darling. Unbe-fucking-lievable! What is that shit ...' His voice becomes fainter then abruptly disappears when I punch the 'end' button.

I toss my phone onto the workbench.

'What did God's gift to the art world do?'

'Gave my details to a guy who came into the gallery asking about Colahan portraits. Presumably the aggro underbidder.'

'Well crap.'

'Indeed. A nice, succinct summation of this turn of events.'

'But it probably has nothing to do with Molly's murder. There's no way anyone could know what was behind her portrait. We agreed the backing paper is contemporary with the frame, right?'

'Right.'

'And if Molly had given the envelope to Colin and asked him to hide it, surely the first thing he'd have done once she was killed would be pull it out and hand it over to the police.'

'Makes sense.'

'So what, Molly peeled back a corner of the paper when the painting was at Colin's house? After it came back from the framer?'

'Either that or the framer didn't put the paper on. Then she'd only have to get the framer's label off the canvas, paper the back and stick the label on. But Molly had to be the one to put the envelope there; it's the only explanation. She might have thought Colin was going to give her the painting anyhow.'

'So if we agree that, one way or another, Molly was the one who stashed the notes, your bloke who's so desperate to buy a Colahan portrait could not possibly know anything about it.'

'Unless she told someone.'

'Why would she? Defeats the purpose.'

'She might have been desperate.' I pause. 'She might have been terrified.'

John stares at me for a moment and I watch as realisation dawns. 'But then why kill her? Say it was the man from her exposé who was lying in wait, if he knew she had all these notes, wouldn't he try to get the incriminating evidence first?'

'Maybe he thought she'd have it on her. Remember all her stuff was scattered across the street. Or maybe she wasn't meant to die.'

John shakes his head. 'But whoever Molly's mystery man was, he'd have to be well into his nineties now, if he's not dead. Sorry Alex, the phone bidder at Lanes, the guy who went to Savage, he must just be a collector. Granted, a slightly more whacked collector than usual, but a collector nonetheless.'

'And what about last night?'

John holds up a hand and pats the air in a placatory manner. 'Clearly that wasn't an old man. Maybe in this case one and one do make three. Did your thug say anything about Colahan? Or Molly?'

'No, he just made a grab for the painting, then swore when he saw the subject matter, dropped it and did a runner.'

'So you just assumed it was about the Molly Dean painting. Why?'

'Well.' I have to think about it. 'I guess because of Rob's weirdness over the underbidder. As well as the fact everything I read about Molly Dean makes me think there was something strange going on. And you probably didn't help with all your stupid theories.' I throw a balled-up rag in his direction but it flops to the floor well short.

'Even if there was a cover-up, it happened nearly seventy years ago.'

'Thank you, Captain Obvious.'

'Look, maybe I got a bit carried away with the whole conspiracy thing, and I agree there was something very wrong about Molly's murder investigation. But, realistically, it's far more likely the guy who shoved you was just a common-or-garden mugger-cum-housebreaker who thought you were a soft target.'

I shoot John a dirty look.

'I only mean that you had your hands full and you were distracted, juggling stuff, getting your house key out. Maybe he thought you had a framed Elvis gold record. Or maybe a laptop – no, too small. Something like that, anyway. Bottom line is, when he saw what the painting was, he didn't come back and work you over until you revealed the location of the Colahan portrait of Molly Dean, did he?'

I can't help smiling at the idea. 'No.'

'So basically, you're highly suggestible, slightly paranoid and a bit unlucky. Oh and there's a nutty collector who probably wants to hand you a fat wad of cash for a painting you've only owned for about a week.'

'When you put it like that ...'

'How about, when this guy calls, you arrange to meet him here? Hogarth and I will hover discreetly in the background in case things go pear-shaped.'

I look from John to my hound who is currently giving himself a back massage by lying upside down in the middle of the room and working all four legs in the air. Discretion is not really something either of them do well. 'Sounds like a plan.'

'Will you sell him the painting if he wants to buy it?' John has returned to cleaning Molly's face, so his back is to me, but I can see he's stopped moving the swab while he waits for my answer.

I drag my good hand across my eyes and down the side of my face. 'The researcher in me wants to hang on to her and keep going, especially in light of her notes.'

'But?'

'But the pragmatist in me says let it go. Particularly if I name a ridiculously high price and he goes for it.'

John puts his swab down and turns to me, folding his arms. If you looked up sceptical in the dictionary, there'd be a picture of the expression on his face. 'And the fact that he'd pay a ridiculously high price without a quibble wouldn't make you suspicious all over again?'

'Oh shut up. You of all people know some collectors pay crazy amounts to get the painting or the conservation job,' I point at his chest meaningfully, 'they want. Besides, nothing allays lingering anxiety like large quantities of cash.'

'You make a fine point there.' John bows his head slightly in acknowledgement. 'So we're agreed? Set up a meeting here, sell the painting, slam the door after the buyer leaves and wash our hands of the whole Molly Dean affair?' He wipes invisible dust off his hands for emphasis.

'That's it. Just as soon as he calls.'

'Or we could follow him and see where he takes the painting.' John waggles his eyebrows at me then ducks behind the easel.

I sigh. 'It's like working with a precocious five-year-old, you know that?'

Hogarth is thumping his tail on the floor, clearly amused by John's antics and I can see the situation is about to deteriorate, but before I can rein the two of them in, my phone rings again. This time, the screen shows a number I don't recognise.

'Alex Clayton speaking.' I use my best professional tone which John always says makes me sound like I'm really pissed off but trying to hide it.

'Yes, hello.' Then nothing but the electronic void of signals bouncing around in the atmosphere.

'Hello? Are you there? This is Alex Clayton, art specialist.'

John edges closer, trying to hear what's going on. I shrug and pull a 'dunno' face at him.

'Sorry, sorry. I was all set to leave a message so it caught me out when you picked up.' The voice is surprisingly normal. I place it in the tenor range, Australian accent with a bit of private school softening the vowels. If this is the mystery Colahan buyer, so far he's the antithesis of scary.

'I was given your number by Damien Savage ...'

I nod to John and give him the thumbs up, then shoo him back to the canvas. If I have a live one on the hook, I want Molly looking her best.

'He suggested you were the person I should talk to about paintings by Colin Colahan. Specifically, portraits by him.'

'Yes, I handle a lot of works by Colahan as well as the rest of the Meldrum circle. His portraits don't come to the Australian market quite as often though. As I'm sure you're aware, Colahan really made his reputation as a portraitist in England, after he left Australia in 1935.' It never hurts to let new clients know you're across the subject, but you have to try to flatter them at the same time. 'Do you collect portraits generally, or is there a specific person who sat for Colahan that you're interested in?'

John is obviously listening because he turns from his easel and gives me the Edvard Munch *Scream* face, hands pressed to cheeks and mouth wide open in an 'o' of horror. Collectors who are chasing a painting of something specific – whether person or event – are often the most obsessive. On the plus side, they usually know nothing about art.

'I'm not quite sure how to answer that. You see, I'm doing this for my father. He's the one who wants the Colahan painting.'

'I understand. Would it be best if we met? Or perhaps I

should meet your father and we could discuss exactly what it is he's after. If it's a portrait of somebody significant, obviously it would be more difficult for me to acquire the painting on his behalf. Having said that, I am acquainted with all the major collectors of Colahan's work, and I can make enquiries. Naturally, things like the Bernard Shaw portrait will not be attainable, Mr ... I'm sorry, I don't believe I got your name.'

'Oh sorry, I should have said. My name's Tom. Thomas Raeburn.'

The name isn't familiar.

'Mr Raeburn.' I say it louder than necessary so John will be sure to catch it.

I needn't have worried. Molly is abandoned on the easel and John is watching me. He screws up his nose and shakes his head.

I press the button to put the call on speaker so John can get it all. 'Would it be best if I met your father? Perhaps saw what else he has in his collection so I can see how a new acquisition would fit in?'

'Well that's the thing, you see. That's why I couldn't answer your earlier question. He doesn't really collect art. In my entire life I've never known him to buy a painting. Then suddenly, I'm over for a visit and he was obsessed. Carrying on and getting himself quite worked up. He's an old man, you know, and that sort of thing can't be good for him. In the end I agreed to try and find what he wanted just to calm him down. I must say – and I tell you this in confidence and only because I don't want to waste your time ...'

I make an encouraging hum.

'I must say I wondered if it wasn't a form of dementia or something, this sudden obsession with a painting. But he seemed perfectly lucid otherwise. Still knew what year it was and that sort of thing.'

There is an expectant pause, but I'm not sure what he's

waiting for me to say. Tom Raeburn sounds perfectly harmless, but I'm sure all the best psychos do. Every time I see a news story about the arrest of a crazed killer, they always interview the neighbours and, without fail, the neighbours say what a nice, polite gentleman he is; and so quiet! Just once I want to hear a neighbour complain about how they were kept up all night by the sound of chainsaws and maniacal laughter. Bottom line, I'm going in with my eyes wide open. 'How can I help you then, Mr Raeburn? What exactly are you looking for? On behalf of your father, of course.'

'A portrait of a young woman painted by Colin Colahan.'

I stop myself from sighing. We need to move this conversation along. 'Fine. Well, a few have gone through the auction rooms in recent years, but I know of several other portraits the owners may be willing to part with for the right price. Do you have any idea if your father has a preference for tone and colour? A blonde or a brunette? Full length or just head and shoulders? Ballgown or more casual attire? Direct gaze or looking away? That's quite important to some people, you know, especially art historians.' I'm being extremely facetious now and John is helpfully rolling his eyes at me to emphasise that fact, but I'm tired of this guy dancing around and I want him to get to the damn point.

'Well I'm not sure about all that, but it's the portrait of one specific girl.'

'Name?'

'Not that specific. At least, Father didn't say.'

'I'm sorry, but we're going round in circles. You say it's a specific portrait but you can't give me any of the details. I'm not quite sure how you expect me to help you. Colahan painted dozens of portraits of women.'

'Oh. It's just that Damien Savage led me to believe you'd bought such a portrait recently.'

There it was.

'And how would you know that was the portrait in question? Assuming I had it. I buy and sell things all the time.'

'Because Mr Savage said you bought the painting at Lane & Co., and that was the sale Father was bidding at. On the phone.'

Finally we get to it. Raeburn senior must be Rob's cranky underbidder.

'I'm a bit puzzled by all this,' I say. 'The painting I assume you're referring to was not auctioned as a Colin Colahan, yet you said your father isn't a collector. How did he identify the artist?'

There is silence. I look at John, John looks at me, and then we both stare at the phone which I'm holding in the air between us.

'Huh. I've no idea. Do you know I can't even think when the name first came up.' Silence again, then Tom comes back with a triumphant note in his voice. 'Father must have seen the painting years ago and remembered it. That must be it. After all, he's only seen the picture in the catalogue, so that's the only thing it could be. He recognised it when he saw it.'

John and I shrug at each other. Raeburn senior may or may not have known the artist, but he must have recognised Molly Dean. And if you knew her, Colahan would be the first name you'd think of. The picture in the catalogue was bad, but if you'd met Molly it would be enough.

'Forgive me for asking, Mr Raeburn, but if your father was so keen to buy the painting, I'm very surprised he didn't go to look at it, let alone bid in person.'

'Oh Father almost never leaves the house.'

'Is he an invalid?'

'He's frail, but he still gets about the house reasonably well. He's just a recluse really. Has been for years and years. And besides, even when he does go out, he can be a little ...

crotchety, and I believe he may be persona non grata in some of the auction houses. He used to collect antique silver, but after a few nasty scenes in the auction room ... Plus he believes all auctioneers are crooks and if they know he's bidding, they bump the price up. These days if he wants to bid on anything he has to get someone to do it for him, or use a different name.'

'The painting I purchased is with my conservator at the moment, and to be perfectly honest I've already offered it to one of my clients, so he has first right of refusal.' John has both hands up and is bowing repeatedly at me. I'm not sure if it's the snooty art dealer tone I've adopted or the bald lie about a client with first dibs, but I've impressed him somehow.

'We're, that is, Father is prepared to pay whatever you ask.'

'That's as may be.' I almost choke on how pompous I sound. 'But I still have to honour the offer I made to my client.' I wink at John. I'm going to push a bit harder. 'Perhaps you'd like to take a look at the painting in the meantime? While it's with the conservator. Just to be sure it's what your father wants. I'm sure if it turns out this painting's not available, I'll be able to source something similar for you.' I hear the sounds of a muffled conversation, one voice quiet and placatory, the other querulous and sharp. Then a scrabble and Tom Raeburn is back on the line.

'That's very kind of you. Would today be suitable?'

'Let's say five o'clock today. I'll check with the conservator that the time suits him, but if you don't hear back from me, consider it confirmed.' John flips through an imaginary diary, then places an index finger on his cheek, tilting his head to one side and gazing at the ceiling. I throw a copy of *Art and Australia* at him.

I give Tom Raeburn the address details and end the call, feeling anxious and excited at the same time.

I turn to John. 'This is either your worst idea ever, or your best.'

John picks up a swab and moves back in front of the easel. 'Just glad I've got a ringside seat for the next bit.'

1930

JUST AS SHE'D EXPECTED, Molly had heard nothing from
Donald Raeburn. When she wasn't over at the Yarra Grove
house, she phoned Colin each evening to check for messages,
but there were none. Nothing from Donald and nothing from
any prospective publishers desperate to read more of her work.
It was plain to Molly that writing this article was the only
chance she was going to get for a long time. She had to come
up with something sensational.

But Molly was putting her time to good use. Working from
the notes she'd made in the Public Library, Molly had compiled
a list of all the names that came up in connection with Donald
Raeburn. She intended to work her way through as many
of them as she possibly could to build up a profile of the
man. Hopefully she would be able to piece together enough
information for an article. The list proved to be quite lengthy,
given that at every social occasion Raeburn's name seemed to
be linked with that of a different woman. In addition to all the
ladies, there were several businessmen, a prominent QC and a
number of professional sportsmen. Raeburn even turned up

at a recent dinner to celebrate the reappointment of General Thomas Blamey as Chief Commissioner of Police. There had been a curious incident some five years ago when Blamey's police badge was found in the possession of a man during a raid on a Fitzroy brothel. But after the attending officers swore the unidentified man was not Blamey, and the Commissioner himself claimed the badge had been stolen, the matter simply went away. Molly's interest was piqued: perhaps she could write about Blamey next. She took copious notes on the scandal before returning her focus to Raeburn.

Armed with her list of Raeburn's associates and acquaintances, Molly spent the next couple of weeks tracking down as many of them as she could. It meant asking for several days leave from her teaching job, a request that was met by ill-disguised displeasure from her principal. Every tiny step she took toward a career as a writer was another blight on her future prospects with the Education Department.

It was easy to make appointments with the various society women and bright young things. She simply telephoned and told them she was writing a piece on the best-dressed women in Melbourne, or the expected must-attend parties for the coming season, and every one of them practically begged her to come and take tea at her earliest possible convenience. Molly even purchased a new frock for the interviews, and clad in her red floral Celanese dress with its flounced sleeves and scarf trailing from the shoulder, she felt quite at ease in Melbourne's most stylish homes. Once she was comfortably settled in the parlour (or on the terrace if the weather was fine), cup of tea and biscuit by her side, it was a simple matter to gently steer the conversation in the right direction.

'I recall you were dressed in one of the Paris models when you attended the Mayor's ball. And Mr Raeburn looked a charming escort …' Or perhaps, 'Having the right mix of guests is so important for the success of one's party. What sort of person is your ideal guest? Someone like Donald Raeburn? I gather he's quite a charming gentleman. Oh but of course you'd know him better that I.' And then Molly would sit back and see where the conversation took them. She didn't want to probe too deeply, but she certainly needed more than platitudes.

The responses she got were quite surprising, but Molly quickly realised she had to allow for the sheer vacuousness of some of her interviewees. One or two simply dissolved into fits of giggles at the mention of Donald Raeburn, but the same thing happened when she dropped the names of other men as conversational camouflage. Comparisons to Rudolph Valentino were not uncommon, as was the use of words such as 'dashing' and 'fast'. But as Molly spoke with more women, and at the same time became more subtle and adept with her questions and delicate hints, she began to see a pattern emerging. And it was a pattern that painted Donald Raeburn in an entirely different light.

At first it was just a couple of little things that almost passed without Molly noticing. A slight change in her hostess's tone, a glance that slid away and did not reconnect until a new topic was introduced, or the sudden offer of more tea. One woman brought a hand to her throat, then changed the gesture to rearrange her pearls. Another unconsciously cradled her wrist, rubbing back and forth, back and forth, with her opposite thumb. Then, noticing these things, Molly also became aware of the frequent quick intake of her hostess's breath when the name Raeburn was mentioned and, when her interviewee did pick up the conversational thread and speak of her date with Donald or their meeting at the Hunt Ball, the woman's voice became brighter, but it was the brightness one associated with a shard of ice, ready to crack the moment pressure was applied. Most significantly, Molly became aware that even those women who spoke at some length about their encounters with Raeburn told her precisely nothing.

Molly dutifully recorded each quote in her notes.

Janice de Vries: 'We hardly spoke, simply danced for a couple of songs and then moved on to new dance partners. He's a commanding lead.'

Phoebe Davidson: 'Oh, he's always telling jokes. Such a funny man! Although sometimes a little risqué.'

Violet Carstairs: 'Yes, I invited him to our last garden party but we're really barely acquainted. It's simply hard these days to find eligible young men to make up numbers.'

The Hon. Amy Roberts: 'I played mixed doubles with him at the club, but all the talk was of tennis. He has a strong backhand.'

After several of these strange interviews with their swirling undercurrents and tensions, Molly was convinced the urbane personality Donald Raeburn presented to the world hid a far more callous heart. Yet each conversation left her more and more frustrated, and as Molly crossed names off her list she began to think the whole exercise was pointless and would result only in a chatty, superficial piece on things that apparently matter to some of Melbourne's most influential women. Sadly, in Molly's opinion, those things did not amount to very much at all.

She had only one woman left to call on and had been debating the wisdom of bothering to chase down any of Raeburn's male acquaintances, but she'd come this far and the alternative was a meek return to her North Melbourne classroom. So it was with great determination but minimal expectation that Molly strode down Collins Street and pushed through the magnificent Gothic portal of the old stock exchange building. Inside, she was momentarily overawed by the vaulted ceiling and regal columns, but the ding of the elevator and a glimpse of its richly panelled interior as the door was being pulled closed reminded Molly of the reason for her visit. She hurried across the marble floor and pushed the 'up' button, then watched as the indicator above the door described a sedate arc counting down from four to 'g'. Once inside the car, the smartly liveried girl operating the lift whisked her swiftly and silently to the sixth floor and Molly stepped out into the reception area of the Lyceum Club, where she had an appointment to meet Constance Jennings. Miss Jennings was something of a celebrity herself, partly due to her philanthropic pursuits, but primarily as a result of her work overseas during the Great War.

Molly gave her name to the girl at the front desk who ran a finger down the ledger in front of her before picking up a phone and engaging in a brief, murmured conversation. 'You're expected and Miss Jennings is ready to receive you.' She turned the book around and slid it toward Molly, then offered her a pen and inkwell. 'Please sign in next to your name and I'll also need to sign you out when you leave the building.'

Molly did as she was asked while trying to discreetly read the names of the Lyceum Club members, then tucked the pen back into its stand.

The girl spun the book back away from Molly and made a note of the time next to the new entry. 'Thank you. If you just head directly through the doors behind me, there'll be someone waiting to direct you to Miss Jennings.'

Molly walked sedately across the thickly carpeted expanse of the reception area and through another heavy Gothic door. On the other side, a girl remarkably similar to the one she'd just left behind took charge. The young woman ushered her through the quiet of the tastefully decorated lounge, where various women were seated alone or in groups, reading, talking

197

or simply cogitating. They headed toward the far corner and a tight cluster of deep club chairs, upholstered in dark burgundy velvet rather than the traditional leather. Two chairs, both empty, were side-on to the room, but one completely faced the corner and, over its back, Molly could see a sleek blonde head. As she watched, a thin curl of smoke rose up and then a hand appeared to one side, languidly brandishing a cigarette in an amber and gold holder.

Molly's escort stepped to one side of the chair and with a deferential nod of her head announced, 'Miss Jennings, your guest, Miss Dean.' The girl then moved aside to allow Molly to take one of the vacant seats.

Molly found herself gazing at a classic profile: sharp high cheekbones, an elegant patrician nose and glossy hair coiffed in a perfect Marcel wave. Constance Jennings was dressed in chic navy and white, a sapphire and diamond brooch gleaming discreetly on her breast.

'Thank you, Doris. Coffee for two, please. Unless you'd prefer tea, Miss Dean?' Constance's voice was low and smooth, and she punctuated the question by drawing deeply on her gasper.

'Coffee would be lovely, thank you.' Molly directed her answer to the girl identified as Doris, then settled herself into the plush embrace of the chair. 'Thank you for agreeing to speak with me, Miss Jennings.'

'Darling, it's Constance, please. Miss Jennings sounds like a dried-up old spinster.'

'Then you must call me Molly.'

'Molly, is it? I approve. Sounds a far more interesting woman than Mary.' She regarded Molly for a moment through the blue-grey haze of tobacco smoke. 'I can't recall reading anything of yours, should I have?'

Although slightly taken aback by the directness of the question, Molly was immediately aware Constance Jennings was not someone who would take kindly to any dissembling or obfuscation. 'I've had a poem published, but the article I'm writing now is effectively a job application. If the publisher and editor like what I give them, they'll offer me a job as a staff writer.'

'And that's your ambition? Journalism?' Constance leaned forward to stub out her cigarette, her eyes never leaving Molly's face.

Molly was about to say yes when a maid approached bearing a tray with coffee and biscuits. She waited while the girl laid out cups, saucers, pot and all the other associated paraphernalia on a low table and poured coffee. 'I'm actually writing a novel.' She wasn't quite sure why she'd revealed that. 'That's my real ambition.' Molly stopped, realising the interview was going entirely the wrong way. She busied herself adding milk and sugar to her coffee, offering each in turn to Constance and receiving two shakes of the head. It was Constance who broke the silence.

'I didn't mean to make you uncomfortable, Molly, and you shouldn't be. Good for you, I say! I've no doubt it won't be long before you're invited back to the Lyceum as a member; you're just the sort of woman this club is all about. Forget your Alexandra Club types. The only reason I'm asking you about yourself is that I like to know exactly who I'm dealing with. And truth be told, I heard a couple of well-heeled ladies talking about you at a fundraiser last week. It made me wonder why you'd want to speak to me. I don't exactly "do" the social scene as they do, and you made no mention of charitable causes when you requested this interview, which is the only link I have with those particular women. So I confess I'm intrigued, Molly.' She paused to sip her coffee, watching Molly over the rim of her cup. 'I'm intrigued to know what it is you're really writing about.'

Molly could feel her cheeks getting warm. For once she was at an absolute loss for words.

'Oh come on. Most of the women in this room,' Constance waved an arm expansively over her head in the general direction of the lounge, 'have spent their adult lives concocting stories and treading carefully to get to where they are today. Even if you're planning on riding roughshod over the masculine powers that be, you have to disguise the fact you're going to do it. I promise not to be shocked or offended, and who knows? I may just tell you everything you want to know. Perhaps more.'

Molly ducked her head slightly, dropping her gaze to her lap and away from Constance's probing eyes. Then, resolutely, her chin came up and she returned the look with as much strength as she could. 'I want to write a piece on Donald Raeburn. He's the real story, but he's refused an interview, and since I started talking to women who've met him I've become more and more convinced that there *is* a story. Every time I manage to work his name into the conversation, it's as though I've committed some dreadful social faux pas. People either ignore the question or bluster through a jolly answer, then quickly change the subject.'

Constance sat back in her chair with an emphatic whump. 'Well that was the absolute last thing I expected you to say. Donald Raeburn, eh? How very interesting. And how very perspicacious of you, Molly Dean. Donald Raeburn is a charming gentleman, good at sports and an astute businessman.'

Molly sighed and her brow furrowed.

'That is, until you catch a glimpse behind his polished veneer or happen to catch one of his former business associates for a quiet word when he's drowning his sorrows. I can tell you a few things you probably won't be able to print. Hearsay, and besides the people involved would most certainly not want their names bandied about. But I can also point you in the direction of some people who may be prepared to give you something solid to work with.' She paused and craned around the edge of her chair, surveying the room. 'I wish they served something stronger than coffee here. The thing is Molly, you must be very careful. Raeburn, despite appearances, is a nasty piece of work. He can be quite ruthless, and he has a lot of powerful friends. Or at least, he's owed favours by powerful people. Take your pick, the end result is the same. You'd be far better off writing the nice society piece you've been using as a smokescreen.'

'I don't want to write about cooking tips or how to beat a rug or why primrose yellow shouldn't be worn near the face. I started on this because I thought Donald Raeburn would have an interesting rags-to-riches story and no one had done it yet. Now when you confirm the story is so much bigger, how could I possibly back away? This could make my name.'

'I thoroughly approve of your ambition, but do tread carefully.'

Molly nodded eagerly.

'In that case, I'll give you two people to talk to, although you'll need to give me a day to speak to them first, let them know you're coming. What they decide to tell you is up to them, and it may be nothing.'

'Thank you. I can't tell you how much I appreciate your help.'

'Don't thank me yet. I'm not at all sure this is sensible.'

1999

JOHN HAS BEEN WORKING hard on Molly's portrait, but he's deliberately left half her face uncleaned so there is a distinct line running through the middle of the painting. It's a good way for the uninitiated to appreciate exactly what it is John does, but we figured it might also put a damper on Tom Raeburn. Who wants to buy something that's only half finished?

At ten to five, Hogarth's ears twitch and he lifts his head. Seconds later we hear the crunch of tyres on gravel.

'Showtime!' John gives it the jazz hands then half untucks his shirt and rumples his hair. 'I've decided to go for the socially inept boffin approach as a foil for your smooth art dealer persona,' he says, although I detect a note of irony when he uses the word 'smooth'.

'Chill buddy.' That's Hogarth's signal to just hang out without necessarily holding a solid stay. He arranges himself into an alert-but-not-alarmed drop and stares expectantly at the door. I'm actually a bit scared. Although I didn't think the voice on the phone sounded like my swearing attacker, what if it's the same guy? Or what if this guy brings the thug along? I know I won't recognise him, so I'll take my cue from Hogarth; he never forgets a bastard.

Peeking out the window, I see a late model Audi sitting smugly in the car park, its tinted windows obscuring my view of the driver. I step back and take a few deep breaths. There's a knock on the door and, for a moment, John, Hogarth and I eyeball each other like this is a B movie and we're all about to run in different directions.

'Coming,' I call, and the spell is broken. John turns back to the canvas, Hogarth takes a moment to scratch his ear, and I step across the floorboards and open the door wide. 'Mr Raeburn?'

'Call me Tom, please.' He's not as tall as I expected, and his light grey hair is in retreat from both temples. He may play golf or social tennis, but his physique isn't screaming assailant so much as accountant. Besides, both arms are also fully functional, so at least I know this isn't the guy Hogarth chased. I glance at my hound to be sure and he has his head on his paws. Okay then.

'Alex Clayton.' Automatically I stick out my hand and shake. I encounter a soft, indoor hand and such a weak grip there's barely a twinge from my injured wrist. Definitely not my attacker. I draw Tom Raeburn across to the easel and clear my throat. 'John.'

'Mmmm? Oh sorry, completely wrapped up in this.' And he thought I could lay it on thick. 'Shan't shake hands.' He brandishes a grubby mitt to emphasise the point, then steps slightly to one side so Tom and I can square up in front of Molly.

'Well, this is the painting I purchased, and from what you've said the painting your father is interested in.' I take a half-step back so he can have Molly to himself. Both John and I are trying to watch his reaction closely without looking like we're staring. I'd like to think I look pleasantly enquiring, while from where I'm standing John just looks shifty.

After a moment Tom inhales sharply and turns to me. 'It certainly looks like the painting he described to me, and I saw the catalogue picture, so I suppose this is it. Although frankly I have no idea about art and can't for the life of me work out what the attraction is.' He must see my slightly startled expression, because he adds, 'I mean, Father's attraction to this painting.' He pauses again and looks at Molly. 'That is, she's a charming looking girl but ...'

'It's okay.' I rescue him from the hole he seems determined to dig. 'I understand what you're saying. Your father is not usually an art collector and you can't get your head around why he's so keen to acquire this particular painting.'

Tom nods gratefully.

'All I can say is I've been doing this for years and I still don't know why some people collect what they do.'

'The eye of the beholder!' John emotes from where he has been standing, quietly arranging brushes.

'Excuse me?' Tom had clearly forgotten about John.

'Art.' John flaps a hand toward Molly. 'The appreciation thereof is in the eye of the beholder. Like beauty.'

Tom's blank expression is like a bucket of iced water. John turns back to his brushes, turning his head in an up-and-over curve that somehow suggests the *artiste* is offended.

'I'm pleased you were able to come and have a look at the painting.' I direct Tom's attention back to Molly and me. 'At least now we know we're all on the same page.'

Tom relaxes again. His sort always respond to a good cliché. It's hypnotic, like listening to a football coach after the team has lost. The more you can say without really saying anything, the more soothed the audience is. Alex Clayton School of Psychology.

'When I told Father I'd managed to locate the painting he was pleased, but very insistent that I repeat my offer to buy, now. He told me you can name your price.'

'I'm very sorry, Mr Raeburn, but as I've already told you, the painting is under offer to someone else and, until that's settled, it is not on the market to you or any other buyer. All I can do is assure you that if this deal does not go ahead, you will be the first person I call.' I'm holding out for a high price, but at the same time, part of me wants to find out why Raeburn senior is so desperate to own Molly.

'I know what you paid at auction, and we're prepared to triple it right now.' He's starting to look a little fevered.

'The answer is still no.' John stops fiddling with his paints and comes to stand next to me, all traces of the dotty artist gone. In the corner, I can see Hogarth has noted the change in the room's atmosphere and is lying very still, eyes trained on our little tableau. 'I'm happy for you to photograph the painting if you wish, so you can confirm it with your father.'

Tom Raeburn shakes his head, but does not meet my eye. His entire focus is on Molly. 'No, it's the right painting.' He rubs the palms of his hands down the sides of his trousers, and Hogarth lifts his nose, scenting the air. This guy is giving off major stress vibes. 'I'm sorry to be so insistent. I do understand, and I wouldn't normally push like this. But Father is an old man, a frail old man ...'

I hold up both hands, a double stop sign. 'It's not negotiable. The best I can do is talk to my client and see if he's made a decision.'

He sighs, 'Yes, thank you.' His shoulders are rounded and his head has dropped forward. 'This will not be an easy conversation.'

'I'll be in touch. Oh and for my records, what's your father's name?'

'Of course, I should have said. It's Donald.'

We shake hands again and, under Hogarth's watchful eye, I see Tom out. Shutting the door, I turn and lean my back against it, eyes closed, while I listen to the sound of his car recrossing the gravel and accelerating away down the street.

'Correct me if I'm wrong ...'

I open my eyes. John is back in front of the easel, but he's not working. He's looking at me with those feverish Mulder eyes again.

'Go on then,' I say.

'If I'm not mistaken, Tom Raeburn is shit-scared of his ninety-something-year-old father.'

'I was hoping that idea was just me, but you saw it too, huh?'

'Hard to miss. Do you think Raeburn senior knew Molly?'

'He must have. But why not say so?'

'So what do we do now?'

'Now? You finish bringing Molly back to her radiant best. I'm going to check on a couple of details about the night Molly was murdered, as well as find out a bit more about Mena Griffiths and Hazel Wilson. I also want to do a bit of digging about Donald Raeburn. Then I'm going to take everything we know to Daphne Lambell and see what she thinks.'

'And then?'

'And then I think we might give Raeburn junior a call and organise a home visit for Molly Dean.'

1930

CONSTANCE'S CONTACTS, ONCE THEY were assured of Molly's intentions, were both willing to talk and sounded as though they would be veritable fountains of information. Provided, of course, their names were kept well out of it.

Molly met the first man at the Robur Tea Rooms, opposite the town hall in Swanston Street. She found him at a table in the back, trying to make himself invisible amid the shining displays of teapots, trays, vases and the variety of other things proudly bearing the Robur company name. He was seated in the corner, surveying the room and the comings and goings of the patrons. But when he stood to greet her, the man ushered Molly into the corner chair, placing himself with his back to the room. He was a tall man with thinning black hair and shoulders rounded as though he carried a great weight. His tie was already slightly askew, but he tugged at the knot as he sat down, pulling it even further off centre. His jacket hung loosely on his lean frame, as though he had lost a considerable amount of weight.

'Thank you for meeting with me, Mr –'

He held up a hand, cutting her off. 'No names, please. Never know who's listening. Perhaps just call me Mr Smith.'

Molly's eyebrows rose. She wondered if the man in front of her had endured a particularly hard war and if this would prove to be a wild goose chase.

'I see what you're thinking and it's perfectly understandable. But I've been through enough. My family ...' He faltered, looked down at the tablecloth for a moment and took a deep breath. 'Donald Raeburn has made our lives almost unbearable. The only reason I agreed to this is that we're moving to Sydney. And something needs to be said.'

Molly pulled out her notebook and set it on the table, just as the waitress in her green apron and orange cap bustled over, her own notepad and pencil at the ready.

'A pot of the Refresher Blend, please.' Molly ordered while her companion dabbed at his face with a handkerchief. Once the waitress had gone, Molly flipped to a clean page. 'I gather you were in business with Donald Raeburn? What sort of business?'

'Import export.' The answer came after a pause and set the tone for the interview. Molly framed each question carefully, lest she cause this anxious man to bolt, and for the first twenty minutes each answer was slow and short: no embellishments, and no real information.

It was only once they were each on to their second cup of tea that Molly decided she was going to have to push to get what she wanted. 'What happened with Donald Raeburn? What did he do? From what you've told me the business was profitable, so what changed, Mr Smith?'

He toyed with his cup for a moment, twisting it around, then raised it to his lips and sipped. When he put the cup back down, it rattled against the saucer. 'I suppose I was naive. I've been in business with other people before and it's all gone

swimmingly. This was the same. We're both gentlemen, well ...'
Mr Smith gazed at the dregs in the bottom of his cup. 'That's
what I thought, anyway. Turns out I put too much faith in the
concept of a handshake and a gentleman's agreement. I found
out Raeburn was importing a lot more than was recorded
on shipping manifests, and a lot of cash was moving through
the business but not showing up anywhere. I realise now he
must've been running a second set of books, but back then,
when I first noticed, I just thought it was an accounting slip.'

Molly remained silent, her eyes fixed on Mr Smith while
her pencil scratched furiously across the page.

'Stupidly, even once I discovered what was going on, I didn't
think Raeburn was behind it. Thought it must be the manager
or the warehouse boss. Of course I went to Raeburn with the
proof I'd uncovered and as soon as I started talking the look
on his face told me just how stupid I'd been.'

'He was shocked that you'd found him out?'

'He couldn't care less that I'd found him out. I think he
was quite delighted. You see, everyone in our employ had
been chosen by him. I was right about the manager, and the
warehouse manager, and probably the woman who came to
sweep the floor, come to mention it. Donald Raeburn gleefully
informed me I was senior partner in a criminal enterprise.'

'Why didn't you just go to the police?'

'My signature was on a lot of the paperwork and he told
me I'd go down for it. He also said he had plenty of friends
high up in the force – how did I think things ran so smoothly
anyway, he asked – and if I even tried to report it, he'd know
and he'd make me pay. And then he started talking about my
wife and daughter. In detail. How they look, where they shop
and play tennis. I may have been slow on the uptake once, but
there was no mistaking his meaning. Shut up or he'd ruin me,
and my family ...'

'So what *did* you do?'

'Signed my interest in the company over to Raeburn and made plans to move interstate.'

Molly put her pencil to her lips, considering what she'd been told. 'How do you know he wasn't bluffing? About his contacts in the police department and such?'

'A few days later I received an envelope in the mail with a photograph of my daughter leaving school. About a week after that, I was at a fundraiser when a senior police officer came up and told me, "Mr Raeburn sends his regards." I've also seen the warehouse manager slipping envelopes to the local constabulary. Once Raeburn was aware I knew what was going on, he made a point of rubbing my nose in it.'

'And what about proof of the illegal activity?'

'I made a list of all the off-the-books shipments I could find, as well as times and dates when things were moved in and out of the warehouse.' Mr Smith slid a few folded sheets of paper across the table to Molly. 'They seem to happen at the same time each month, so if you've a mind you could get someone to keep an eye on the place for you and see what happens.'

There was a loud burst of laughter from a table toward the front of the cafe and, at the same moment, a car backfired in Swanston Street. Mr Smith flinched, then jumped to his feet. 'I have to go.' He threw a few coins on the table. 'This was a bad idea. I thought it would help if I told someone, but I've probably made it worse. Raeburn crushes anything that gets in his way. I'm sorry, I shouldn't have involved you.'

Molly watched from her seat by the wall as the man hurried through the cafe, ricocheting off a table and stumbling over the threshold before being absorbed by the crowd of pedestrians and disappearing beyond the edge of the plate glass window.

Her second contact would only meet out in the open, so Molly found herself in the Botanic Gardens with a similarly anonymous gentleman. They walked slowly around Guilfoyle's Volcano, the rest of the gardens and the city of Melbourne spread out below them, and as they did so Molly heard another tale of shady business dealings, this time involving drugs and alcohol and culminating with her informant being threatened with a gun and beaten. Not by Raeburn apparently, but by a man claiming to deliver a 'message'. Once again, the only evidence he could provide was insubstantial, although Molly found herself convinced by the man's haggard expression and darting eyes.

Later, when she sat down and compiled her copious notes, Molly realised that, essentially, she still had nothing. It didn't matter what shady deals were being done, which police were paid off or even how many women Raeburn had forced his attentions on, she still had no solid proof and nothing any decent publisher would touch. Molly had no illusions about watching the comings and goings at a warehouse, and she was loath to simply turn everything over to the *Truth* and let one of their established male hacks follow up on her notes, or craft something rich with innuendo but short on names and details. Molly knew she was out of her depth with a potential criminal story as large as this.

Time was running out; she had to produce an article for *Table Talk*. The sensible thing to do was forget about Raeburn, forget about the police, and instead write about one of the people in Colin's circle: Fritz perhaps, or even Betty Roland. Betty would make an interesting subject and a few snippets of lurid gossip would help to liven up the article.

But before she became reconciled to taking the easier option, there was one more thing Molly had to try. If she wanted to be taken seriously as a journalist she needed to follow the story. Although the thought of it filled her with deep misgivings, Molly had to speak to Raeburn again.

THIS TIME WHEN SHE presented herself at Raeburn's house, Molly had an appointment. She'd telephoned a week earlier and been quite surprised to receive an answer in the affirmative. If Donald Raeburn was now prepared to grant her request for an interview, Molly had no doubt everything he told her would be self-serving and bear only a passing acquaintance with the truth, but at least she might get some direct quotes she could use and an article she could submit to a publisher.

Standing on Conniston's front porch, Molly took a moment to check that her seams were straight and her hat sat at just the right angle. St Kilda Road was busy with traffic and pedestrians, everyone with somewhere to be but not necessarily in a hurry to get there. Molly was oblivious to the passing parade; all her attention was focused on the man behind the glossy black door. When she rang the bell, the door swung open so quickly she wondered if the taciturn manservant had simply been standing there, waiting for a task or watching for her. Momentarily discomfited, Molly steeled herself for the imminent encounter. It was too late to back out now. Head high, she swept into the vestibule and made directly for the drawing room.

'This way if you please, Miss Dean.'

She swung around. The man – had Raeburn called him Dickie? – was standing by a door on the opposite side of the staircase. As Molly moved to join him, he knocked twice and pushed the door open without waiting for an answer. She passed close to his starched shirt front and heard the click of the latch behind her.

Donald Raeburn's study was everything the drawing room was not. Panelled walls, heavy chairs and a dark red carpet conspired to give the room a brooding, old-world quality, its masculine aura heightened by the scent of tobacco, leather and something more ephemeral that teased the senses but remained unknown. At the far side of the room, Donald Raeburn sat behind an oak desk so massive it looked as though it might be an ancient monument, an immovable monolith where long-dead people once came to worship. In a corner near the door, a grandfather clock marked the passage of time. Molly listened to the steady pulse of its pendulum as she waited for Raeburn to acknowledge her, but for several minutes he did not look up and continued to write, or at least made a show of doing so.

Finally Donald Raeburn capped his pen and dropped it on the desk, raised his head, and sat back to look at her.

'Why don't you come and sit down, Mary Dean.' It wasn't a question.

'It's a pleasure to see you again, Mr Raeburn.' Molly's voice sounded high and forced to her own ears. She made her way across the carpeted expanse toward the desk and sat down. The chair was low, and she found herself in the uncomfortable position of having to look up to meet Donald Raeburn's eye.

'Let's not beat about the bush, Miss Dean. I hear you've been asking about me, probing into my affairs.'

This was not what Molly had expected and she felt her

stomach suddenly grip with anxiety. 'Well, that is, yes. I ... I have been speaking to people about you. I told you I thought you'd be perfect for a profile piece, but when you didn't contact me after we last spoke, I decided to come at the article another way.'

'I will be quite clear. I do not wish to be the subject of an article, society piece or otherwise. I do not want you to talk to anyone – *anyone* – about me or my business dealings.' Raeburn placed both palms on the desk and leaned forward, looming over Molly. 'There is no story here. Do you understand?'

Molly could feel the button back of the chair pressing into her spine. She knew she should probably just make her excuses and get out, but she could also feel her prospects slipping away with the story. 'Please Mr Raeburn, I hadn't intended to go behind your back. Why, that's precisely why I'm here! So that you have the chance to confirm and clarify some facts. So that I'm sure everything is correct. For example, your friendship with Chief Commissioner Blamey.'

Raeburn slammed his fist onto the desk, causing Molly to jump and cower back in the chair.

'Enough! I do not intend to confirm, deny or even discuss anything. This ends now.' His voice became low. 'I've checked up on you too, Miss Dean. I know you're trying to move up in the world. That can be hard. So many people don't make it. Things happen, an accident of fate, a malicious rumour perhaps, and a life is destroyed before it's even begun. Don't cross me, Miss Dean, I will not be your ticket to greater things and if you've done your research – and I think you have – you'll know that I don't turn the other cheek.'

Molly looked down at her hands, seeing them wrapped tightly around her notebook but unsure when she'd taken it from her bag. She tried to start a sentence, but the words caught in the back of her throat and all that came out was an inarticulate half-gasp, half-squeak. She swallowed, tried again. 'I see.' That was better, only a slight quiver. 'I'm sorry to have bothered you.'

'You can see yourself out.' Raeburn picked up his pen and bent his head, then looked up again when Molly didn't move. 'Or should I have Dickie escort you out?'

Molly stood, her eyes wide and blinking fast as she fought to hold off tears. She made for the door, conscious of keeping her steps slow and measured. With her hand on the knob she turned back toward Raeburn, wanting to have the last word, to salvage some dignity. Molly gasped. Raeburn had come out from behind his desk, seemingly without a sound, and was now standing a few feet behind her, arms folded, the malice in his eyes so strong she could almost feel it forcing her from the room. Molly spun around and fled from the study, across the vestibule and out the front door. She clattered down the steps without stopping, using one hand on the gatepost to swing herself into the street.

Standing at the window, Donald Raeburn watched her go, one corner of his lip lifting ever so slightly. He was about to turn away when another figure caught his eye. A man, hat pulled down low over his forehead, was hurrying across St Kilda Road. His curious gait marked him out as he dodged between the traffic, angling in the same direction taken by Molly Dean. He stumbled to a halt in front of Raeburn's fence and stood, staring down the street, anger creasing his ruddy face. Rising up onto his toes, he tilted his torso from side to side, craning his neck, clearly trying to track the progress of someone up ahead. Giving up, the man turned toward the house and found himself staring straight at Donald Raeburn.

Their gazes locked and Raeburn's eyes narrowed. Then, simultaneously, both men turned to stare at the point where Molly Dean had vanished into the crowd.

1999

LAST NIGHT I WENT back through all the photocopies and notes I've made about Molly's death. There is definitely no mention of anyone called Raeburn, and the case against Adam Graham seems stronger each time I read the details. Graham admitted to following Molly in the past, and witnesses said a man with a strange gait was dogging her footsteps. But then Ethel Dean had also followed her daughter on occasion. Could the man with a strange gait have been a woman disguising her appearance? The more I think about the murder, the wilder my theories become. But it's when I start a list of people who knew Molly would be at the theatre on 20 November that I get a shock. Betty Roland wasn't in the theatre party that night, but it was she who gave Colin and Molly the tickets to *Pygmalion*.

This morning, to round out the research, I zip back to the State Library. I start by looking up Donald Raeburn in the *Australian Dictionary of Biography*. Born in 1903, he's listed as a merchant and importer. The entry details a tough Collingwood childhood but glosses over how he became successful and vastly wealthy by the age of twenty-eight. Given that 1920s

Melbourne had quite a few gangsters and racketeers like Squizzy Taylor, I have my suspicions. It doesn't explain how Raeburn fits into Molly's story, but it does mean he could be the subject of her notes. At least he should still have enough money to pay for the painting. I move on to the newspapers.

This time I look for any useful information on the murders of Mena Griffiths and Hazel Wilson. I soon confirm Mena was killed three weeks before Molly, Hazel just over a month after. Both Mena and Hazel were murdered in Ormond, just a couple of suburbs along from Molly Dean's Elwood address. All three had stockings around their necks, but Mena and Hazel died from strangulation, while the coroner had deemed Molly's death to be the result of her catastrophic head wounds. Yet according to several articles, the pathologist who performed the post-mortem examinations noted similarities between the three cases, as did the police. Journalists seemed divided on whether there was a single maniac on the loose or if the last murder was the work of a copycat.

I skim through papers, trying to find out if anyone was found guilty of Mena and Hazel's murders. There were plenty of suspects for Mena, none for Hazel. Questions were asked about the competence of police. Finally, I find a series of jubilant articles – a man was arrested for the murder of Mena Griffiths. The trial was set for November 1931, and I'm about to jump ahead to see what the verdict was, when another headline catches my eye. I fiddle with the knob on the microfiche but it takes me a moment to bring the text into focus. Then I feel sick. The Mena Griffiths case shares another appalling similarity with the murder of Molly Dean. All charges were dropped before the trial began. An alibi that had been previously dismissed was now held up as rock solid. And I can find no further reference to an arrest or trial for the murders of Mena Griffiths or Hazel Wilson.

Leaving the library I almost stumble down the steps. I thought this bit of research would make things clearer, but my head is buzzing and I'm more confused than ever. I need to talk to Daphne.

∂

I find her in the Hillview gardens, among the rhododendrons. She's perched on the seat of her walker, just to one side of a reproduction Coalbrookdale iron bench. Those things always look attractive, but after five minutes they're bloody uncomfortable. I make a sacrifice for the greater good and sit down.

'Alex! What a lovely surprise. I'm glad you found me. There's a singalong in the activities room, so I'm in hiding.' She closes her eyes and sighs deeply. 'But enough about my sparkling social life, what brings you here?'

'Does the name Donald Raeburn mean anything to you?'

She frowns. 'There was a wealthy Melbourne family by that name, but that was years ago.'

'Nothing connected with Molly's death?'

'Not that I recall. Why?' The frown deepens, making hills and valleys of her forehead.

I fill her in on Tom Raeburn's visit.

'Dad never even mentioned the name Raeburn. I'm sure of it. Not in all the years he talked about the case.'

'Do you think it's possible he spoke to Raeburn early on and dismissed him as a suspect?'

'It's possible, but improbable. He talked over everything, again and again.' She shakes her head emphatically. 'No, your Mr Raeburn can't be Molly's murderer.'

I feel some relief, even if I can't quite share Daphne's blind faith in her father's abilities as a detective.

Now I pull out Molly's envelope and tell Daphne what it is and where we found it. Her hand trembles a little as she reaches for it, and she only holds it for a moment before handing it back.

'I haven't got my glasses. You tell me what's in it.'

I can see the chain for her specs disappearing beneath her lemon-coloured cardigan, but I don't comment. Instead I tell her everything Molly had to say.

'Based on what she wrote,' I tap the envelope into the palm of my other hand, 'Molly was scared of this man, of what he might do.'

'But would he have killed her? Over what? Certainly, it sounds like Molly had done her research, and I grant you there are salacious details there and evidence of criminality. But from what you've said there's nothing to suggest Molly feared for her life. She was a woman trying to make a name for herself in Melbourne in 1930. You could destroy her in a dozen ways without laying a finger on her if you had the right contacts, and the person in Molly's hidden notes clearly had contacts.'

'You're right. It's one thing to be an intimidating and nasty man, but another thing to ambush a woman and beat her to death.' I shake my head.

'And if this Raeburn was involved, why did Dad never mention him? I don't understand.' Daphne's skin has gone a chalky white.

'Maybe he wasn't involved. There's every chance he's just a collector.' I don't want to bring up the idea of a cover-up, but there's something I need to know. 'Why didn't your dad keep going after Adam Graham?'

'He never got the chance. After the aborted trial, he and Jerry O'Keeffe were pulled from the case. It wasn't his choice.' Daphne grips the sides of the walker, her knuckles turning white.

I don't want to upset her, so I move on. 'Anyway, I wanted to ask you about Mena Griffiths and Hazel Wilson.'

'What about them?'

'I know you said they weren't related to Molly's case, but the police and the coroner seemed to connect them.'

'Oh no, Alex. They're nothing to do with Molly.'

'Don't dismiss the idea too quickly, I mean, there were some similarities, and their murders were never solved.'

'But that's what I mean. They were solved. Or at least a man confessed. It was years later, about 1936.'

'What?' I hadn't even thought to search more than a couple of years after the crime.

'Yes, he confessed to those and two other murders, but not Molly's. He described the four killings in great detail. They hung him the same year.'

'Oh.'

The sun goes behind a cloud and Daphne shivers, drawing her cardigan tightly around her shoulders.

20 NOVEMBER 1930

MOLLY WAS AT COLIN'S house when her portrait was returned by the framer. She had spent the previous night with Colin and decided to stay for the day, content to get on with her writing while Colin painted. Each uninterrupted moment she could devote to her novel or poetry was another reminder why she had to push ahead, give up teaching and escape the toxic atmosphere of the Milton Street house. Even Donald Raeburn's threats failed to dampen her zeal, and Molly used the anxiety gnawing at her psyche as inspiration for a new poem. She had already taken every scrap of information on Donald Raeburn and his associates – every note, conversation and suggestion of police corruption – and distilled it into a single, eleven-page document. Molly doubted now whether she would ever have the courage to take it to a publisher, but the thought of putting all her work aside, of yielding to Raeburn's intimidation, was anathema to her.

'Molly darling, come and see.' Colin had spirited the painting away the moment it arrived, still wrapped securely in brown paper and string. Molly knew he'd chosen the frame's moulding personally, making several trips to the framer to ensure the gilding was not too bright, the wash just so. 'I'm waiting in the studio. It's time for the big unveiling!'

'Coming.' She tucked her notes into an envelope she'd taken from Colin's desk and placed it into the front of her notebook. From Colin's rarely used study, she hurried through the house to the studio where he was waiting, too excited to sit. The paper wrapping was a crumpled ball on the floor and Colin had placed her portrait on his easel before draping it in a red throw rug taken from the chaise.

'Sit down, sit down.' He danced around her like one of the boys from her class at the Queensberry Street School. His excitement was infectious and she bounced as she sat in the same chair she'd occupied for her portrait sittings.

'Should I be taking notes? Renowned artist Colin Colahan unveils his latest masterpiece?' She mimed opening an invisible notepad and poised a non-existent pencil.

'You mock.' Colin placed a melodramatic hand on his heart. 'But this really is a masterpiece. And besides, this painting does not need to be reviewed, because it's not for public sale. I'm far too fond of it for that.'

Molly smiled at his flirtatious behaviour. 'Go on then. Show me.'

With a flourish, Colin flipped the blanket back and away, letting it fall to the floor behind the easel. They both gazed at the painting.

The frame he had chosen was simple and elegant. Dark burnished gold, straight sides and little rounded flourishes at each corner, almost like elephant's ears. It was a lovely frame, but its beauty was in the way it enhanced Molly's portrait, made it seem as though it was the centre of the room, as though all eyes should be on Molly Dean.

'It was amazing before, but now, seeing it finished and

framed ... How did you do that? Make me look so, so ...' Molly circled her hand in front of her, unable to conjure up the words.

'I didn't make you look anything. I just painted what I saw.'

'But what you did with the light. I can see how it has direction, how it falls, but at the same time it's as though the whole picture is sort of lit from inside.'

Colin smiled. 'You like it then?'

'Like it? I adore it. You're incredible.' Molly jumped out of her chair and threw her arms around Colin. 'Thank you.'

'Thank you for being such a wonderful model.' Colin glanced over her shoulder at the mantel clock. 'Good grief! We really must hurry and make ourselves presentable before the others arrive for dinner. Oh, and the Skippers have said they're happy to drive us into town.'

Molly stepped back, still holding on to Colin's arms. 'I did want to talk to you, but I suppose we can do that tomorrow morning.'

'Oh, Molly ...' Colin ran a hand through his hair. 'The thing is, I have a lot to do to finish these paintings for the joint exhibition. I was planning on working all night after the theatre. It'll be no fun for you being here. Perhaps you ought to stay at Elwood tonight.'

Molly flushed. She knew he was telling the truth about the show, but it hurt to be sent packing. 'I shan't get in your way,' she said softly.

'You know it's not that. I love having you here, but you need to make at least a token appearance for your mother's sake. Just for the time being, until things are more settled. And besides, you know how antisocial I become when I start burning the candle at both ends.'

'It's fine.' It wasn't. 'Anyway, I must change. I don't want to keep anyone waiting.'

'Sometimes I simply need to organise my thoughts and attack the work, no interruptions.'

Molly turned abruptly and left the room. As the clock struck the half hour, Colin hurried in her wake. They had only twenty minutes to dress for dinner.

Molly changed quickly into her green crêpe-de-Chine with the satin-trimmed insets, then made a check of the bedroom. There was no need to pack anything. She was in the habit of leaving half her things at Colin's anyway. But she did need to do something about her notes. It would not do to have anyone find those, and pawing among Molly's possessions in her absence was just the sort of thing Sue or Betty would love.

Leaving Colin to fiddle with his collar and studs, Molly went to the study to retrieve her possessions. She added her notebook and a few loose pages to her already crowded bag, but the envelope and its contents were another matter. Having her mother find it was an infinitely worse prospect than anything that could happen in the Colahan household. Clutching it in one hand, she looked around. Tucking it into a book was no good. All Colin's friends dipped in and out of his library. No other place in the study presented itself as a likely prospect, so Molly moved quietly out of the room and toward the studio. She could still hear Colin in the bedroom, and she held her breath, hoping he wouldn't hear her, or be ready too soon.

The studio, once she was standing in it, seemed equally bereft of hiding places. A vase was just as likely to be used as an ashtray or be pressed into service for a still life, a sofa cushion would reveal its secret with a telltale crinkle if sat upon. Everything else, well who could know which box of paints Colin would use, or which cupboard he would rummage through as he prepared for the upcoming show? Then her eyes fell on the newly unveiled portrait. Colin wasn't going to sell it, not yet anyway: her notes would be safe for a while. She hurried over to the easel and turned the painting so its back was on show.

'Bother.' Molly frowned. She had thought to tuck the envelope in the back of the stretcher, but the framer had papered over the exposed canvas. Yet as Molly reached to turn the painting over again, her hand brushed a corner of the paper. She peered more closely at it. One edge had not properly adhered to the wood of the stretcher. It was not much, but it might just be enough for her to slide the envelope in.

Working carefully and as quickly as she could, Molly teased at the loose edge with a fingernail, slowly widening the gap until it was big enough for her purpose. She slid the envelope through and was even able to give it a bit of a downward push before she felt it stop. Molly picked up the canvas and tilted it side to side in an experimental fashion. The envelope did not shift and she sighed with relief.

'What on earth are you doing?'

Molly almost dropped the painting. How long had Colin been standing there?

'I wanted to see who the framer was,' she said, not meeting his eye. 'But then I noticed the paper was loose.'

Colin came up beside her and looked where she was pointing. 'Must have been hurrying to get the job done. I can fix it in a jiff and then we'll organise some drinks.'

Colin stepped across to his work table and reached for a small pot at the back. 'Bit of rabbit-skin glue will do the trick.' Picking up a brush, he returned to the easel and took only a moment to dab some glue on the stretcher and press the paper back into position. Dropping the glue pot on the table, he used a rag to give his hands a quick wipe.

'Now come on, Molly darling, the others will be here any minute.' He crossed to her and placed his palm gently against her face. 'Don't be angry, please. You know how important you are to me.'

Molly placed her own hand over his. 'It's okay. Well, it's not, but I understand. Probably more than anyone I understand what it is to need the space to work without having to worry about others. Just promise me we can talk properly soon?'

'Promise.'

Dinner was a brief but lively affair, dominated by talk of the night ahead. Molly got on well with Lena Skipper and Belle Leason, and she soon found her anxiety fading into the background as they chattered about plays and playwrights and the state of arts in Australia. Shortly after seven they set off for the city, driving in convoy up Victoria Street and trundling through the evening crowds before parking in Exhibition Street. The group gathered on the footpath, and after agreeing to meet under the clocks at the end of the evening, reformed into three parties. Molly, Colin and the Leasons set off for the Bijou in Bourke Street, eager to see the Gregan McMahon Players' production of *Pygmalion*. Mervyn Skipper turned for Collins Place and Kelvin Hall, where he was to attend *The Seekers,* a comedy written by the young Aubrey Danvers-Walker. As this was a charity event, supporting the Alfred and St Vincent's hospitals, he'd felt obliged to attend, but Lena was keen to see *Arms and the Man,* so she and Norman Lewis accompanied Molly's group down to Swanston Street where they could catch a tram to the Playhouse. Bets were made – about the quality of the various productions and whether the actress playing Eliza Doolittle would really swear on stage – until the tram finally arrived and Norman's repartee was lost in the cacophony of a Melbourne night.

It was close to eleven o'clock by the time the cast of *Pygmalion* took their final curtain to thunderous applause.

Molly had laughed along with the rest of the audience and delighted at Bernard Shaw's witty dialogue, resolving to get a copy of the play as soon as she could to properly study the parry and thrust of each scene.

'Did you enjoy it?' Colin gathered her close, looping his arm through hers as they moved slowly through the departing crowd and stepped into Bourke Street, the Leasons a few paces behind.

'It was a delight.' Molly bumped her shoulder gently against him. 'Shaw is an absolute genius to have interpreted Ovid in such a way.'

'And the sanguinary adjective, as the press have called it?'

'Well you won the bet! But truly, I'd hardly have noticed it at all if those wowsers in the audience hadn't gasped and tutted. Of course that's what they came for, so I suppose they have to feign moral outrage.'

'You're right. They've paid money specifically so they can be scandalised, and tell all their friends just how shocked they were.' He glanced over his shoulder at the Leasons, following not far behind. 'You're a bit like her, you know.'

'Who, Eliza? Should I be insulted?'

'No, I just mean you're a woman who's going places. Who's prepared to work hard to achieve her dreams. It's an admirable thing, Molly. One of the things I love about you.'

'I hope you don't see yourself as Professor Higgins!'

Colin laughed. 'Hardly! You don't need anyone to tell you what to do, Molly. And I hardly think I'm a good example.'

Molly was silent as they crossed Flinders Lane and walked past St Paul's. 'Colin, I —'

'There's Mervyn under the clocks. Wonder if he's been waiting long?' Colin increased his pace, pulling Molly across Flinders Street.

The Leasons caught up at the steps of the station, and it

was only a few minutes before Lena and Norman came into view, battling upstream against the tide of pedestrians leaving the city. It was 11.30, and although the dance halls and clubs still pulsed with life, no one was keen to extend the evening. It was still a long drive to Eaglemont for the Skippers, while the Leasons had even further to travel to their home in Eltham. So after quick assessments of their respective theatre experiences and promises to get together for a proper dinner next week, the group disbanded and Molly, Colin and Norman found themselves alone in the anonymous crowd.

Faced with the prospect of returning home, Molly felt her resentment begin to resurface. She didn't really expect to move in with Colin, but neither did she expect to get her marching orders. 'I wish to God I didn't have to go home tonight. I need to talk to you, Colin. I want to discuss my plans with you.'

'I know, Molly. And we will, but let's wait until the weekend, shall we? When we're both fresh and there's plenty of time?'

Molly crossed her arms and sighed. It was not what she wanted to hear. She needed to talk now. But before she could formulate a reply, Norman, who had been standing a few discreet steps away, called out, 'Colin, our tram's coming!'

'Go and catch your tram then.' Molly tried but failed to suppress a small pout.

'Oh no, I'll see you on your way first, Molly. I certainly don't want to just dash off and abandon you in the city.'

'Don't be silly. I'll be perfectly fine. And that's the last tram of the night. You don't want to miss it.'

Colin hesitated.

'Go on, I'll get the train to St Kilda. I've just got time to make the platform.' She stretched up and gave him a kiss on the cheek, followed by a gentle shove.

Colin smiled, then bounded down the steps, just managing to swing up into the tram on Norman's heels. Molly watched as he found a place to stand, then turned to look out at her as the tram clattered down Flinders Street toward East Melbourne. She raised her hand in a small wave.

Molly's train was half full as it left Flinders Street Station, but she easily found a seat. She adjusted her red beret so it tilted low over one side of her forehead, blocking out the carriage and her fellow passengers. They rattled slowly across the Sandridge Bridge before branching off from the Port Melbourne line and picking up speed. Gradually, as the train passed through South Melbourne, Albert Park and Middle Park stations, the carriage emptied and Molly was alone with her thoughts. She was determined to present an article to the *Table Talk* editor: the piece she had in mind would be perfectly suited to the magazine. It was not what Molly had planned, but this article was just the first step. It would be impossible to simply turn her back on her teaching without some means of support while she worked on her novel, and journalism was an attractive proposition.

The possibilities ran through Molly's head, the speeding train providing a soundscape of urgency that the rocking motion failed to dispel. As the end of the line approached and the train began to slow, Molly turned to stare out of the window, but all she could see was her own pale face reflected back against the darkness of the world.

The lights of St Kilda Station suddenly replaced the blackness, and Molly's image disappeared. At the same moment, she realised it was imperative she speak to Colin as soon as possible. Molly needed his advice, but more importantly, she needed his support. Stepping down onto the platform, Molly made straight for the public phone box outside the station, oblivious to other stragglers descending from their carriages or moving toward the street. Pulling the door closed behind her, she picked up the earpiece and leaned in.

'Operator.' A man's voice.

'Hawthorn 5176, please.'

'One moment.'

Molly rested her back against the glass and wood of the wall, rummaging in her bag for coins while she waited for the operator to connect her call.

'Insert your coins, please.'

She obeyed, listening to the ping echo down the line.

'Go ahead, please.'

'Hello?'

'Colin?'

'Molly? What's happened? Are you all right?'

'Yes, no. I don't know. I needed to talk to you and we didn't get a chance. When I got off the train I realised you'd be home by now so –'

'Molly, it's just gone midnight. I promised we'd talk and I meant it. What's so important that it can't wait?'

'My life!' Molly's reply caught in her throat. 'I have a chance with journalism, but it means giving up teaching and that seems like such a big step. But it may be my only chance, and I can't keep going on like this with Mother in that house, and –'

'Molly, Molly, hold on for a moment, stop!' Colin raised his voice to cut across her. 'I can hear how wound up you are. You'll make yourself ill if you go on in this way. Please. We're both tired, and this is a very big decision. Go home and we'll talk about it tomorrow.'

'Colin –'

'Tomorrow Molly. It's only a few hours away.' He softened his voice. 'Goodnight now. It will be all right.'

'Goodnight.' Molly's voice sounded peevish even to her own ears, but it was too late. Colin had broken the connection.

Molly turned, pushed the door open, and stepped across to a bench where an older woman in a large hat was seated. She flopped herself down at the opposite end, suddenly exhausted. The woman glanced at her as she sat, then turned back to the street, discreet or disinterested, Molly didn't notice.

Molly sighed and rubbed her eyes. Colin clearly had no idea this decision would change her life. She looked around. There were still a few people out and about in addition to herself and her fellow bench-sitter. Most of them were on the move, none of them in a hurry. Over near the boot kiosk, a man in a suit stood immobile, facing Molly and the station as though waiting for someone to arrive. From where Molly sat, his face was lost in shadow with only the occasional glint from his eyes betraying the direction of his focus.

Suddenly Molly sprang up and dove back into the phone box, coin already in her hand.

'Operator.'

'Hawthorn 5176 please.'

'One moment. Insert your coins, please.'

This time she spoke first. 'Colin, I know it's late. I wish I was there with you so we could talk about this properly, but I'm not. That was your decision.'

'Molly, I explained why I needed a bit of time to myself.'

'Well, you told me. I'm not sure that what you said explained anything, but it doesn't matter right now. I don't want to talk about that. You and I and whatever we are — that's not why I'm calling.'

Colin was silent for a moment and Molly hoped she had given him pause for thought. She was not one of those women who resorted to pleas, threats or tears.

Then he let out a short laugh. 'I can't believe you're calling me again after midnight, Molly. You are the most impetuous creature I know, and I absolutely adore that about you.'

Molly felt herself smile and soften in response to his words, but then she straightened her back. 'I'm calling to tell you I've decided. I wanted to discuss it with you, but ... Anyway, I'm going to do it. The school year is almost done, so I'm going to hand in my notice, work out the year, and then devote myself 100 per cent to writing. The journalism job is there for the taking, and I know I can do it. I wanted you to be the first to know.'

'Molly.' The line crackled and he paused. 'Molly, I think you'll be a wonderful writer, a great journalist.'

'But?'

'But don't be too impulsive. Don't throw away teaching just like that, not until you at least get your foot in the door with writing.'

'How can I make a go of writing if I'm shackled to the Education Department?'

'Perhaps you could be a relief teacher or some such? I don't know, but just think about it carefully. We'll talk, I promise, but sleep on it now, please?'

Molly was silent for a moment, trying hard not to cry, nor to let her voice betray the fact tears were close. 'Fine. I'll see you at the weekend then.'

'We can look at it from every possible angle and make a plan.'

'I suppose so.'

'Are you all right?'

'I'm fine. I should go now or I'll miss the last tram.'

'Just sleep on it, Molly, and it will be okay. You're going to be famous.'

Molly's mouth twitched. Of course he'd try to flatter her now. 'Goodnight, Colin.'

'Goodnight, Molly, sweet dreams.' Once again, it was Colin who ended the call.

1999

I PHONE JOHN FROM the car before I leave Hillview.

'Daphne has never heard the name Donald Raeburn in connection with Molly Dean.'

'Not surprising. The whole thing seems to have been a massive cover-up.'

'Are we back to your conspiracy theory?'

'It makes sense and you know it.'

'At the moment I don't know anything, but I'll call Raeburn junior and organise a time to show his father the painting. I'm assuming you're in.'

'Is the atomic weight of cobalt 58.9?'

'Is that a yes?'

'Of course it's a yes. I've got about another hour of work on the painting though.'

'Okay, I'll set it up for tomorrow morning then. Does that work?'

'Yeah, but how are you going to play it? I mean, would you sell Molly to him? And if the answer's no, how do we politely back out the door with the painting once we're there?'

KATHERINE KOVACIC

John has a point. 'I didn't really have a plan beyond getting in there and eyeballing Donald Raeburn, maybe confronting him with Molly's notes, but that is a fairly significant detail.'

'Rather.'

'Well what's your plan then?'

'You could name a ridiculous price. Oh wait, you've already sort of done that. I could feign sudden illness.'

'Or ...' I raise my voice to drown John out before he can make any other stupid remarks. 'Or, you could stop working on the painting right now. Then we just say it needs further work, and I never sell anything in that condition, blah blah, your reputation, blah, blah. Then we get the hell out.'

'I could muss it up a bit.'

'Not helping, John.'

'Sorry Alex. I think I'm a bit nervous about the whole thing. We – well, mostly you – have been running around unravelling the story behind Molly's murder, but it was all so long ago. I didn't really expect that we'd end up facing down the person who may well be the killer.'

'That's still up for debate. We certainly haven't got enough proof of anything to go to the police.'

'Even if we did, what would the cops do? Investigate a ninety-plus-year-old man for a seventy-year-old crime? Assuming they didn't just hustle us out the door, given our complete lack of solid evidence, wouldn't there be a statute of limitations on stuff like that? Or Raeburn could just say Molly had an active imagination and that would be that. Except for the bit where his pricey lawyers sue the crap out of you. I mean, you could talk to the police, but I think – unless you just want to walk away – this is really the only option.'

'Agreed. I'll make the call now and be at the studio in about twenty minutes.'

238

'No rush. If I'm not going to work on Molly, I might even tidy up the studio a bit.'

'Sure you will; knock yourself out. And before you get too attached to your cover-up idea, I've discovered a couple of other things we need to discuss.'

'Intriguing. I'll be waiting.'

I jab the button, ending the call. Outside the car, I can see the wind has picked up a bit, pushing swollen grey clouds across the sky to a point where they begin to back up and insulate the world, obscuring the sun and the infinite blue beyond. I think of the colours Turner would have used to paint that sky, or Constable. How would Tom Roberts have captured the elements of this gathering storm? The patches of light and dark that now dapple the ground and the agitation of the trees. I know I'm procrastinating, but thinking about art is very calming. Bringing my attention back inside the car, I scroll through the numbers on my phone, select the name Raeburn, T, and press the button with the ironic icon of a rotary dial phone receiver. I clear my throat as it starts to ring.

'Thomas Raeburn.'

'Mr Raeburn, it's Alex Clayton.' My voice sounds strange in my ears. 'Good news. My client has decided against the painting, so as promised I'm giving your father first right of refusal.'

'He definitely wants it.'

'We haven't agreed on a price yet and it's still undergoing cleaning.'

'I've been asked to tell you that you can name the price.'

'We can finalise that when I deliver the painting. I'm anticipating that the conservator will have finished the work by late tonight, barring any sort of emergency. That means I could bring it round tomorrow morning, say about ten?'

'I'm more than happy to collect it. In fact, it might be simpler.'

'Nonsense. It's part of the service.' I'm grasping a bit, so I decide to play the trump card. 'Besides, I want to make sure your father is completely happy. I'd hate to be the reason you found yourself in a difficult position.'

I hear him swallow. 'Perhaps you're right.'

Raeburn senior must be scary as hell when he's worked up.

'Excellent. Where am I delivering the painting?'

'Number 13 Bannock Avenue, Toorak. I'll make sure the gate is unlocked.'

'See you at ten, then. I'm looking forward to meeting your father.'

'Yes, see you at ten.'

The phone is still against my ear when the line is cut and it's another few seconds before I drop it onto the passenger seat. John isn't the only one who's nervous. I twist the key in the ignition and the engine doesn't so much roar to life as excuse itself in a very Gallic manner, accompanied by the prolonged shrug of the suspension. I feel quite cold all of a sudden, so I crank on the heater and leave it blasting all the way to John's studio.

'I still think Adam Graham looks good for it.' I'm sprawled in the yellow basket chair. 'But I need to run a couple of things past you.'

'Go on.' John hands me a coffee and moves to the other chair.

'First, I found out – well, Daphne told me – that someone else confessed to killing Mena and Hazel.'

'That rules out the random psycho theory then.'

'Well there was a psycho, but he had nothing to do with Molly's death.'

'Melbourne must have been a lovely town in 1930.'

'I know. It still leaves the spate of non-fatal attacks on women unsolved. I don't know if they're related to anything, but they were very close to Molly's house and they stopped after her murder.'

'So back to Adam Graham or the man Molly was writing about. And I'm going on record and saying I think she *was* writing about Donald Raeburn.'

'Well I agree we can rule out the idea of an unknown killer. I mean, what are the odds Molly Dean would be the victim of a random attack when she already had a vicious mother, Adam Graham stalking her, some very jealous acquaintances and eleven pages of explosive material on someone who sounds like a crime boss?'

'Let's call him Donald Raeburn, shall we?'

I sigh. 'Would you just listen for a moment?'

'Fine. Tell me what you've got.'

'I was thinking again about the idea that the killer could be a woman.'

John raises his eyebrows but I hold up a hand before he can speak.

'What if the man in the coat and hat following Molly was a woman? The strange gait the witnesses described could be because it was a woman trying to walk like a man.'

John takes a breath but I move my extended hand sharply, pushing the air in front of his face.

'I'm thinking either Ethel Dean, in which case she was probably in it together with Graham ... or Betty Roland.'

'You think this tops my Donald Raeburn conspiracy theory?'

'I found out Betty Roland gave Molly the theatre tickets. She would have known Molly would be coming home alone.'

John shakes his head. 'First, Ethel Dean. If Graham was the

killer, she might have known something, but I don't think she dressed as a man to follow Molly home. Why do that when we know he was happy to do her bidding on that score?'

'You don't think he was lying in wait and Ethel was …' I trail off. 'Okay, maybe that is a bit of a stretch. But what about Betty Roland? Possible rival for Colin's affections?'

John gets up and rummages around in his bookcase for a moment. When he turns back, he's already flicking through the pages of a yellow hardback. It's Betty Roland's biography.

'Betty Roland could not possibly be involved. The police questioned her, like they did everyone in that social group.' He turns the book around and thrusts it toward me. 'Read that.' He taps a spot halfway down the page.

I scan the text. Betty Roland was 200 miles away from Elwood on the night Molly was murdered. I snap the book shut and sigh. 'So tell me your theory then.'

'Theories!'

'Whatever.'

'Number one. Donald Raeburn killed her and paid off the police.'

'But if we assume he's the man in Molly's notes, he was powerful enough not to need to kill her. Threats and intimidation would have done the trick. Plus I think Percy Lambell wouldn't have spent the rest of his life agonising about the case if he knew who did it but had been bought off. I think Daphne's right about her dad – he must have been squeaky clean.'

'I agree about Lambell, but Raeburn could have bribed someone higher up the food chain. And he might have killed Molly just because he was a sadist and knew he could do it and get away with it. Or maybe it was a warning to others not to cross him.'

I screw up my nose. 'What's the second theory?'

'Molly was getting too close to a police corruption story so the cops – not Lambell – eliminated her.'

I shake my head. 'I hope there's a third theory.'

'Adam Graham did it.'

'What?'

'Yep.' John nods. 'But Raeburn paid him to do it. Somehow their paths crossed and they realised they had a mutual interest in Molly Dean.'

'That's a huge reach.'

'Ahh! But remember how Adam Graham was so relaxed after the committal, he fell asleep in the police cells? And how his enormous bail was posted immediately by a stranger?'

'That was a retired farmer. I don't remember his name.'

'Doesn't matter. We know from experience Raeburn likes using false names.'

'You really have a thing about Raeburn.'

'Molly hid those notes for a reason.'

'But she doesn't name Raeburn.'

John snorts. 'You said yourself it was too much of a coincidence for Molly to have all those nasty people in her life and still get murdered by a random stranger.'

'What's your point?'

'It's also too much of a coincidence for her to have written about a powerful and intimidating man and for just such a person to be trying to buy her portrait seventy years later. Unless it's the same man.'

'I'm not sure about any of these people anymore.' I fold my arms. 'But I guess we'll find out tomorrow.'

THE NEXT MORNING, HOGARTH and I collect John and Molly from the studio just after nine. Last night's storm has blown itself out, but it will be a few hours before the sun manages to erase the lingering traces of damp from the glistening streets. Hogarth is aware that we're on edge, so he does what any self-respecting wolfhound would do under the circumstances: sits bang in the middle of the back seat and inserts his head between John and me in the front. Occasionally he drags his tongue across my cheek in a reassuring manner. I'm going to need to exfoliate the rest of my face to catch up.

'Is your wrist still bothering you?' John nods toward my hands on the steering wheel.

'I overdid it a bit yesterday, the bandage is just for extra support. But never mind about that. Your Raeburn theories made me paranoid, so I ran off three copies of Molly's papers last night.' My voice sounds loud. 'I didn't want to bring the originals, and I stuck one copy in the post to Daphne, and another to your home address.'

'Good, good.' John looks across at me. 'I keep telling myself this is an old man we're going to see, but I'm shit scared.'

'Let's call that a healthy degree of caution. It doesn't sound quite so bad then. It will be okay. I'm freaking out too, but we agreed we can do this. We need to do this.'

'Can we have a code word? If things are getting too, I don't know, psycho-killer-ish?'

'We won't need one. We're just going to go in, show him the painting, drop a few broad remarks about Molly's murder and her notes, and see what happens.'

'Okay. But if I mention Max Meldrum, you can take that as a sign that I'm about to bottle it.'

'Duly noted.'

I flip on the indicator and we swing into Bannock Avenue. It's the sort of street where the air feels like it's freshly piped in every morning. Nature strips are mown with military precision and there is not a single car parked on the narrow road. It's a vista of high walls and imposing gates, like some sort of medieval battlement that has been gussied up by an assortment of decorators, all trying to outdo each other without tipping over into tackiness. Except for number 13.

Number 13 Bannock Avenue appears to be the house time – not to mention paint and landscaping – forgot. Whatever the tall fence was made from, the whole thing is dense with vines. Not an attractive russet-coloured Boston ivy or something delightfully floral and aromatic like wisteria or honeysuckle, but the sort of vine for which the term 'creeper' is particularly apt. The leaves are thick and dark, and the tangle of tendrils stretches up and out from the fence, looking for somewhere new to attach their suckers. They crowd in on the gate, or rather the solid door that crouches midway along the property line. Beyond the top of the fence, tall cypress trees and what looks like the top of a monkey puzzle tree crowd together, fighting toward the light. The upper storey of a Victorian house, rendered grey, is just visible. If I was a kid, this is the sort of place I'd run past on my way home from school.

'Talk about setting the scene. This place is straight from central casting.' I roll the car to a stop directly across from the gate.

'Does it strike you as deeply ironic that it's number 13?' John leans around me to get a better look.

The gate shifts slightly as we watch, and both John and I crane forward, holding our breath. Nothing. 'Tom said he'd make sure it's unlocked. They must have chocked it open and the wind is catching it.' I'm not sure if I'm saying it for John's benefit or mine.

'Sure, the wind.' John licks his lips. 'How about a couple of rules? No opening any closed doors at the end of long hallways, and if we hear any music in a minor key, we get the hell out.'

'Sounds reasonable. At least there's no trouble getting Hogarth into the garden.'

'What about the house though?'

'Depends. When they open the door, I'll go first with the painting and try to keep the attention on me, then you get Hogarth to tail you in and ask him to chill in the hall. And try to leave the door off the latch in case we need to beat a hasty retreat. Crap, it's giving me the heebie-jeebies just thinking about going in there.'

'I reckon it's time we stopped thinking and just did this or we'll be here for ever.'

'You're right. Let's go.'

We clamber out of the car and I retrieve Molly from the boot and wrap a blanket around her while John grabs Hogarth's collar. We regroup next to the rear bumper.

'Have you got Molly's notes?'

I know I do, because I've checked a dozen times already

this morning, but now John has asked I have to pat my pocket again. It's like when I'm on the way to the airport and someone says, 'Have you got everything? Passport?'

'C'mon.'

I start across the road with John and Hogarth close behind. The gate is indeed propped open with a brick, and as we pass through I make sure there's no chance it can be blown shut. Inside the fence, the garden is wildly overgrown. There are glimpses here and there of its former glory: a fragment of path now meandering into a solid wall of green; the lichen-covered face of a statue peering out from a dark corner; and, to one side of the house, a swimming pool. The design just visible in the broken line of tiles is enough to show the pool was probably the last word in sophistication back in the 1950s, but today the water is dark, black and overlain by a thick blanket of algae and scum. I don't want to think about what might be on the bottom of that pool.

Two chipped and worn steps lead up to a porch where the original Victorian tiles – or most of them – form a geometric pattern in tan, black and ochre. Leaves from a decade of autumns are scattered across the surface and piled up where the wind has driven them. A bay window juts out to our left, but shutters obscure the interior. On the other side of the window, a suite of once-elegant wicker furniture is slowly collapsing in on itself, the victim of damp, rot and small things that like to chew.

We position Hogarth away from the door and I press the bell. Nothing happens.

'That's a relief, because based on what we've seen so far, I was expecting something discordant, followed by dragging footsteps, and either Lurch or Vincent Price on the other side.'

'Again, not helping, John.' I eye off the doorknocker, but it looks as though anything too vigorous would send it crashing to the ground, so I rap firmly on the wood with my good hand. Somewhere in the house I hear a door open and a light comes on, flooding through the fanlight and the etched ruby glass panels that bracket the entrance. Rather than being welcoming, it just serves to highlight the pervading gloom. The door opens. No creaking hinges, but it sounds as though something large was dragged out of the way before the locks tumbled. Tom is standing there and I immediately step forward with the painting in front of me, blocking any view he might have of Hogarth.

'Mr Raeburn. Good to see you again. I've brought John with me as he was unable to finish the cleaning and he wanted to be on hand if you or your father have any questions about the process.' I'm talking fast and walking forward at the same time, but I almost falter as I step over the threshold and catch my first glimpse of the interior. The hall is jammed with a bizarre conglomeration of stuff. Antique stuff, yes, but not like delicate gilt Louis XIV chairs and Italian torchère sort of antiques. Far more random. A suit of armour sits next to a nineteenth-century pedal-operated dentist's drill, while a Black Forest hall stand, all gnarled branches and grumpy bear, cosies up to a teetering pile of yellowing magazines so tall I'd need to reach over my head for the topmost copy. And that's just the beginning. There is enough room to pass single file down the middle of the hall, but only just, and everything is covered by a layer of dust so thick it looks like a scientific experiment in progress.

'Father is incredibly paranoid about security – won't have cleaners or gardeners on the property – and he's also become a bit of a hoarder.' From the tone of his voice, I can tell Tom Raeburn knows this is the understatement of the millennium. 'He has plans to gift his possessions to the museum.'

What museum? The Museum of Mouldering Crap? I hope I didn't say that out loud. Tom doesn't react, so I think I'm safe.

On the plus side, the narrow aisle means he has to walk ahead of me into the house, so it's easy for John to slip Hogarth in behind us. I make a mental note to treat Hogarth for fleas before I let him back in our house. Then I make another note to do the same for myself. I glance over my shoulder and see John is only a few steps behind and I catch a glimpse of shaggy grey fur behind him. Hogarth won't be thrilled about letting me out of his sight in this strange place, but there should be lots of interesting rodent-type smells to keep him occupied.

'Does your father live here alone?'

'Ordinarily my son comes in every day to help or take Father to medical appointments. He and Father are incredibly close. But he dislocated his shoulder earlier this week playing football, so he's out of action.' Tom Raeburn is talking over his shoulder so he doesn't notice John and I gaping at each other. I'm thinking that dislocation has nothing to do with football and a lot to do with Hogarth.

We pass three doors that are firmly closed, although I can see a key in the lock of one, and a staircase on our left, leading up into the darkness. There's a grandfather clock on the landing of the stairs and I can hear its deep and ponderous tick. I peer up and am surprised to see it shows the correct time.

Tom notices my interest. 'That clock is indestructible. It has a double chime so loud you can hear it from almost anywhere in the house. Used to drive me mad when we were kids and it would be chiming through the night. Father refused to silence it when we went to bed, always said he found it reassuring in the small hours. Of course, I always thought you'd be asleep in the small hours if it wasn't for hearing that thing boom out twenty-four notes at midnight ...'

John and I have stopped walking and are staring at Tom, who has become slightly flushed. Clearly growing up in the Raeburn family has caused a few lingering issues.

'Anyway, that's all long ago now. Father is waiting in the small sitting room.' Tom takes a couple more steps and pushes open a door on his left. A wedge of light angles out, creating planes and deep shadows among the hallway's detritus. He stands aside so John and I can go in first, then follows us, somehow failing to notice Hogarth.

Despite its cavernous appearance, the sitting room is stuffy and overly warm. There is a gas fire that looks as though it's been there since the turn of the century, its Bakelite knob worn and yellow. Judging by the scattering of burned match heads in front of the grate, the gas supply must be temperamental in a way that encourages the user to stand well back and throw matches until, one way or another, something ignites. Heavy velvet drapes cover all the windows and seem to absorb light from the room: the overhead fixture is blazing but doing surprisingly little. Bookshelves line two walls and are jammed full. I can see everything from leather and gilt spines to gaudy paperbacks, the latter often lying horizontally on top of the former. Additional piles of books and newspapers are arranged to create pathways between islands of furniture: a breakfast table and chairs close to the window, a desk near the opposite wall.

Nearer to the fire is a massive leather chair. Based on the rest of the decor, I was expecting something like a nineteenth-century chesterfield, possibly with stuffing poking out of the back. But this is state of the art and the size of it screams American, like an upholstered cousin to a 1950s Chevy. The footrest is popped and I know that with the push of a button this baby will slowly lift and tilt until the occupant is delivered gently into the upright position. From where we are gathered to one side of the chair, I can see the footrest supports two bony, liver-spotted ankles, spanning the distance between tartan trousers and blue woollen slippers, while on the arm of the chair a hand rests, so shrivelled it looks like a witch's fetish. On the far side and a little in front of the chair, a claw-foot walking stick stands waiting for the grasping hand of its owner.

Tom steps to the front of the chair. 'Father, this is Alex Clayton and the conservator. Miss Clayton, my father, Donald Raeburn.'

I pass Molly backwards to John and step forward, bandaged hand extended. 'Mr Raeburn. Pleased to meet you.'

The man in the chair was once big and powerful, that much is evident from the length of his legs and the width of his shoulders, but it's as though he's been pressed between the pages of one of his many books. His skin looks tissue-thin and his sparse white hair floats away from his skull, as though each strand wishes to escape. If it weren't for his gaze, I'd describe Donald Raeburn as delicate, but from inside the shell of his body, green-brown eyes stare at me shrewdly, glittering with something more than mere interest or intellect. He may be old, but Raeburn senior is not someone to be taken lightly. He holds his wizened paw out to me, not far, just enough so I have to step in and stoop to complete the handshake. His hand rests briefly in mine without gripping, but somehow the touch doesn't feel weak. It feels contained. I begin to wonder how frail Donald Raeburn really is. After all, his son did say he could get about, he simply chooses not to.

'Do you have my painting?'

Okay, no small talk, and apparently no chairs or refreshments. I'm guessing visitors are a rare occurrence Chez Raeburn.

'I have brought the portrait, yes.' I see his eyes spark in response. 'But an unforeseen problem means it hasn't been fully cleaned. You can inspect it today and if you still want to buy it and we agree on a price, John will finish the cleaning and we'll get Molly Dean back in her frame and delivered to you.' I throw her name out there deliberately, just to see what happens.

252

So far, all my conversations with Raeburn junior have been about a portrait of a woman. The name Molly Dean has never been mentioned. I can't see Tom, so I hope John is watching for a reaction, and I hope it's as good as the one I get from Donald Raeburn. When I say her name he stiffens, just for a moment, and if I wasn't looking closely I would have missed it. His lips twitch and I think he's about to speak, but his son jumps in and kills it.

'I'm sorry, what name did you say? Have you identified the sitter?'

I step back and half turn, so I can eye both Donald and Tom. John is standing very still.

'Yes, I have actually. Her name is Molly – or Mary – Dean. She was Colin Colahan's lover, but unfortunately she died not long after he painted this portrait.' I stare hard at Donald Raeburn. 'That was another reason I wanted to discuss the painting with you personally. Molly Dean died a very violent death, and not everyone would be happy to have that sort of portrait hanging on their wall.'

'Do I look like a sentimental man?' His voice, like his body, has all the patina of age but none of its feebleness. It sounds like a whip designed to lash lesser humans into submission. 'Show me the painting.'

'As I said, cleaning is a work in progress.' Next to my thigh, and hopefully out of Donald Raeburn's line of sight, I make an upside-down stop sign with my hand. I don't want John to unwrap Molly just yet. 'It looks quite odd out of its frame and with half her face still dulled by old varnish. I wouldn't normally show it to a client at this stage, but your son said you were quite insistent.'

'Show. Me. The. Painting.'

I splay the fingers of my hidden hand and hope John notices. I want Molly's face to be the coup de grâce of this little encounter. 'Just before we get to that, there's one other thing I need to mention.' I glance at Tom but he's looking quite relaxed, hands in pockets and rocking back on his heels. 'When we removed the frame to clean the portrait, we found something. Something we believe Molly put there herself.'

'How fascinating!' Tom is definitely not a player in this game.

'Yes, it was quite fascinating.' I'm watching Donald Raeburn closely as I speak, but other than those fierce eyes he's giving nothing away. 'It was a sheaf of handwritten notes she'd made, probably while preparing to write an article about somebody.' I turn to the son. 'She was an aspiring journalist and author, you know.'

Tom Raeburn nods and looks genuinely interested, but I've already turned back to his father. His scrawny hands have flexed into claws on the arms of his La-Z-Boy and I can see the rapid rise and fall of his chest beneath his navy cardigan and hear the agitated rasp of his breathing.

'The really funny thing about all of it, is that Molly's notes could almost have been written about you, Mr Raeburn.'

'What?' It's Tom again but I ignore him. John moves forward so he is standing slightly behind on my left. He is holding Molly in front of his chest, but she is still hidden under the blanket. I wait, hoping Donald Raeburn will say or do something, wondering how far I'm going to have to push before he does.

'Father?' Tom steps around John and me and moves to the side of Donald's chair. 'What's going on? Did you know the woman in the portrait? Why didn't you say so?'

'Shut up, Thomas.'

Tom's jaw snaps shut like he's just been slapped and he takes a half-step back from the chair, out of reach.

'It seems from these extensive notes that Molly Dean was

working on an article about your father.' I turn my focus back to Donald. 'She'd spoken to a lot of people about you. Business people, women on the social scene, a number of Melbourne's movers and shakers of the day. You *really* don't remember Molly?'

Donald's hands have now curled into fists so tight his knuckles are turning white. 'I met a lot of people back then. You can't expect me to remember one girl, a reporter at that. Reporters make things up all the time.'

He hasn't flat-out denied knowing Molly, so I decide to hit Donald Raeburn with everything I've got. 'Why would she make up a story about talking to you? Twice? Why would she say she'd spoken to all these other people, heard all these other snippets? If it was all imagined, who'd publish it? And why hide her notes?'

'I want the painting and, as part of the transaction, I want the notes too. Now. Today. Thomas, get the cheque book.'

'The notes are not for sale. They're important historical documents. And you know what? I think the painting is off the market too. Looking around I don't think it would hang well with the rest of your collection. I think you may regret your decision to take on Molly Dean, and I'd just hate for that to happen.'

While I've been talking, Tom has sidled closer to John. 'What am I missing here?' he murmurs. John looks at me, eyebrows raised.

'Your son wants to know what's going on,' I say. 'Do you want to tell him?'

There is silence except for the rasp of Donald's breath and the hiss and pop of the gas fire.

'I can quote directly from Molly's notes if you like, or just give Tom the big picture version and let him draw his own conclusions.'

Donald's chin comes up and one side of his lip curls ever so slightly. 'I've had enough of this. Get out. Thomas, see them out.' His voice is like iron and Tom turns to comply, the habits of a lifetime kicking in. John and I don't budge.

'Hang on Tom, don't you want to hear the story?'

Tom stops, and his head swivels from me to his father and back again, his mouth open like a sideshow clown.

'It's the tale of an aspiring young author who was apparently looking for the story that would launch her career.'

'Get out.' Donald's voice is louder, angrier, but unlike Tom I'm unaccustomed to taking orders, least of all from aggressive men who think they own the world and everyone in it.

'She decided to write about Donald Raeburn. A brash young man who'd hauled himself up by his bootstraps in record time to become a real source of wealth and power in 1930s Melbourne. But Donald Raeburn Esquire didn't give interviews. She asked, but he knocked her back. So she started talking to other people. And she started to hear things she hadn't expected. Secrets and rumours, sure, only she was hearing the same stories from all sorts of different people. And all those stories were drawing a very different picture of Donald Raeburn. Molly suddenly found herself with a far bigger story.'

John is pressing his elbow insistently into my side. This is way more intense than I thought it would be, but I've come too far to stop. I look at Tom, his eyes are wide.

'Here.' I pull the copy of Molly's notes from my pocket and hand it to him. I have to give the papers an extra flap before he takes hold. 'She wrote it all down and I photocopied it for your father, but perhaps you'd like to read it first.'

'Give those to me, Thomas.' Donald is deathly calm, his icy tone brooking no argument.

Tom grasps the papers tightly to his chest, the crumpling

sound cutting across the air like a sudden burst of radio static. 'What happened?' His voice is a bare whisper.

'After hearing all those stories, Molly decided to do what any good journalist would do. Get confirmation. She went back to Donald Raeburn and asked again if he'd be prepared to talk to her. Only this time, she didn't claim to be writing a society puff piece, she probably told him at least some of what she'd found out about his business dealings. About the way he made his fortune. And some other things she'd picked up from the women he'd dated. He threatened her then threw her out.'

'The lies of jealous people and Melbourne old money who thought my shiny new pennies weren't good enough. Nothing was ever published. Not a word.' Donald has found a more reasonable tone although it has not lost the superior edge. 'I'll sue you if any of it gets out.'

'Can't sue me for Molly's words if they should happen to find their way to the press,' I shrug.

Tom has uncrumpled the notes from his chest and is reading the top sheet. His face seems to be getting whiter as I watch, and he's only on page one. He glances up at me then slowly turns to his father. 'How much of this is true?' Donald Raeburn ignores him, so Tom turns to me. 'Is this true?'

'All I can tell you is that, from what I've read, Molly clearly believed it was true, and she was meticulous about cross-checking the various details she uncovered. She was also worried enough about what she'd found to hide these notes. It's just a pity they stayed hidden for so long.' I speak quietly. I feel sorry for Tom, caught in the crossfire.

'What happened after my father threw her out? Why didn't she write the article?'

'Do you want to tell your son, Mr Raeburn?'

'Nothing to tell. She made up lies, I sent her packing. End of story.'

'Except it wasn't the end, was it? Oh and thanks for confirming the details so far.' I look at Tom again. 'Molly Dean was brutally murdered less than a week later. They never found out who did it.'

'Rubbish! They had a man bang to rights!' Donald is almost spitting.

'Except a mysterious stranger posted £1000 bail within minutes of charges being laid. Oh, and they conveniently let the man go on day one of the criminal trial, charges dropped, just like that. No more questions, no more investigation, no more suspects. I think either that man was set up,' I lean a bit closer to Donald Raeburn, 'or perhaps someone put him up to it. Paid him and assured him that if the police came knocking, the problem could be made to disappear. Someone with the connections to have a murder investigation buried and make the files disappear. Someone with a lot to lose if Molly Dean published her article.'

'What did you do?' Tom is staring at his father and shaking, but whether with shock or rage, I don't know. 'What did you do?'

But all he gets in reply is the harsh, increasingly wet sound of Donald Raeburn's breathing.

It's time for us to go, but there's just one more thing. I nod at John. 'You wanted Molly's portrait, well take a good look. I don't know whether you paid Adam Graham or whether you killed her yourself and he was just the idiot who ended up in the middle of everything, but I know what Molly uncovered, and that she was terrified of you.'

John has pulled the blanket from Molly's portrait and now he thrusts it forward into Donald Raeburn's face. 'Look at her face.' John's voice is icy. 'Do you remember how badly she was beaten? The stocking tied so tightly around her neck? It's been nearly seventy years but we all know, one way or another, you killed her.'

I put a hand on John's shoulder and gently push him backwards, away from the chair, away from the heat, toward the door. We need to leave.

'They're right aren't they? You killed that girl.' Tom's pallor is gone, replaced by a deep flush that extends up from his neck and across his entire face.

I start turning toward him, but suddenly Donald Raeburn lurches up from his chair and grabs my bad wrist. His strength is frightening and I'm almost blinded by the pain as he increases the pressure.

'Bitch,' he snarls.

'Alex!' John yells.

Somehow I grab Raeburn's little finger and bend it back, forcing him to let go. He falls to the floor and I quickly back away.

'Thomas, get me up.' Donald Raeburn extends a hand to his son.

Tom shakes his head slowly. He is rooted to the spot, eyes wide. When Donald reaches toward him again, he flinches and recoils.

John has the door open and hustles me out into the hall where Hogarth stands, alert. His ears relax visibly when he sees me, but as John and I step past and head for the front door, Hogarth scents the air exuding from the sitting room and a low, primal growl rises from deep in his chest.

'Let's go, Hogarth,' I say, and with a last look over his shoulder, Hogarth falls in behind us.

'Thomas!' Donald is yelling from the sitting room. 'Thomas!'

We pass through the front door and I can still hear Raeburn senior shouting as John slams it behind us.

21 NOVEMBER 1930

SHE CLUNKED THE PHONE'S earpiece down and pushed her way out of the red booth. Fighting back tears, Molly stumbled from St Kilda Station into Fitzroy Street. Now, after midnight, only a few hardy souls shared the night.

'Sleep on it! Think about it carefully!' Indignation gave way to frustrated muttering as Molly rounded the corner into Grey Street. The last tram was just rattling past the St Kilda Coffee Palace, too far away to catch now.

Molly let the tears come and they flowed unchecked as she slowly began to trudge in the tram's wake. The books in her bag seemed suddenly to be made of lead, dragging her down, keeping her back. She was not usually given to crying, but the disappointments of recent days were somehow magnified when played out against the backdrop of life in her mother's house. At Colin's home, among the artists, dancers, musicians and ever-changing cast of Melbourne's creative set, anything seemed possible. No more Opportunity School, only opportunities for her: journalism, poetry, one day a novel.

Molly turned into Barkly Street, the shop lights beginning

261

to fade behind her. Pulling out her handkerchief, she mopped her face dry. Tears over. She needed a new plan. Tugging off her favourite red beret, Molly let the night breeze wash over her. As she moved into the residential streets, the commercial odours of dust and engine oil were gradually replaced by a rich tapestry of night blossom, clipped lawn and the occasional hint of eucalyptus.

She sighed loudly, the sound attracting the attention of a couple of men, clearly on their way home from a late drink in one of St Kilda's less salubrious establishments. Molly flicked her eyes in their direction, assessed and dismissed them.

Crossing the intersection into Mitford Street, Molly felt her resolve hardening and in response her pace quickened, making her seem like a stop-motion animation as she moved between the light puddled around the street lamps. She rounded the corner into Dickens Street.

'Not bloody likely!' She laughed. *Pygmalion*'s notorious line was the perfect response to every plan her mother had for her. No more. This time she would go and not look back. If Eliza Doolittle could do it, Molly Dean could do it, and she didn't need anyone to tell her how.

A sudden screech made her snap her head to the right. A man, sharply outlined by the light behind him, was framed in a first-floor window. His arms, raised as if in surrender, still grasped the edge of the pane he had thrown open. Their eyes met, and Molly was preparing a pithy rebuff, when his gaze suddenly shifted down the street and he withdrew from sight.

Primed now, Molly half hoped her mother would be lying in wait as she often was. Although it may be better to hold off until morning and present her plan rationally, part of her hungered for confrontation. It didn't really matter. Despite the late hour, Molly knew tonight there would be no sleep as she mapped out the next stage of her life, the first step to truly greater things.

She turned without thinking into Addison Street, a landscape obscured by night, but with the path familiar to her feet.

A whisper of sound behind her, the brush of fabric on fabric, a sudden rush of air, excruciating pain as something cracked into her head. Molly fell against a fence, then to the path, bag still over her arm. She clawed the ground, opened her mouth to scream, but could barely suck in air.

Another blow, head again, metal on bone. Molly stopped moving.

A hulking shape loomed, grabbed her ankles and dragged her from Addison Street into a cobbled lane, a Stygian red river of blood marking their path. A shoe fell in the mouth of the laneway, her bag came adrift, books tumbled, papers fluttered. In the darkness of the lane, he began tearing at her clothes – petticoat first, then the stocking, knickers.

Molly groaned, gasped. Her hand fluttered weakly, seeming to move toward her head before falling back to the cobbles.

She didn't feel the stocking going around her throat, was barely aware as it became tight, tighter. Her dress and chemise were pushed up, exposing Molly's breasts, and the petticoat was tied around one arm, but Molly's conscious mind had already abandoned her pain-racked body. A barely audible gurgle emanated from deep in her throat.

This seemed to enrage her attacker. The response was swift and brutal. The tyre iron swung again and again.

Molly was still now, silent. Crouched over her, breathing heavily but trying to keep quiet, her attacker shifted the tyre iron to his other hand. He was not done yet. Minutes passed, with only the sound of his heavy breathing disturbing the night.

Somewhere, the harsh sound of a man drawing hard on the

last of a cigarette. How close? Sounds travel differently at night.

The assailant stood. A moment's hesitation, a last, lingering look at Mary Winifred Dean. A backward step and the shadows embraced him. He had returned to the darkness and Molly was alone.

There was a moment when Elwood, or maybe all of Melbourne, held its breath. Then Molly began to groan.

Each tortured breath, each infinitesimally small rise and fall of her broken chest, produced a low lament of pain and anguish. It was the primal sound of the mortally wounded.

In the front bedroom of number 5 Addison Street, Beatrice Owen felt the hairs on the back of her neck rise. Never one to quail, she twitched the curtain and pressed her face to the window, eyes wide and straining against the dark. A shadow flicked past the fence.

'Fred! Fred!'

'Bea? Wassup?' Her brother's voice was thick with sleep.

'Someone's out there! I saw someone!'

'Go back to sleep.' Even from across the hall, she heard the creak of the mattress springs as he settled back in. 'Yer dreamin', Bea.'

Doubting but wanting the reassurance, Beatrice turned toward her bed, but a soft whimper had her spinning into the hall and at her brother's door.

'There's something hurt out there. Get up! I'm not going out by myself.'

'I swear, Bea.' Fred pulled on his dressing gown. 'I'm working in the morning.' Slid his feet into his shoes. 'You gotta stop reading those penny dreadfuls!'

He stomped down the hall, flung open the door and stood, scenting the air like a bloodhound. Beatrice pushed past him and stepped down the path. At the gate, she froze.

'Holy heck, Fred!' He was by her side in an instant.

'Strewth!'

Just beyond the pickets lay a woman's things – hat, bag, shoe – and a jumble of papers, as though their owner had suddenly been plucked from the world, too quickly to gather her possessions.

Wrenching the gate open, Fred had only taken two steps when his brain linked the input from nose and eyes. The sharp ferrous tang he'd first detected from the verandah was emanating from the viscous trail that led into the lane.

'Go inside, Bea. I've got to phone the coppers.' His voice was harsh with fear.

1999

IT'S A FEW DAYS after our visit with Donald Raeburn, and Hogarth and I are standing just inside the North Road entrance to Brighton General Cemetery. John has taken his car to collect Daphne from Hillview, and I'm expecting them to join us any minute. I've just finished updating Mum about Molly's story, and I drop my mobile back into my bag. There's a gentle breeze blowing, enough to make the few nearby trees whisper softly to one another, but not so much that I need a coat. My face is turned to the sun, eyes closed behind my sunglasses. I have a bunch of carnations tucked under my arm and Hogarth is leaning against my leg, happy to be out and about.

'We made it.' It's John.

I open my eyes. He and Daphne are coming through the gate at a steady pace. John is matching his stride to Daphne and her walker, and judging by their relatively jaunty approach she's having a good day. Hogarth steps forward to meet them, tail waving in a gentlemanly fashion.

'When you said you didn't want us all squashed into one car, I didn't quite appreciate your point.' Daphne strokes Hogarth's

267

head and gives his ear a rub. 'But now it makes perfect sense.'

'Good to see you, Daphne.' I give her a peck on the cheek. 'I'm glad you could come.'

'It's a wonderful idea and I wouldn't miss it. Dad would have wanted me to come too.'

'It's not far and I have a map. Shall we go?'

We start down the road into the cemetery. I suppose we could have driven closer, but this feels right, a more mindful approach. It's a weekday morning so the place is quiet except for a few birds and the background susurration of cars on the roads outside the cemetery walls.

'Have you heard anything more from the Raeburns?' John thought, once he'd had a chance to regroup, Donald Raeburn would come out guns blazing.

'Not a thing. I never saw who attacked me, so I can't prove it was Tom's son, and as for Tom, well ... I don't know whether he really has the guts to stand up to his father, but I'd like to think it's possible. And there did seem to be a hint of backbone in there.'

'Yeah.' John shrugs. 'But family and a lifetime of habits are powerful things.'

'I don't care. If Tom can live with that, I really don't care. We achieved something though. Donald Raeburn knows the past has caught up with him. It would be great if he could be called to account, but there's not much we can do about that. Besides, by the sound of him, he'll pop his clogs fairly soon.'

'I hope it hurts when he does.' Daphne smacks the handle of her walker for emphasis.

John and I both stop and stare at her.

'What? Just because I'm old doesn't mean I'm soft. Anyhow, that seems to be the way of it. From what I've seen at Hillview, the nasty ones always seem to rot on the inside or have a massive, painful brain bleed, something like that.'

'Gee, it's all sweetness and light in retirement living, isn't it?' John looks at Daphne admiringly. 'Can I paint your portrait sometime? I want to catch the steel in your eyes.'

Daphne gives him a playful swat on the arm and we start walking again.

'I wish Raeburn would give us a deathbed confession,' I say. 'I'd really like to know exactly what the story was with Adam Graham.'

John snorts.

'I still think Adam was involved,' Daphne replies. 'All that evidence, and the strange way he and Ethel Dean behaved about Molly. He had to have been there.'

'Your dad seemed fairly certain it was Graham who actually killed her, but had no idea about Raeburn's connection to Molly. We're never going to know for sure though.'

'What about those other girls who were attacked at about the same time? Surely that wasn't just coincidence?' Daphne asks.

'I don't know, but from what you remembered and the other little bits I could find out, I think that was someone else. The girls were usually grabbed around the neck, but not throttled, and a couple of them were hit with a blunt instrument, but not seriously bashed. And there were a few bags stolen. I suspect Molly's killer was trying to make her attack look like it fitted with the others.' I shrug. It's as good as I can get. 'And those attacks seem to have stopped after Molly's death. I can only assume the man responsible for those got scared he'd be blamed for Molly if he tried it again.'

There's silence for a moment, except for the crunch of gravel under shoes and wheels.

'What are you going to do with the notes?' John asks.

'Get them published. I thought of writing something myself, trying to resurrect my academic career, but then I realised that would be doing Molly a disservice. Maybe once Raeburn senior is dead I'll pass the whole thing on to a newspaper and let them run with it.' I stop and look at my map. 'Down here.'

We peel off the main road and start making our way between the rows of graves. 'This is really quite a fitting spot,' I say. 'There are lots of artists here: Fred McCubbin, Septimus Power, Emanuel Phillips Fox... Not to mention writers like Adam Lindsay Gordon and Marion Miller.'

The path is narrow and a bit uneven so we move slowly. I read a few headstones as we pass by and feel an echoing pang of sorrow for all these dearly beloveds and sadly misseds, most of whom have now been joined by those who wrote their epitaphs. Then, without fanfare, we are there in front of a sad little plot edged in bluestone and granite, like a medieval fortification in miniature. There is no headstone, just a small weathered plaque.

John helps Daphne to reposition her walker so she can sit down, then he and I carefully pull out the weeds that have taken hold in places across the dry earth. It doesn't take long before the plot is clear, but I realise we have no vase for the flowers. I'd kind of assumed there would be more here, that what followed Molly's dramatic death would be bigger and more, well, monumental.

Daphne reaches into her cavernous bag and pulls out a large plastic tumbler, the sort of drink container they give to the sick and infirm. 'I brought it just in case. Hillview won't miss it.'

I take the cup and leave John and Daphne while I look for a tap. Hogarth follows me a little way then breaks off to snuffle around, tail in the air. When I return, slopping water over my shoes, the two of them are silent. John's hand is on Daphne's shoulder and her hand sits on his. Unwrapping the flowers, I try to arrange them, but the cup isn't really designed for that, and I have to let them be. I press the makeshift vase into the crumbly soil, twisting it around a few times to bed it in and help it counter the height of the flowers. Then I step back to Daphne's other side.

'Where's Molly's portrait?' Daphne is looking up at me, squinting a little against the sun.

'Molly is now installed above the mantelpiece in my living room, and that's where she's going to stay.'

'You're not going to sell her?'

'Not for a long time, if ever. I know so much more about Molly now, and she deserves to be remembered for who she was, not how she died. It doesn't seem right to parade her around or turn a profit. Especially when the story is revived.'

'What? Alex "what's it worth" Clayton is hanging on to a painting for sentimental reasons? That's a first.' John stares at me.

I shrug and push my sunglasses more firmly onto my face.

'But after the past couple of weeks, well …' John turns back to Molly's grave as he speaks. 'I agree, Molly deserves some peace.'

We stay like that for a while, not speaking, until Hogarth trots up and breaks the spell.

'Come on then,' I say, as John and I help Daphne up and set her walker on the path. 'Why don't you come back to my place and visit Molly?'

I turn toward the gate, and we set off. Around us angels weep tears of stone, but Hogarth is bounding ahead in the sunshine.

AUTHOR'S NOTES

THE EVENTS IN THIS novel are based on the 1930 murder of Mary 'Molly' Winifred Dean. I have imagined her conversations and day-to-day activities based on what is known of her life and aspirations. While Alex Clayton and her contemporaries are all entirely fictitious, most of Molly's close associates were real people. The exceptions are Donald Raeburn and those people that are part of his story. Donald Raeburn was created solely to provide a sense of closure to Molly's murder and is entirely my own creation. The way in which Adam Graham's £1000 bail was immediately paid by a mysterious benefactor and the surprising way the whole case suddenly evaporated suggested powerful forces at work, and I envisaged Raeburn as the holder of that power.

I have attempted to remain true to the immediate facts regarding Molly's murder. Documents relating to the investigation of Molly Dean's death did indeed go missing.

The details of Molly's relationships with her mother, Ethel Dean, and with Adam Graham were reported widely in the press during the coronial inquest. So too was Molly's desire to pursue a career as a writer, and her relationship with the artist Colin Colahan. Her final night, from the calls placed to Colahan, to the people who saw her walking home, the nature of her injuries and the placement of the stocking and underwear, adheres to the facts laid out before the coroner's court. I have merely provided thoughts for Molly that seemed appropriate to her mood and what was apparently said during the final phone call. Molly did tell Colin Colahan and Norman Lewis that she 'wished to God' she didn't have to go home to Milton Street that night.

Detective Harold Saker initially assisted Percy Lambell at the crime scene, but was replaced by Jerry O'Keeffe at 9 a.m. on 21 November. I have assigned Saker's brief role to O'Keeffe.

The lines from the poem 'Merlin' are Molly's own. The poem was published in 1929 in volume 1, number 2, of the short-lived Melbourne journal, *Verse*.

At one point during the investigation, newspapers reported that police were of the opinion the murder was committed by a man, but that a woman was directly associated with the crime. This couple were supposedly known to Molly Dean, had objections to some of her associations and had threatened her accordingly. While these articles do not name Adam Graham and Ethel Dean, the inference is clear.

The evidence against Adam Graham, such as his unusual gait, bloodstains on his suit and his history of following Molly (at Ethel Dean's behest) is all fact. However, there is nothing to indicate he knew Molly would return to Elwood that night. The criminal case against Graham was dropped by the prosecution on the day it was due to commence, presumably due to the circumstantial nature of the evidence. I could find no account of any further investigation into the murder of Molly Dean.

Colin Colahan was deeply affected by Molly's murder and

left Australia several years later to pursue a successful career in England and Europe. He is known to have painted two images of Molly Dean, a portrait (location unknown) and a nude titled *Sleep* (private collection). In the narrative I have inferred the nude was painted first, but the opposite is true. *Sleep* was still in the artist's studio, unfinished, at the time of Molly's murder.

Percy Lambell appears sporadically in the newspapers throughout his life as a member of the Victoria Police Force. He served a distinguished career keeping the streets of Melbourne free from crime. I don't believe he had children, but I'm sure they'd be just as proud of him as the fictitious Daphne.

ACKNOWLEDGEMENTS

THANK YOU TO Toni Jordan and Paddy O'Reilly for your pushing, cajoling, critiquing, inspiring and extensive hand-holding, and to Rob McDonald for being the voice of reason and an enthusiastic cheer squad. Thanks also to my agent, Sally Bird, to Charlotte Cole, and to Angela Meyer, Clive Hebard and all the incredible team at Bonnier Publishing Australia, for believing in Molly and helping to bring her to life. Mum and Dad, thanks for everything.

QUESTIONS FOR READING GROUPS

As a young woman in 1930, do you think Molly was naïve or gutsy to consider giving away her career as a teacher to try to become a writer? Why?

Why do you think Alex was initially reluctant to sell the portrait?

Should Alex have sold the painting when she first had a chance?

When do you think Alex became more interested in unravelling Molly's story than in simply increasing the value of the painting?

Do you think Ethel Dean knew something about what happened to Molly?

Was Adam Graham involved in Molly's death? What makes you think so (or not)?

What do you think of John's theories? Was Molly's murder the subject of a cover-up?

'A crap marriage is a great motivator for getting to work bright and early, and John's wife, well … I did try to warn him: now I'm just waiting to pick up the pieces.'

Alex and John are close friends. Do you think Alex is hoping for more?

Do Molly and Alex have anything in common?

Could Alex have handled the meeting with Donald Raeburn differently? Should she have gone to the police?

The reader knows from the first chapter that Molly Dean is murdered, yet this does not actually happen until almost the end of the book. How does this affect the reader's feelings towards Molly?